AMERITOPIA 2075

COREY L SIMMINS

Dedicated to the memory of
CPL Nicholas Olivas
who told me as he left my
classroom, "I will go off to fight,
so you can stay here and teach."

Special Thanks:

To my wife and children,
who allowed me to neglect them
for five months.

My Students: (past, present, and future)
You are that which propels me

To my first three editors, Bobbi Jo, John and Colin – Thanks!
To my second edition editor, Sarah, your destiny has materialized.

Homage:

To Ernest Shackleton who taught me how to lead
To George Orwell who taught me how to think
To Herman Melville who taught me how to write
To John Steinbeck who taught me how to cope
To Aldous Huxley who taught me how to question
To James Joyce who taught me how to craft
To George Leigh Mallory who taught me how to strive
To Jonathan Swift who taught me how to eviscerate
To Winston Churchill who taught me how to speak
To Tennessee Williams who taught me how to suffer
and
To Robert Falcon Scott who taught me how to die
I thank thee all.

CHAPTER ONE

Mr. Moore said he would walk the referral down himself. Murray Moore stood up from his desk in a semi-agitated state, glancing around his room, exhaling in a manner that when younger, drove his mother to madness for she always knew that he teetered on the brink of fits of rage. He loathed any student who forced his hand into writing a referral. It served as a mark of shame on his classroom management skills and aggravated him towards hysteria that any young student could possess such a temperament of cluelessness concerning the world so as to *not*

literally plop out of the womb and realize that being born in the "Disney World" country on the planet should motivate the dolt to perk up in class and comprehend the need to edify the mind. Generally a sarcastic admonishment resulting in a swift verbal kick in the pants motivated the worst of his students; however, today seemed to manifest to Murray that his normal teaching style would not suffice.

Standing, he ambled toward the classroom door, casting a furtive glance at the room's myriad flags draped upon the wall. He loved those flags. He adored the flags almost as much as his *1984* mural outside his classroom in the hall on the wall. Stepping through the door into the hall, he viewed the visage of George Orwell glowering with the words "Big Brother" above his face and "always watches you" below. Usually, when only a few minutes into his plan period, Murray would stride down the hall at his usual brisk pace; a pace so brisk that daily, he nearly ran over students, forcing him to bob and weave through the phalanx of pubescence, pontificating the preponderance of obesity in the country. However, with time wasted composing the referral, he found himself fifteen minutes into the class period with the halls barren and thus his brisk pace unimpeded. Striding down the hall, he thought of getting coffee only to mutter "bloody hell" under his breath, for he realized his cup sat idly back on his desk, wasting that which had already been poured. Cutting left at the teacher's workroom, he moved toward the center of the building's stairwell when he glanced up gazing upon his colleague's mural near his door at the far end of the building boasting the classic "Uncle Sam" image in World War II uniform with that now nearly century and a half old slogan "Uncle Sam Needs You" under his pointing index finger and penetrating stare. Murray decided that he needed a mental relief from the day, and the best medicine for stress would be a good old fashioned political showdown with his fellow teacher and best friend, Jacob Wilde.

This interesting friendship started ten years earlier when Murray began his teaching tenure at Mayfield High School. Murray felt obligated to strike up a conversation during their first week in the building when he discovered Jacob shared the surname with one of his favorite historical figures Frank Wild—the right hand man of

Antarctic explorer Ernest Shackleton. Possessing an undying admiration of Sir Ernest Shackleton, an Anglophile's love for the Age of Heroism, and a penchant for all things Antarctic, Murray felt compelled to introduce himself to the other (at the time) young teacher in hopes of striking up a conversation about his new school and his old love, Sir Ernest. The friendship of the two budding pedagogical neophytes blossomed instantly, for Wilde taught American Civics and Government and Moore taught Language Arts with little care for grammar, less concern for most stereotypical literature, and a fervent interest in novels possessing a theme steeped in sociological and/or political topics. The two teachers quickly found common ground in their intellectual passions and became the best of friends with interests that led them in multifarious conversations concerning life, the universe, and everything. Early on in their friendship, Moore convinced Wilde to read George Orwell's *1984* and *Animal Farm* just to generate endless political and historical conversation. Furthermore, Wilde's interest in the Federalist Papers, the Declaration of Independence, the Constitution and so on and so on, led the two men into divers conversations on politics while draining numerous adult beverages during periodic camping weekends. The debates, explorations, and at times, tempestuous tirades on governance shaped the two men into more than mere friends; they evolved into intellectual compatriots. At times, when teaching went from a passionate calling—almost a cultish desire to convert the students to a philosophy—to a drudge of endless grading and essay examination, it seemed that the personal connection between these two intellectuals made their existence as teachers bearable in the worst of times, divine in best of the times.

Finding himself caught glancing at Uncle Sam to his left and Jacob Wilde's door to his right, Murray Moore contemplated a final thought prior to bursting into Jacob's lesson. Should he turn this referral into the principal or do what he did with most—pitch it, castigate the student the following day, and finally, hold the violation over the kid's head until the end of the term? When this type of moral conundrum exhibited itself, Murray always found that time spent with Jacob generally sorted it out. Moore decided to engage in the one activity that always, no matter the depth, would lift him from his educational nadir—interrupt Jacob Wilde's class to engage in political discourse.

Over the course of the years, Murray would oftentimes kick open Jacob's door and blurt out a controversial statement as if Wilde were not teaching class and the two men were actually the last men on the planet. Murray would toss a line out impugning the value of a belief or a political party, Jacob would counter the claim, and off they would go. The irony for the students—as both educators full well comprehended—centered around the fact that in their naïve belief that the teachers had strayed off course, much to their surprise, they found themselves gaining insight into American politics and sociology to the likes they would not have attained in a regular class setting. Generally, Murray would fling open the door, puff out his chest, stand akimbo, then profess some universal truth to be debated. Today, he entered more subdued and placid; Jacob turned as the door creeped uncharacteristically open and Murray skulked unsuccessfully into the room, for despite his best effort, all noticed his entrance. Wilde, shocked at the passivity of his fellow teacher and usual intellectual combatant, went on with his lesson as if nothing out of the ordinary occurred.

"Alright guys and girls, now that the quiz has concluded, we shall cover the material in its entirety." He glanced inquisitively toward Moore as if to ask, "What?" only to receive a gesticulation indicating to proceed with the aforestarted lesson. Wilde proceeded without out a superfluous explanation—for the two men understood one another in much the same manner as a catcher and pitcher in baseball. "I shall begin with an easy question, tell me about L.O.F.I."

"Lord of the Flies Island!" shouted a myriad of students with one louder than the rest.

"Gregg!"

"Yeah?"

"You remember the rules; no blurting out the answers."

"Sorry, but I think others answered, too."

"You were the most vocal. That being said, now you are on the hot seat my friend. Can you share with the class the origins of Lord of the Flies Island?"

"Uh, yeah."

"Did you read the Net posted assignment last night on the class page?"

"Uh, yeah."

"Alright then, give me some information. Share. Prove you are a valuable asset to humanity, a productive, thinking citizen."

"Uh, okay. It should not be called L.O.F.I. They called it something else."

"Wow!" Clearly agitated by the student's lack of serious effort, Wilde walked away from Gregg shaking his head thundering on, "Clearly you cheated your way past the Secondary School Assessment your freshman year and have slipped through the high school cracks. Why did you cheat? Afraid to lay a brick? Operate a machine?"

Murray chuckled internally; this exhibition of student/teacher repartee served the purpose of transforming his sullen manner into a more chipper mood. The verbal castigation of students by Wilde rivaled his own; the difference being he preferred to passively enjoy Wilde attack his students, as opposed to being the active participant eviscerating his own students. However, whenever they hammered a student for lassitude, both Wilde and Moore reverted to the Secondary School Assessment students took toward the end of their ninth year which determined each student's final three years in the public school system. Modeled after the Army's ASVAB test, this examination placed the students, based upon aptitude, into vocational track learning: bricklaying, carpentry, welding, etcetera or into the college preparatory high school.

"Mr. Moore!" Wilde barked at him.

"Yes, sir," Murray responded in their normal bantering manner when they invaded each other's classrooms using the other as a sounding board for a student's pathetic performance. This "good cop/bad cop" routine entertained the students and most importantly, Murray and Jacob.

"Mr. Moore, young Gregg here can't seem to generate an answer of a sufficient level to suit the good citizens of the United States and the community of Mayfield, Ohio who selflessly put him through a college prep education in hopes to determine which intellectual career he shall pursue: two-year, four-year, or pre-graduate level college. What should we do?"

"Well Mr. Wilde, I could send a student to grab a toilet brush, and I could demonstrate to him how to use it."

"Too late! He passed the Secondary School Assessment. The government doesn't like to be wrong. He must be ready for college. Too late for vocational training. He must use his mind."

This routine Murray and Wilde performed class after class, semester after semester, and year after year. They had a cast of historical characters from which to choose. Whether Wilde visited Murray or vice a versa, one teacher would toss out the question, the other teacher would provide the example, and this chatter could be used to ridicule a student, mildly admonish a student, explain or clarify a message for a student, or in general, entertain all of the students.

"Well, he could Lawrence Oates himself," Murray submitted grinning ear to ear.

"Ahhhhhh," Jacob drew out a long exhalation of a vocalized pause then continued, "Brilliant. Gregg, Lawrence Oates, do you know him?"

Gregg, wishing his current location anywhere but class, racked his brain, but this obscure name never crossed his ears like the history of L.O.F.I. – the United States Federal Penal Colony System – which he should have read. He would read next time. Before Gregg could embarrass himself, Murray Moore violently leapt from his desk, stood at a military attention and snapped himself into a traditional British Naval Salute belting out in his best British accent, "I am just going outside and may be some time," then began to walk across the front of the classroom in a limping manner, all to the amusement of the classroom for they noticed Mr. Moore suddenly had shed his shoes and hobbled from the classroom toward the boy's restroom located across from Jacob Wilde's room.

"As Robert Falcon Scott's doomed British Antarctic Expedition trudged ill-fatedly back from the South Pole in 1912," Jacob Wilde cut into the conversation, "Captain Oates, stricken with severely frostbitten feet, the ravaging effects of scurvy, and a most assuredly doomed future, young Captain Oates realizing that he became a drain upon the team, knowing that he would never live, and that his continuance of slowing down the expedition along with eating their dwindling food supply, decided to take the noble approach to the situation and walk off into the -40 degree Antarctic blizzard to his frozen demise in order to offer his comrades, his countrymen, a better chance of survival."

At that moment catching his cue, Murray thrust his head back into the classroom repeating, in a now comedic fashion, his previous statement in perfect hoity-toity British English, "I say dear chaps; I am just going outside and may be some time."

"You see Gregg," Wilde broke in, "there are times in society when men of that society must realize that they are nothing but a drag upon society, the community, and country as a whole and that it would serve all best if they, or in this case you, just went out and committed honorable suicide."

"Tis the noble thing to do," bantered back Murray.

Here, Gregg completely ashamed and bearing the glares and stares of his classmates reluctantly admitted, "I didn't read the assignment Mr. Wilde."

"Really," smiled Wilde, "I would have never suspected. Did you fail to read the material because you couldn't find the assignment? Ah no, I sent it to your phone's email along with posting it upon the class website. Lassitude! Unacceptable. Read."

"Mr. Wilde?" A hand shot up from the back of the room.

"Yes, ma'am."

"I can answer the question. I read."

"Brilliant, please continue." Jacob Wilde appeared smug; Gregg chagrined. "Continue, please, Miss Sarvak."

"The United States Federal Penal Colony System became fully instituted after the Great Compromise of 2025. Currently the government has two penal colonies; one on the island of Guam and the other on America Samoa."

"Thank you. Gregg," Wilde glowered at his faltering student, "Pay attention. Miss Sarvak, could you explain the nickname along with the Great Compromise of 2025?"

"Yes Mr. Wilde, the nickname of L.O.F.I. developed when people through social media sites and general conversation began addressing it as such based upon the 20th century novel by British author William Golding. At first a pejorative by opposition groups, it quickly grew into the common term by the public and politicians alike. As for the Great Compromise, I read it, but I don't quite understand it. The posting stated that Democrats and Republicans came together and hashed out a deal of such magnitude as not witnessed in 300 years of American history. I don't quite understand the political party stuff," Sarvak finished, looking worried.

Jacob Wilde smiled that smug grin any teacher would exhibit when a student can belt back a response on that level. He continued to scathingly scowl at Gregg who continued to prove time and time again that the current state of education and its academic testing and placement system had yet to achieve utopian status, though close. Wilde began to respond as Murray stood up. "Well class, the dissolution of political parties occurred not long after the Great Compromise of '25. Though nearly fifty years prior to our world, the ramifications of dissolving the political parties has proved stunningly efficacious—illustrating the beauty, pragmatics, and dynamism of the Founding Fathers' documents and earlier sentiments of Thomas Jefferson, who cautioned America against political parties." Wilde, finally noticed Murray sidling toward the door, "Must you leave Mr. Moore?"

"I need to drop this off in the principal's office."

"Yikes! A referral? Someone commit murder?"

Murray blushed a bit; the lack of referrals sent to the main office served as a matter of pride to all teachers but none so much as the Wilde-Moore braintrust. Both adhered to the premise that any teacher worth his or her salt never found it necessary to apply to the office for assistance in classroom management. In a History of Education class in his college days, Murray remembered the scoffing tales told by professors with statistics to match the complete lack of control in the American educational system prior to the 2025 compromise. The lack of control and discipline manifested itself in pathetic standardized test scores and national embarrassment in a global comparison. Today, the instructor rarely found it of dire importance to write up an official referral to have a student disciplined in the American secondary college preparatory high schools. These schools were inhabited by the most promising intellectual minds of the nation. Furthermore, even though the vocational schools tended to have the rougher, less intellectual type, those schools abounded with students engaged, for a job awaited them upon completion of their training. In a post-compromise era started in 2025, America had vaulted to an economic dominance that had not been seen in the previous centuries. As World War II propelled the United States to the top of the economic food chain, the Great Compromise of 2025 solidified the hold due to radicalized moderate policies.

"Worse," Murray emphatically stated then headed toward the door. "I can catch up with you later. Bummed that I will miss the lecture on political parties; let me know which the class deems more pernicious. I know the one you adore, you flag waving Jingoist." Murray waved the referral in the air and sauntered out of the classroom door and pulled it shut just as he heard a student cry out, "Please define Jingoist, Mr. Wilde."

CHAPTER TWO

Murray Moore blasted his way down the hall at a torrent of a pace realizing that his planning time rapidly dwindled down. Though the pit stop into Jacob Wilde's class cost him precious minutes, the respite served crucially to defuse the internal bomb ticking toward explosion caused by dealing with the human piece of offal who caused him to have to find a referral sheet and then sit and compose the report. L.O.F.I. always made him chuckle when he heard it; now it sat there hanging off in the horizon as a possible destination for the sack of human waste and it gratified Murray. Gloom from the likes of his earlier frustration with a miscreant student and Wilde's current exasperation with the Gregg kid oftentimes washed themselves away, knowing that the citizens who chose the wrong path in life and had become unproductive had to look down the barrel of Lord of the Flies Island. Oftentimes, the malevolent students would resort to a life of crime, and then find themselves bound for the United States Federal Penal Colony on the island of Guam. This scenario played itself out with near certainty; for a future in the United States required a diploma from an accredited university, community college, high school, or vocational training center. Without one of the four, a student would not be hired for a legal occupation—a life of freeloading, homelessness, family dependence, and squalor seemed certain. Though most teachers laughed at the thought of this final "detention" if you will, the reality manifested a far more bleak future for the student. This lawless island became the final resting place of America's detritus; as the inmates landed at the Andersen Air Force Base on Guam, they were handed a week's worth of Meals Ready to Eat (MRE) then escorted to the top of the Great Wall of Guam and made to walk the retractable plank bridge over the moat to the top of the Hadrian's Wall. From that moment on, the inmates found themselves in a human survivor scenario for the remainder of their lives. Feeling gratified and mellowed, Murray lost some of the urgency to rush downstairs to the office to meet with the principal and engage in a conversation that would reflect a level of shame on his part. This proved most fortuitous because his reverie which now transcended to euphoria became broken when a student spotted him from the Media and Information Center. Emerging from the research area of the Media and Information Center, the student hailed his instructor.

"Mr. Moore!"

Murray admired this student, no two ways about it. His penchant for literary allusions and predilection for pedantic speech had created an interesting habit: he had taken to addressing his students as Alphas in praise and admiration for Aldous Huxley's *Brave New World*. Though he offended the softer-minded, more magnanimous instructors, Moore never failed to call a dolt an Epsilon if the opportunity manifested itself. He felt a certain "cock of the walk" in his own abilities. After all, he taught the most advanced students in America's public schools, and his students would ultimately prove the best in the world. What, with the world beating down the American doors to get their students into America's public schools, why wouldn't Murray ebulliently display his arrogance and pride for his students? Besides the fact that his students reflected the upper crust of American intelligentsia, it also exuded a stock of global promise. America's immigrant history proudly demonstrated an open door policy for the masses, but never in history had immigration been so honed and perfected. Every semester, a glob of students entered his class and he would laughingly joke, "My God, it looks like the United Nations at lunch time." He found nothing more exhilarating than a class that manifested America's most dominating color: bi-racial. Though a minority white man himself, he still felt a certain sense of pride that America had been founded and run by "a bunch of white guys" for a couple of hundred years. However, this feeling proved less racial and more relative; kind of like rooting for America during the Olympics, or the underdog, or someone from your hometown for some award. Consequently, not having seen a "white president" but once in his lifetime did not bother him in the least—consciously or subconsciously. America's melting pot finally came to fruition, and Murray often contemplated that Martin Luther King Jr. may have been flabbergasted himself if he had arrived in America in 2075. America's breaking down of social marital mores led the mixture of white, brown, black, and yellow to become a steady chocolate.

Geneticists had attempted to sociologically and categorically pigeon-hole America into racial groups; however, due to the nearly indefinable motley mess of chromosomes, statisticians within the American government just utilized bi-racial for the catch-all. So whether Sub-continent Indian and White mixed, or Hispanic and Black mixed, or African and Hispanic mixed, or Asian and whatever mixed, it all came out to chocolate, hence bi-racial. When Murray would look out at his classes, he would chuckle, for he could see that one student's Oriental emerged more than another, or that a student's black features trumped the Hispanic ones. Black students with French surnames and Indians with outdated Caucasian names and the scores of Oriental Christinas resulted in an often inner guffaw for Murray. Classes generally looked chocolate with overtones of designated racial groups while some in the room possessed the rare "pure bloods," for lack of a better word. Full blooded Whites, Blacks, Hispanics, and Orientals were more a novelty, along with the steady stream of foreign students from abroad. The full pendulum swing of America's view on race, from institutionalized racism to universal acceptance, manifested itself in the treatment of these "full-blooded" students when they decided to mate; if they married someone of the same race, most people said, "Keeping it pure, I see." If they married someone of another race, most people said, "Welcome to the club." Neither phrase reflected a derogatory tone—just a statement of fact. America had become a color blind society; how could it be otherwise? The coagulation of the global gene pool had resulted in the most economically dynamic society the planet had ever witnessed. Everybody loved a winner. With that, Murray Moore responded to his Indian-American student panting exhaustively as he emerged through the Media and Information Center.

"Ehsaan Shahnawaz! Good morning. What can I do for you my young Alpha?"

"Sir, you are so kind to stop and speak with me during your busy schedule. I so wanted to inquire about a particular passage read in our novel."

"You mean Heinlein's *Starship Troopers*?"

"Yes, sir!"

"Well Ehsaan, ask away." Murray's student typified the immigrant experience to America, especially from the Indian sub-continent. Murray had no doubt that young Ehsaan fully understood the policy that had, in Moore's opinion, become the pivotal cornerstone of competitive education: Ehsaan's parents, educated professionals, had applied for visas, green cards and ultimately had acquired citizenship; all according to policy. Acquiring citizenship proved to be a simple formula for any immigrant—no matter educational level: the United States government assigned immigrants their occupation, for none gained entrance unless America needed a position filled. If the immigrants performed the job well, they stayed; if not, deportation a certainty. With the world's population lined up to gain entry into the United States, the government, nor the people, tolerated unproductive immigrants. So whether they entered the country as a fruit-picker, construction worker, engineer, or doctor, it did not matter. The first stage in naturalization came with adequate work history. Stage two then fell upon the children of the immigrants. Immigrant children had to obtain a degree from either vocational training, high school with community college, or finally, high school with a university degree. When stage two had reached completion, all of the immigrants gained citizenship. The only hitch stemmed from the rare, but plausible, multiple child families. If an immigrant family had multiple children, only one needed to complete the terms of education for the child and the parents to be granted citizenship; however, if a sibling of the family failed to perform his/her educational duty and failed to graduate, that child would not be granted citizenship and thus be deported. That left the family in an awkward position: stay in the richest, most productive country on Earth with an education and a job, or return home with a wayward child to God knew what future. Very few went back with the failed children; adoption and procreation provided far too easy an alternative replacement.

"Well sir, if I may so boldly ask, explain the significance of reading a 20th century novel of a futuristic meritocratic society with racial and ethic equality? America has evolved into the land of racial and social equality."

"Mr. Shahnawaz, you must remember that Heinlein released his book a decade prior to the Civil Rights Act and Dr. Martin Luther King Jr.'s speech on the Lincoln Memorial steps. Though our Founding Fathers' documents have existed since the late 1700s, the citizens did not always practice those principles," Murray patiently replied, for his student had only been in the states for a year, and though reading comprehension, mathematics, chemistry, and biology offered him no resistance, coming to a full understanding of the American social strata along with its history would take longer to master.

"I am sorry to have troubled you sir; I should have checked the copyright of the book and cross-referenced it with the major dates of the Civil Rights Movement. I apologize."

"Ehsaan, no worries. Keep up the good work. I will see you in class." Murray took leave of his student, contemplating how he exemplified the classic immigrant story: dutiful, industrious, and inquisitive. John De Crevecoeur would still be writing of the glories of America if around in Murray's world of 2075. Throughout America's history, many immigrant groups struggled with personal and cultural identity, finding it difficult to assimilate or gain acceptance. Immigrants from India seemed to circumvent all those hassles; whether a Patel or a Desai, smooth, productive transition into the melting pot of America proved simple. From the Irish, the Scots, the Germans, the Italians, the Africans, the Orientals, and the Hispanics, all have washed up on the shores of America—some involuntarily, some forcibly, some desperately, but most eagerly. Throughout history, each group seemed to have encountered some cultural resistance, for man's instinct seemed to cause him to warily and forebodingly glance at his new neighbor; however, in the past fifty years immigration reform from the Great Compromise appeared to have smoothed the troubled waters. The collaboration utilized by the Fighting Moderates during 2025 and the decade after served to give Washington D.C. the proverbial kick in the pants politicians needed. When the radicalized moderates seized D.C. in '25, their ability to solve a political and social dilemma by bringing the antagonists together and knocking their heads about proved most efficacious for the legislative process. Murray recalled learning in a college course, along with hearing Wilde expound upon it during his lecture, about the head moderate Johannes Schmitt, a Senator from Tennessee. His "Abstinence from Ignorance" campaign electrified the American voter, for he publicly censured colleagues and politicians for their circuitous speeches filled with vacuous platitudes. Once the penal system took hold, along with the great compromise in education, immigration seemed simple, especially to Schmitt. He exhibited palpable disdain for party-line partisan politicians. He condemned the intractable plan some had for removing all illegals who resided in the country, but equally had empathy for those who bemoaned the drain placed upon the social safety net, schools, hospitals, and ultimately the taxpayer. His famous speech haranguing the partisans for their insular viewpoints broke the scenario down for the common voter—amnesty now, L.O.F.I. later. It worked. All citizens eventually registered with an American identification card which carried their virtual life's story in an imbedded data chip. All Americans, legal or illegal, submitted and thus were awarded their privileges and rights along with the card; the illegals began the path to citizenship based upon their work and children's academic achievements. After the initial period, a lockdown ensued. This audacious move forced all Americans to present their cards for everything from jobs and credit card transactions to entrance into school. No card, no nothing. Anyone caught inhabiting the country without a card would be labeled illegal, and deportation immediately to L.O.F.I. The United States sent enough of its nefarious characters to the island that immigrants patiently waited in their countries of origin as America evolved into a pseudo-sports franchise; citizens performed well, wanted to be a team player, contributed to society productively, or out of the country they went. Early in the process, religious groups, civil rights groups and the like protested but as American productivity soared beneficently, crimes decreased rapidly, and the economy roared robustly—along with the many speeches by Senator Schmitt in which he ostensibly stated to the citizens who objected "go to hell or go to L.O.F.I."—all of the tumult waned. The world's population comprehended America's policy; every American expelled to L.O.F.I. meant an immigrant received a green card.

Murray started for the office, glanced up at the clock, grumbled under his breath, then headed back to classroom, for the end of his planning period quickly approached. As he neared the door, once again the words, "Mr. Murray!" rang out followed by, "I hope you are hungry." Coming up the final flight of stairs to the landing near his door, Kelli, another Alpha, bounded up, dangling a bag in front of her.

"Ahhh, Ms. Niehaus, the morning bagel arrives, and none too soon." This diurnal ritual had accentuated the morning for most of the school year. Not being a man of frills, Mr. Moore enjoyed the banal, plain bagel, generally with his reheated coffee, for he never got five minutes to drink it in peace. Upon completing her genial and amiable salutations, Kelli whisked herself off to class ebulliently demonstrating all of the qualities a teacher dreams of in a student.

CHAPTER THREE

"Excessive bail shall not be required nor excessive fines imposed, nor cruel and unusual punishments inflicted."

UNITED STATES BILL OF RIGHTS **1789**

Murray Moore folded the referral and placed it gently into his jacket pocket. *That will have to wait,* he thought. Class would start in five minutes; he wanted to make sure his lesson plans were arranged and ready to go. Murray thoroughly enjoyed teaching his class, Modern Society as witnessed through Science Fiction. The class allowed him to discuss modern politics, social reforms, technological advancements and the like, all cloaked in great works of literature. He became captivated by any novel that spoke truth in the face of falsehood concerning any modern day or recent historical date. His class's current exploration of Heinlein's *Starship Troopers* caused him to become exhilarated by the world of meritocracy—especially the aspect that service gained you the right to vote. Though Moore's modern America did not require military service for full citizenship, it did seem to guarantee that America would be educated. He greeted his students as they entered his classroom in his genial and jovial manner. As the clock struck the top of the hour, marking the starting time, the students settled into their individual seats pulling out their computer tablets in the usual manner. Moore already felt better about the referral after the visit to Wilde's class along with the brief interlude with Shahnawaz and Niehaus in the hall. He successfully put the paperwork in his jacket pocket out of his mind enabling him to segue from the periodic aggravation of the occupation to the ecstasy of teaching.

"Alright class, I asked you to analyze the similarities and differences of our own national reconstruction with that of Heinlein's societal reconstruction in his book. You were permitted to use any internet source. How did we do?" Murray enjoyed the exercise for it afforded him the opportunity to tie literature to the real world. While he waited for the students to pull up their essays on their computer tablets, he pulled his chair over to his desk, fumbling with miscellaneous clutter that always seemed to occupy his work area.

"Scheer, Tunnell, Schlegel, and Chappell, why are you four gentleman out of your desks and hanging out the back window?" Murray found himself instinctively inquiring emotionlessly for this generalized the extent of discipline problems in high school—off task. The whimsical and capricious meanderings of these four students frequently required the proverbial boot in the backside. Zealous about the intellectual, the esoteric, and all things quite "nerdy," these four often drifted mind and body from one topic, or place, to another. He often wondered about what interesting adventures they would pursue as adults.

"Mr. Moore the police are in the teacher parking lot. I think they are arresting someone." Murray abhorred classroom interruptions given the amount of material he found himself required to teach, all in preparation for the high school exit exam. Said exam determined whether the students would be sent to one of the many national universities for a bachelor's, master's, or doctoral degree or to one of the many local community colleges for training in any of the variety of specialized jobs required in the American economy. He reflected. The stakes on the tests were high; a poor score in the ninth grade meant a trade school—plumbing, carpentry, or any other form of necessary manual labor. A high score, on the other hand, sent you to a countywide mega high school where three more years of rigorous academics determined a student's post-secondary options. Murray barely remembered taking the ninth grade test, but he did remember the party his parents threw for him when he scored well enough to make it to his county's mega high school. Murray's experience in high school proved more vivid; he remembered the instructors pushing each of their classes, the frequent field trips to local professional businesses such as: hospitals, medical treatment centers, banks, along with entrepreneurial businesses, engineering and architectural firms, fire and police stations, and so on. During one of these trips, they actually toured Mayfield High School in Cutler County, the adjacent district. It served a most strange and engaging enterprise for he had not viewed teaching as a profession until he left his own school to travel to a then strange institution. Until his Mayfield field trip, education as a career had never occurred to Murray; he had not realized that teaching in America garnered the respect of the nation. He always respected his teachers; he valued their skill and intellectual prowess, but the trip solidified his pursuit in life. Murray knew at that moment that he would strive to be a teacher if he scored high enough on his secondary exit exam to gain entry into the university; he figured if he did not score well enough, community college would offer him the chance to be a fireman or business manager.

Murray reached the window where the boys were gawking, not fully realizing that he had risen from his desk; the boys' story proved accurate. In the staff parking lot two police cars sat nose to nose; an officer had a young man clutched by the arm leading him to the back of a squad car. Moore immediately recognized his former student being laid face down on the trunk of the car and searched. Sam Wolfe, the boy's name, dropped out of Mayfield at the beginning of his senior year. Murray recognized the signs: flagrant disregard for the rules, the desecration of his arms and neck with ribald tattoos, repudiation of national school orthodoxy, and the infusing of rancor into any class he attended. Though Sam Wolfe proved more the anomaly than the norm, drop-outs did occur. Generally, the students got into drugs or alcohol, became despondent, started trouble in school, and then faced the administrators. The choice became simple: rehabilitation and remedial training, removal and placement in the vocational school, or drop out. A student choosing rehab could test back into high school; any relapse into drugs proved intolerable and automatic expulsion ensued. Americans loathed deadbeats. Dropping out might as well have been a death sentence. Welfare did not exist; you worked or you starved. Everyone knew and understood that. With education guaranteed from primary school all the way through a doctoral degree, America had developed intolerance for those not willing to "toe the line" and contribute to society. Occupational certitude made it nearly impossible to be unemployed, though in rare times of economic slow downs, unemployment guarantees kicked in. In his lifetime, Murray could hardly recall anyone using unemployment. The economy rolled and rolled.

"Well boys, you may recognize that malcontent Sam Wolfe. He sat in this very room in the fall. He chose to drop out," Murray reminded them.

"Mr. Murray I thought he started taking drugs?" an inquisitive Schlegel piped in.

"Taking drugs, selling drugs, all the same." Before he could continue, Wolfe broke free from the police as they extricated a bag of some narcotic from the inside of his pant leg. He escaped their grasps and took off down the parking lot through the cars. "Stupid," instinctively stated Murray. The police did not react in a hasty way. The officer that did not pull the drugs from Wolfe's pants simply opened the back car door and let out the K-9 German Shepherd, and the hopeless race commenced. "Stupid," Murray repeatedly blurted out. By this time, the entire class had pressed itself up against the back window. Generally, this would infuriate Moore, but he always recognized a teachable moment; this would segue right into the day's topic. Down in the parking lot, the same officer that had unleashed the hound closed the door and pulled out his taser as the accosting officer popped the trunk, dropped in the narcotics, closed the lid, then turned with his fellow officer and began to trot in the general direction of the canine which had already nabbed the Wolfe kid.

The immediate future for the culprit presented an ominous fate, and that fate dripped with palpability. The dog attack proved potent and Sam Wolfe flailed on the ground as the police patiently approached allowing the dog to thoroughly throttle and maltreat the now criminal—running from the law in itself served as a felony. A strike in the three strikes to L.O.F.I. system; in fact many hip hop artists for decades had worked this type of lingo into myriad rap songs. Strike two most certainly would be narcotics. So many drugs were legalized during the era immediately following the Great Compromise that doing anything or selling anything illegal proved pure folly. If Wolfe had any other felonious convictions, he could be gone by week's end. All police stops being videoed, not only from the car but also the helmet cameras of the officers, guaranteed there would be no avoidance, acquittal, or mitigation of this crime. Society had decidedly said "no" to certain behaviors and running from the law manifested one such behavior. By now the police stooped over Wolfe as he screamed for respite from the shepherd; he received his reprieve as the dog let go, hopped over, and observed as the officer delivered the coup de grace of apprehension, a full barrage of voltage. Sam Wolfe's back arched as he convulsed; the officer disengaged, and his quarry lay silent. The second officer rolled the motionless boy over, manacled him, then headed back to his police vehicle. The officers always blasted the runners. First it ensured total compliance, and second, it provided a deterrent for any bystanders.

"Totally Awesome!" Chappell elatedly exclaimed. "I would pay money to see that again." Tunnell and Scheer, both possessing a modicum of temperance, glanced at one another and simultaneously uttered, "Reprobate." Schlegel wallowing in his own impetuousness seemed unable to decide whether to "high five" his cronies or state something constructive, so he just opted to giggle, moving around in a tight circle like a dog pursuant of his own tail. Murray, in his most affable manner, began to wave his arms much like the proverbial shepherd attempting to move his flock.

"All right boys and girls, the circus has concluded. How about some class discussion?" This futile warning provided the necessary break for the class to begin meandering back to their individual seats. Outside, the German shepherd received its reward, and Sam Wolfe accepted the fact that being hogtied and tossed into the back of the cruiser would be the best he would get for the rest of the day. Murray dropped the blinds in his room in front of the stragglers hoping against hope to catch some juicy follow up. Moore headed for the front of class as the rest of the students settled into their desks and back to retrieving their electronic Heinlein essays.

"Well, what did we learn today?" Murray's instincts kicked in for he hoped to take the activity outside from the student's own world and compare them to the nearly 120 year old piece of prophetic science-fiction literature. A hand shot up.

"I think the author would approve of our justice system," volunteered Kaminsky; another immigrant student to the United States.

"Why?"

"Well, for one, Robert Heinlein supported swift and expedient punishment, even public floggings. In the book, he likened it to training a puppy that urinates on a rug. He would rub its nose in it."

"What about the United States Penal Colony System? Any place for that in Heinlein's novel?" Moore continued.

"He doesn't state anything concerning the matter. He has executions and floggings. I am not sure on L.O.F.I.; I mean the penal colony system," Kaminsky continued.

"Well Justine, conjecture. Thinking would be required."

"I guess he would take it as the alternative for a death penalty. He promoted.one; we do not. We outlawed all forms of death penalty."

"When?" Another hand shot up, Murray nodded in recognition.

"After the Great Compromise!" shouted Jake Tunnell.

"Correct!" Pleased with the discussion, Murray finished the thought, "During the Great Compromise period, anti-death penalty liberals, along with right-to-life religious groups opposed the hardcore conservative 'kill them all and let God sort them out' factions. The compromise called for the United States Penal Colony System, along with the shutting down of every major high security prison in the county. The economic savings were immense. Housing an inmate costs the equivalent of a working man's annual wages—for a death row inmate nearly three times the cost."

"Why so much on a death row inmate Mr. Moore?" inquired Kelli Niehaus, one of his rare Caucasian students, but an immigrant.

"Can anyone clarify?" Hands shot up throughout the classroom. "Toren Chenault, you have the floor."

"Yeah, Mista Moore, all that stuff cost so much because of the lawyer fees and court costs. Total waste of money."

"Excellent. There you go class, another example of compromise improving the lives of the country. In the 20th and early 21st centuries, America found itself spending more on prisons than on education. The governmental budget ballooned for correctional facilities that housed the worst scum of society providing them with healthcare, food, shelter, and educational opportunities. After the economic collapse of Europe in 2015 and the subsequent floundering of the Chinese juggernaut, the world found itself in economic chaos and ruin. The United States found itself the rudder on the Titanic, though last to sink, bound to go down. The citizens began to evaluate, raise hell, and then form radical groups." Murray noticed a hand and acknowledged Zoe Anderson.

"That makes sense then. The government closed the prisons and shipped the inmates to Guam."

"Exactly! The billions of dollars spent on prisons found itself subsidizing education and health care. After all, why should an inmate receive 'free' health services when at that time in America, millions of working adults went without it?"

"Mr. Moore. What about cruel and unusual punishment?" spoke up a voice that Murray recognized immediately as Alex Seifert.

"Well, we have totally drifted from language arts and literature into your civics studies. Hasn't Mr. Wilde covered this? Allow me to draw back to our novel. As the character Dubois states in *Starship Troopers*, 'for punishment to be effective, it must be cruel and unusual' otherwise, it would not be punishment. Hence, Guam, the prison system, the wasting of money on citizens who ostensibly proved to be a detriment to society all led to the 30th Amendment, the revocation of citizenship when a criminal has proven his/her antipathy for the rule of law, hence the three strikes felony rule. I am sure that Mr. Wolfe, who we saw apprehended and shackled today, will find himself soon in citizenship limbo—a criminal without a country." Looking up at the clock, knowing the lesson plan had been blown out of the water, Murray felt satisfied, for the outside world's efficacy proved its sensibility in his classroom. With that, the bell rang, and the class scurried out. And so it goes.

CHAPTER FOUR

After the bell rang dismissing the students, when Murray Moore awoke from his class euphoria, he found himself transformed at his desk into an ignominious instructor. His metamorphosis, precipitated by the referral still in his pocket, required him to perfunctorily head toward the principal's office at the first opportunity. He loathed the meeting with the principal over the referral; his pride hung in the balance. As the other class periods began to wend their individual ways in and out of his room, Murray felt a stronger sense of abasement that he knew would not abate until he took the report to the office himself to face the "music." The day concluded, Murray hesitatingly fiddled around his desk waiting to see if the plethora of students who generally stormed his room at day's end would appear. Today's parade proved paltry since spring break had just ended and not much in the manner of work had been assigned yet. Murray answered a couple of questions, pulled the parchment from his pocket then looked above his half-mooned spectacles when he heard the steady shuffle that he instinctively knew to be the gait of Jacob Wilde.

Wilde exploded in through his open door in his normal bombastic—yet oblivious—manner and served up his quotidian salutation of, "Anything shaking?"

"Ah, I still need to take this bloody referral down to Bobby Feinauer's office."

"Hey, I can walk with you."

The friendship between the two men ignited the moment Moore began his tenure at Mayfield. As a neophyte to the district and the public school system, he found himself traveling and his first assignment took place in Wilde's room. The friendship blossomed out of their first interactions. Wilde taught American Government and Civics, and he had placed in his midst a comedic teacher of American literature. Wilde quickly ascertained that Moore's knowledge of literature had been accentuated with a profundity of understanding in the realm of American history, warfare, and social structure—though his comprehension of the intricacies of American governance reflected a shallow nature. He immediately forgave the callow nature of Moore's complete understanding of his own personal forte for two reasons: first, most language arts teachers possessed an unhealthy and slightly erotic love of William Shakespeare, and second, this "weakness" in Moore's intellectual repertoire would give them something to discuss. He knew the nature of Moore's passion for pedagogy—immersive; plus, after sitting in on a class one period and a student queried him as to why he didn't possess a Shakespeare poster on his wall like the other teachers, Moore's candid response stunned the room, "I wish old Billy-boy would have died in his crib much like his two older siblings!"

Though in Moore's early periods in Wilde's room, Jacob would have to constrain himself, for Moore would ridicule and lampoon 20th century liberal politicians for their insistence on the "gray area" in matters. After the Great Compromise of 2025, much of the political fervor began to wane, especially a decade or two after the implementations. Once the bulk of Americans came to the realization that the logos of the compromise offered more than the ethos and pathos combined, the squawkers were silent or silenced. When the herd galloped gracefully down the path, it took a fool or a zealot to stand in front waving his or her arms; such action often got the impromptu leader killed. Moore manifested a more black and white nature—a four legs good, two legs bad kind of guy—but that philosophy stretched back a decade.

Jacob reminisced upon the day he felt compelled to commit a coup in Moore's class while Murray taught his class some novel (a title Wilde had forgotten) that revolved around the death penalty, which at the time still legally existed in the United States. As teacher etiquette required, teachers had to vacate their respective classrooms while a traveling teacher taught. Moore, early in the relationship, told Wilde he could disregard that order; "utilize your desk" he stated. Moore never used a one-dollar word, when a two- or twenty-dollar one would suffice. When questioned on the matter, Moore would elucidate upon that fact that, "Proles and Epsilons used Anglo-Saxon vocabulary; why would I descend down the declivity of decadence to be understood by the rabble?" Speaking in alliterative phrases or mild and major redundancy never fazed Moore. He reveled in it. He insistently expressed himself in that manner especially if the timing would be considered less than apropos. However, on this particular day, Jacob witnessed Murray flapping his wrists in the most vivacious manner, as if attempting to take flight, proclaiming, "Look at me, I am a liberal; I don't want to execute murderers and rapists. I want them to enjoy cable, free education, health care, and a gymnasium." This level of jocularity regularly exuded itself from the very pores of Murray while he taught; he became vehemently obsessed when he would engage in rants during his lectures. Students loved his classes even if they abhorred his views. Nothing clandestine about his nature; he jubilantly performed for his classes; in fact, he referred to teaching quite often as performing. Jacob had to give him credit; students learned while being entertained. Wilde once told Moore, "I feel I am only missing red floppy shoes and a horn!"

As he reflected upon the first coup he committed in Moore's class, Jacob recalled Murray, a veritable lecturing virtuoso, gesticulating around the room flapping his wrists, vilifying the liberals of nearly a century ago, and he felt he must become a virtual interlocutor and risk upsetting the delicate balance between educators as friends and educators as interlopers. Moore possessed a particular "je ne sais quoi" which allowed him to insult everyone but offend no one.

"Uh, Mr. Murray, if I could interject," he remembered bravely and tentatively interrupting.

"By all means Mr. Wilde, do you have something to add? Perhaps your great, great grandpa lived the life of a pot smoking hippie from the 1960s?"

"Hardly, I just had one question. What about those who had been convicted of a capital crime only to be exonerated by exculpable DNA testing decades later when the technology emerged?" Wilde remembered Murray unflappable in his response, "No one innocent resides in prison. They may have not committed the crime of their conviction, but to dream they were randomly chosen and plopped into the big house lies in a realm of absurdity. They were guilty of something—if not just association. Birds of a feather, Mr. Wilde. Birds of a feather." Then back to his lesson as nonchalantly as if Jacob's point served up to the class for critical thought delved in nothing more than pure speculation. Though Jacob loathed Murray for his notoriously limited spectrum of critical thought in political matters reducing the issues to pure black or white, he found his conviction and his classroom persona admirable. Nevertheless, over the years as Murray grew as a teacher— though he would never admit the fact—Moore began to explore the gray areas of the past century prior to and immediately after the Great Compromise of 2025.

As Murray and Jacob entered the main office, for they walked silently each lost in thought, the secretary glanced up, eyes widened with a smile, then Laurie Savage stated, "Just the two men that Mr. Feinauer requested to see. He just went into his office; I just picked up the phone to 'all-call' you two through the system."

"Well this can't be good," Jacob muttered furtively glancing at Murray.

"Hmm. Agreed," retorted Murray. Both teachers sauntered into the principal's office as Bobby Feinauer sat down in his chair,

"Gentlemen, unbelievably quick. How in the name of...?"

"We were heading down to see you," interjected Wilde. "Or should I say, Murray here needed to see you. He can't handle his classes you know."

"Codswallop!" Murray Moore exploded.

"Once again my friend, you continue to use those insane words."

"Firstly, any erudite logophile could appreciate codswallop. Secondly, I handle my classes just fine thank you. Some students have no business in school."

"No one wishes to be a," Wilde paused, "whatever you just said."

"Well gentleman, that happens to be the precise reason for my calling for the two of you." He leaned forward into his desk, pressed the elbows down with his hands folded up near his chin. "I would like to know your future career plans."

This seemed a strange question to both, for currently Jacob and Murray were in fact engaged in their respected future plans, or so they thought. Murray's nonplussed manner at that moment must have manifested itself upon his countenance for the principal continued, "Mr. Moore you appear flummoxed. Anything wrong with the head of a public school asking his two best educators their future plans? I ask because you two exhibit qualities that may go beyond the classroom. You both currently teach in the monk fashion, which most Americans prefer to the family option."

The monk fashion of teaching developed about thirty to forty years prior after the schools moved into their respective post-compromise phases. High school core subject teachers—math, science, civics and language arts—were offered greater pay to remain single and live in the school. Some schools provided dorms, others trailers for accommodations and still some used nearby boarding houses. It purely depended upon the building layout. At Mayfield,

31

a gargantuan edifice, when high school sports received the ax as being a superfluous appendage that distracted not only the students from their studies, but also administrators and community leaders from their duties, the district had plenty of room to convert the auxiliary gym into a rather capacious collection of living quarters—providing a central lounge adjoined to quaint, austere bunk rooms. Students no longer became fixated with games, and districts no longer wasted precious resources on such frivolities as facilities, fields, turf or coaches. During college, Murray bought into the orthodoxy of the monk life for an instructor. The federal government could not, or would not, require all teachers to live single lives residing on campus, for so many educators had been married with children at the time of the conversion. To Murray, the monkish lifestyle epitomized that which all educators should embody. The idea that an educator needed to be at the beck and call of his students twenty-four hours a day only seemed practical. Nearly 2100 years of Catholic Church history had demonstrated how demanding priests to be unmarried and live on church grounds gave the man one, single purpose in life—cater to and tend to his flock. If a priest's charge reflected the eternal salvation of his congregate, then the teacher had good cause to be charged with the earthly intellectual edification of his student; therefore, having a robust coterie of core content teachers in the building and on school grounds made sense.

Granted some high schools had students living in the dorms, some kept certain sections of the buildings open for the teacher to be near if students came for help or extra instruction, much like a priest sitting in the confessional awaiting parishioners to come in for confession. Whatever the practice, teachers attended all events in the building. Couple that practice with each monk teacher carrying a personal social media mini computer, and students could contact teachers perpetually. After all, a student's learning has never been confined to the hours of eight to three; moreover, how efficacious can a teacher be that runs home to his or her children and spouse? If Bobby Feinauer needed to inquire as to his future marital plans, Murray did not see the necessity.

"Let me cut to the chase boys. As you know, I will not be here forever; in fact, there has been some talk of moving me to the central curriculum and direction office which handles the southern part of the state." In pre-compromise days, generally each city had its own high school. In post-compromise, mega high schools began to coalesce out of the numerous splintered town schools—those being used for specialized vocational training. Realistically, four to six of these mega schools came under the guise of one superintendent. "Basically boys, this school will need a new administrator. A few schools will, as a matter of fact, and I think you two gentlemen have all of the qualities: knowledge of content, enthusiasm for the profession, and undying admiration of your duties to convey the founding tenets of this great country of ours to the next generation of thinkers."

This accolade of being nominated for a principal position reflected the highest honor. Teachers did not apply for a principalship; principals were recruited much like a secret society membership. If you had to inquire, you were not invited. Principals reflected one of the highest positions available in pay and prestige in the United States—equivalent to being a CEO of a major multimillion dollar company. Not to be taken lightly, Murray and Jacob each gave the other a furtive glance as if to confirm the reality of the situation. Both felt thunderstruck at the prospect. Describing a principal's salary as lucrative would reflect a gross understatement, but the privilege and honors were not matched by any occupation, none better than the annual trip to Washington D.C. during the school summer hiatus when all the principals of the nation met in the capital and were granted a small audience with the President of the United States.

"I don't know what to say," Wilde offered as Moore sat bewildered.

"Say nothing. You can't answer that question at the moment. Careful consideration must be taken. The training represents a unique opportunity to explore your individual dogma along with the minutiae that makes this country tick. As you know, principals are all chosen from monk teachers. You must complete the training successfully, surpassing numerous hurdles; consequently, once completed, men, you will have one of the most important and rewarding occupations this country, the greatest country on the planet, I might add, has to offer." He gave Wilde and Moore a cursory glance. "Take the evening off, go out tonight, reflect on this, discuss it, and come speak to me when you are ready to provide me with an answer. I am laying the world at your feet lads; you must choose, but choose wisely."

CHAPTER FIVE

"Be not afraid of greatness: some are born great, some achieve greatness and some have greatness thrust upon them."

WILLIAM SHAKESPEARE TWELFTH NIGHT

Murray, fully gruntled concerning the proposition, headed back first toward the common dorm then switched gears to the workroom area. He had a bunk in the partitioned dorm area with the other monk teachers—twenty-seven of the one hundred or so teachers—but he far preferred the back room between his classroom and adjacent classroom. Between each set of classrooms existed a space divided in half. The front half opened into the hall and served as an office for the two teachers to share and the students to meet them during tutoring sessions. The back half became the storage area or dump or pell-mell collection of the flotsam and jetsam of a public school building. Murray transformed the back storage into his own private hovel, reading lounge, and personal library.

Most teachers shared the back storage equally or had material assigned there from the department chair. Murray's abhorrent partner exemplified all that the public saw as lacking in an instructor. When Murray studied at the Northern Kentucky University, great emphasis had been placed on understanding the types of teachers that caused great consternation in the public eye, poor test scores by the students, and a generalized distrust of education as a whole. In the post-Compromise Era, these teachers ultimately succumbed to the weeding out process that propelled the American public school into the achievement envy of the globe. However, Sammy Reed, the anachronistic relic from antiquity, manifested a dung heap of apathy. His very survival long indicated that somewhere in the school system, Sammy must have a relative that protected his job. Murray envisioned Sammy, younger, deciding to be a teacher in the pre-compromise days—a figure that probably chose to be a teacher for summers off and the various breaks. Being too ignorant to compete in the work world with a real job, Sammy Reed served as the incarnation of the phrase "those who can, do and those who can't, teach." Due to his deleterious affect upon the realm of education, Murray Moore abominated him and his very existence, thus he established no sense of camaraderie with the man. Students viewed him as a phony and fraud; Moore could only assume that the administration simply had not caught on to his "flying under the radar," and he hid his ineptitude.

Oddly enough, Sammy Reed remained oblivious to this level of antipathy. Though an anathema in the eyes of Moore, Murray remained quiescent and allowed the students to judge the capable from the fraud; meanwhile, he silently commandeered the back room into his own personal oasis. He adored the room; though not aesthetically pleasing to most, Murray decorated the hermitage to reflect the scriptorium constructed to assemble the Oxford English Dictionary—the veritable Bible of lexicon. Being a logophile along with an Anglophile, he dubbed his seclusion "Little

Britain." From floor to ceiling, books reached for the sky. Murray chose the backroom, which had access to the rear of both his and Sammy Reed's classrooms, as an opportunity to block Reed's access to him by shoving a bookshelf in front of the aperture leading into Reed's room. This served as a silent affront which he gladly attributed publicly as a necessary evil to fulfill his own personal Jeffersonian library. Moore arranged "Little Britain" with such zeal and alacrity that the very notion of going there to opine excited the very synapses of his intellect. Not realizing it, he had skipped the common room with the other monks lounging or pontificating and found himself entering his classroom intent on making it into his cerebral abode.

Every time Murray opened the door to "Little Britain" he felt compelled to reconnoiter his exquisite environ. Aside from the copious books that hung from ceiling to floor—including the barricading of access to Reed's room—there stood a small musical unit that allowed his portable iPod to plug and play. Centered in the small room, a chair, draped with a six foot by nine foot Union Jack that tucked into all of the crevices and spread over the arm rests and hung to the floor, sat there waiting for Murray to recline. He cruised around his reading chair glancing at the various classics lining his walls—items read, along with items needing read—glorious, almost divinely inspired text, such as Jonathan's Swift's *Gulliver's Travels* down to overrated blowhards such as Charles Dickens, along with erudite geniuses such as Samuel Johnson's dictionary to entertaining series such as *Harry Potter, Lord of the Rings*, and the *Chronicles of Narnia*. No greater place of honor could be found for novels than the center of the back wall offset by British flags and there sat the works of George Orwell, Aldous Huxley, Joseph Conrad, James Joyce, and Virginia Woolf – Gods among mortals! Murray glimpsed through the blocked door window seeing the paltry collection of rags upon Reed's shelf, which exhibited a paucity of literature and preponderance of trash from adolescent vampire love novels to self-hackneyed tales of a heroine with indecisive mind and accurate bow. Reed's execrable choice in reading only affirmed Murray's contempt, causing him to peruse the room looking for something to cover up the opening in the window into that half-wit, sorry-for-an-excuse educator's room. Murray sat in his Union Jack draped chair and thought.

Call me principal. A few class periods ago—completely forgetting the cause of his discontent—having little thought of his future, and nothing beyond his classroom to interest him in life, Murray thought he would have to bow down to humiliation and request help from the administrative arm of the school. With this reprieve, Murray accounted it high time to get to his chair as soon as he could. As he sank in and contemplated the proposition presented to him, he reflected. In his ten-year teaching career, Murray never contemplated the principal role—that represented a different breed of educator: loners. Most principals came from the monk teaching ranks; if not monk, still single. Many teachers who lived the monk life eventually tripped up and wound up married, still taught but saw their efficaciousness wane, especially if they chose to procreate. Murray thought about marriage once—seriously dated a girl in college. His opinion on the matter vastly deviated after an epiphany attending a bachelor party of a friend. The guys had spent all day preparing the "big surprise" for him, first a trip to the local Walmart, then to the hardware store, then down to the local vocational school to see the industrial arts instructor. When his friends arrived, they sat him in a chair and told him in the most compelling manner to be still and close his eyes that they had a gift for him in the other room. Beguiling this friend took no special cunning, he lacked sharp wit to begin with, but opening a door and fallaciously yelling out "you can bring her out" only ensured that his eyes would remain closed. As adroitly as two more of his old high school classmates could manage it, they slipped a dog collar around his neck and padlocked it. Now, this dog collar, woven through a rather robust link in a chain attached to a bolt and drilled into a cheap ten pound bowling ball, served as a hilarious joke, for the evening promised clubbing and bar hopping, using the friend as bait for free drinks. When the victim opened his eyes, much to his chagrin, the dancing girl that he had engendered in his mind dissipated, his face visibly demonstrated his crestfallen nature. Murray remembered thinking of the hilarity of it all; the jocularity it caused in every establishment they entered; and finally, the epiphany it evinced. The ball and chain served less as gag of frivolity and more of a premonition of doom; from that moment on, marriage found itself pushed to the back of his mind, then finally out. Inundated with fear and then loathing of marital commitment and feeling as if perched upon a precipice precariously clinging, he discovered his relationship with his fiancée permanently sullied. It soon ended. At the university when Murray discovered higher pay for monk teachers, his resolve became solidified.

Now, Murray Moore faced an immense decision: principal. The very offer reflected a level of adulation unattained by Murray to that point of his career. Principals were a different breed; none married. Principals held complete sway over a school building much like a captain over a ship. Generally possessing an antiseptic persona, a principal's incontrovertible power presented itself time and time again. Required to be stoic and staid, principals possessed an "all business" haughty air to them not to be tinkered with. When a teacher became a pariah to his or her colleagues, the principal wielded the power to ax them—no ifs, ands, or unions—they had been dissolved as another victim of the Great Compromise. Teachers at times would irreverently remark, "Lack of performance will set you free." However, the truth of the matter could be quantified; ineffective teachers were sacked with regularity. Principals never worried about accommodating for their teacher's personal lives and all that rubbish; education became big business, and big business demanded results, and results came from test scores. The late 20th and early 21st centuries' willy-nilly approach to education had been smothered, then choked out by educators, per the demands of the populace, expecting that America remain top dog in everything in the world—especially education. Their world existed with high prestige, unmitigated privileges, and lucrative pay. Being a capitalist at heart, Murray heard the almighty dollar calling and decided he would explore the option so long as Jacob Wilde also chose the path. He didn't feel he had the nerve to go it alone.

Murray opined dreamily for an undisclosed amount of time before he became aroused by that unmistakable shuffle of feet that could be no one but Jacob Wilde. He gawked into the window through the books, saw Moore reclining and burst into the room with his perfunctory, "Anything shakin?"

"Just thinking about Bobby Feinauer's offer. I don't know much about the field; heck, I thought you had to be 'Teacher of the Year' or something to get that gig."

"Are you kidding me? The Teacher of the Year popularity contest represents nothing more than a fallacy of good teaching rarely awarded to the assiduous. Don't get me started!" Jacob Wilde regularly chastised these honors in the most caustic manner, finding no value in them at all. "Come on! If Teacher of the Year had any merit, we would be candidates annually. Think about it. Will it be Moore or Wilde? Wilde or Moore? One of the biggest reasons I loathe Teacher of the Year stems from the fact that I abhor phonies." Murray knew once Jacob began to rant Caulfield-esquely, he would quickly need to switch topics.

"Jacob, Bobby said if we took the offer, the training would be extensive, arduous, and yet pragmatic. What does that mean?"

"Haven't you read up on principal training?"

"Well, uh…okay, no. I have not. You know I delve into the inner workings of the government with the same amount of alacrity as a cat at bath time. I read the minimum on bureaucracy; that my friend belongs to you."

Jacob always took umbrage when any one, especially Murray, demonstrated the least bit of apathy towards the intricacies of the American government. He ate, slept, and dreamt in congressional terminology. Where Murray ebulliently could erupt into a barrage of magniloquence, Jacob prided himself on knowing that the President Pro Tempore represented the third in succession to the President after the Vice-President and the Speaker of the House.

"Murray, the preliminary introduction and interview process starts at Miami, Oxford. If you pass the screening, you attend some classes, then a trip to L.O.F.I.; think man, L.O.F.I. Can you flippin' believe that! L.O.F.I." The United States Federal Penal Colony System on Guam Island, a.k.a. L.O.F.I., enthralled Murray by name alone. Being an Anglophile, a lover of literature, and a fan of Golding, the fact that this acronym caught on in the past and became part of the common lexicon—even entered into the

Oxford English Dictionary edition 2055—L.O.F.I. produced in Murray an ethereal bliss that only other idiosyncratic intellects could appreciate.

"You are kidding me?" served as Murray's best response.

"I am incredulous! You know nothing."

"Shut up Piggy!" Murray responded, "Or I will rap that conch upside your corpulent cranium." Here, Murray, knowing that Jacob had the upper intellectual hand on him concerning the requirements for principal training, resorted to his first defense; literary allusion and grandiloquence. Whereas Moore failed to be enamored by the political megillah of America, when Murray spoke in polysyllabic phrases infusing it with literature, Wilde's countenance quickly transformed into that of Robert Falcon Scott's famous photo at the South Pole when he realized that a dog-eating Norwegian, Roald Amundsen, beat him to glory leaving him with a nearly 900 mile, ignominious death march back to king and country.

"What in the hell? Piggy?"

"Geez! You get all excited about L.O.F.I., but have you read *Lord of the Flies*? No, of course not. Anything artistic flabbergasts you. The character Piggy, like you, reflected a know-it-all without any common social sense."

"I have heard of the book."

"How could you not have read it? It would serve as a great transition in your civics and government class," continued Murray.

"Alright, I will try to read it. If we survive that next phase, the team-building in the Grand Canyon, we move on to L.O.F.I." Murray's mind became fraught with visions; how fortuitous! He had always wanted to see the Grand Canyon.

"What do you do at the Grand Canyon?" seemed to be the best Murray could muster up intellectually to this new-found bit of adventure.

"I am sure you have to hike. I am sure we are not flying there just to take a picture," Jacob exhibited great forbearance here with Murray's lack of knowledge.

"How do you know this? I thought the principal team building training rotated?" Murray posed this query for he felt sure that he knew about the rotation.

"I looked it up!"

"Already?" Murray Moore knew he had to accept. Though his commitment to the idea and ideals of being a principal had been equivocal up to this point; the accolade of nomination required at the very minimum consideration, and if you put that with not one, but two trips—the first to the Grand Canyon and the second to Guam—Murray could not logically produce a reason not to further investigate. As for Jacob and Murray, this could be their finest hour.

CHAPTER SIX

"The best argument against democracy would be a five-minute conversation with the average voter."

WINSTON CHURCHILL

Murray and Jacob lilted down Oxford Millville Road heading toward Miami University for their individualized interviews concerning their eligibility for the United States Principalship Certificate. Both educators were flummoxed by the rapidity with which the process had advanced. Murray recalled stopping back in Feinauer's office to tell him that he accepted the opportunity to go forward in the process.

"Well, Murray, the government does not dither. This year's candidates are being scheduled to train. You must first pass an interview. The review board, comprised of a rather eclectic group of intellectuals, will review your college transcripts, the question-naire you completed, along with a letter I composed to them con-cerning your technique and personality. They will conduct the rest." Murray found it queer that he answered a myriad of questions that appeared to have nothing to do with running a high school or teaching a class.

"Furthermore, Murray, I like your classroom management skills, your devotion to your career, the monk life you chose, and your level of intellect displayed perpetually." Moore remembered the referral he had brought down that had yet to be addressed. Its existence antagonized him; Principal Feinauer continued, "By the way, Jacob related to me a concern of yours over a referral. I will take it. What would you like done?"

"He told you," Murray initially responded, then concluding that Jacob had done him a service, "Well, off the record, I believe that human piece of offal should be put on a raft and pushed out to sea, maybe towards Cuba. On the record, I feel confident to leave the matter to your discretion."

"No problem, I will handle him. As for your interview, under-stand that they are individualized per candidate. You and Jacob will not receive the same questions. The panel acquainted itself with your background. The only coaching that I will provide lies in this: be honest. Do not answer what you think they want to hear; speak from your soul upon the issues and leave it at that. If your answers do not suffice and you ostensibly fail, do not fret. Better to be weeded out early as opposed to too late." All throughout the discussion, Feinauer appeared far more animated than his usual phlegmatic persona. His beseeching of honesty seemed to burnish an image in Murray's mind.

Murray, glancing over at Jacob as he drove, felt compelled to inquire as to his thoughts concerning the interviews. "Any idea what they will ask?"

"The most plausible tactic lies in the winsome manner in which they ask questions extremely familiar to your teachings. However, their analysis of the minutiae in your response can and will bring down upon you the wrath of the committee." This type of response from Jacob unnerved Moore. As a matter of fact, the duress incurred by the interview had become rather stressful. Throughout his career, Moore had been adamant about keeping teaching jocund; he always juxtaposed his position with that of the principal and felt that teaching afforded the educator latitude, while the principal's post contained a plentitude of stress. This entire episode with Bobby Feinauer had Murray completely discombobulated.

"What do you think of all this?" Murray's biting nerves washed away all grandiloquence, especially when speaking privately with Jacob.

"You mean the principal interview? Man, I have been waiting my entire career for this. Why?"

"Not sure what I think about it." Murray's resolve, inspired by Wilde's determination, began to wane.

"Are you nuts?" Jacob's reproachful tone nettled Murray. "When you are the principal, you are the man! D.C. conferences, meeting Senators and Congressman, audience with the President. Are you nuts? We have been living for this!"

"You are probably right." Murray hoped his less than resolute response would provide Jacob the ammo to convince him of the beneficial nature of this quest.

"Hey man, you can't go at this interview or process in a timorous fashion. This represents the real deal. We are like the town detective gaining an interview with the Central Intelligence Agency; we are going to the major leagues here."

"I am good; just thinking out loud." Murray now taciturn hoped to find a way to bring the conversation to a close. Maybe his nerves were playing tricks with him. Elephantine decisions in life always posed a stumbling block for him, and this could be a potential career game changer. He much preferred putting the strenuous pressure on his students, not have that type of career pressure applied to him.

One of Murray's favorite exercises occurred during the first day of class. The bell would ring in every class in the building and the bulk of the teachers would email the class the rules, the assignments and all of the other inane refuse from their computer files. Murray, more a maverick, enjoyed a "shock and awe" approach. He preferred to offer a break from the norm, teach them something tangible, and of course, shove it up their noses doing it. He would wait for the bell to ring before presenting himself, explode out of the backroom (a.k.a. "Little Britain") whistling "God Save the Queen," swagger through the room, out the front classroom door, stop, turn, and say, "Well, come on!"

Students never need much cajoling to leave a classroom, and in fact this lesson generally reflected the only time Murray did indeed take his class from the room. Moore would proceed down the hall to the wall outside the restrooms where he had the names painted with the mini-biographies of Mayfield's "finest" students. He felt a list of high school drop outs and other pariah that left Mayfield to end up in L.O.F.I., or worse, apropos painted outside the lavatories. He referred to it as "Poetic Symbolism." This proverbial wall of shame exhibited the country's ne'er-do-wells—the excrescence of the community, the blemishes that had to be expurgated from life. He always began with a speech.

"Greetings young Alphas. My quotidian task throughout this year shall be like that of Jesus. I am to show you the light, the way. I am not here to hornswoggle you into following a road less traveled or more traveled. In front of you, painted upon this wall, reflects a veritable lollapalooza of losers in life." He recalled this year as particularly amusing for not only did the excursion provide a reminder to students their fate if they failed to succeed in school, it also served as a trenchant lesson demonstrating the efficacious nature of America's immigration policy. He glanced out into the crowd of young, fresh faces and purposely picked a Mulan-esque looking young lady to lay the groundwork of portents to come. "You, your name?"

"Diane Shao."

"Born here Ms. Shao?"

"No, Chinese."

"Parents didn't want you to live under an oppressive regime where women have little rights and the people have little voice, eh?"

"Not really. Catholic nuns found me on a dock in Shanghai in a cardboard box. My parents left me for dead."

"Wow. A tragic start to life; unfortunately, a start not uncommon in China, especially for girls. Let me guess, some evil American organization brought you to the States and put you up for adoption."

"Uh…my adoptive parents wanted to give me an opportunity for a good education."

"Sure, sure. Women are abused around the planet, America and Europe the exception. I would like you to pick a name off this wall of shame. Any name. Then read it to your classmates."

"Uh…okay."

"Go ahead. I know a plethora exist from which to choose. Please, Ms. Shao, pick and read."

"Alright. Andrew Adams."

"What about him?" Murray inquired.

"Andrew Adams attended Mayfield from 2064-2066. Graduated bottom of his class. Covicted of larceny and trafficking. Three strikes. Sentenced to life on L.O.F.I."

"Well read. Thanks." Murray scanned the hall, looking for another student to exemplify his point; he found one based upon the countenances to further his point on multi-culturalism. "Your name?"

"Samantha Chang."

"Please, Miss Chang, pick a name and read."

"Sure, Iain Warrell-King attended Mayfield from 2071-2073. Expelled. Found dead in Churchill Woods 2074. Cause of death: homicide."

"Well done, two for two. You see folks, these names represent the refuse of our society. All share two things in common: poor students and untimely deaths." Murray felt this lesson, though reprehensible to some, served as a trenchant lesson about life. "One more please, you," he called out to a tall, robust looking lad a solid half a foot taller than himself, "Your name?"

"Matt Van Houten"

"Well, Master Van Houten, judging by your accent, or lack there of, you were born in the states. How about your parents?"

"Born in Germany, near Freiburg on the French border."

"I would have packed up and moved also with the western wind blowing the stench of France over my village. Pick a name please and read."

"Certainly, Kyle Medley. Attended Mayfield 2069-2072. Dropped out. Found dead in Great Miami River. Cause of death: suspected suicide."

"Thank you Master Van Houten. Would anyone care to tell me what fails to appear on this wall of shame?" Moore knew that his lesson, shocking to some, reflected a tenable reality when it came to a student's comprehension of his/her society. "You miss, your name?"

"Lina. Lina Ran."

"Forgive my Oriental ignorance, from which country does your family hail?"

"I am part Cambodian, Chinese, and Thai. A mutt," Lina coquettishly grinned.

"Well, Ms. Ran you are a genetic mess. Mutt would be a most apropos term. What don't you notice on this wall?"

"There are no Oriental names," Lina pronounced.

"Well, I beseech all, please tell me, anything else."

"I don't see any foreign names up on the wall," commented Diane Shoa.

"No German names for sure," interjected Van Houten.

"Very good. My young Alphas, my students for this year, this wall exemplifies two things. First, the value of the immigrant as a team player. People from all over this globe come here and participate to the full extent of their abilities, reflecting the greatness of this nation. Furthermore, as you can see from the cornucopia of names up and down this wall, if you fail to get educated your fate will be unpleasant." His lesson worked well with names of foreign persuasion; however, the other group that never makes the wall, the Mormons, proved a tad too difficult to peg down. No matter their walk of life, socio-economic status, race, color, or nationality, Murray Moore had yet to meet a Mormon he didn't like.

Murray Moore suddenly found himself disturbed from his warm reverie by the parking of the car. His rumination of earlier in the school year had placed him in a dreamlike trance all the way to his arrival at Miami University Oxford. Jacob Wilde observed him, saw the uncomfortable look upon his countenance then inquired, "You ready? You alright?" Murray complied. He felt a tad apprehensive, but ready nonetheless. Besides, if all went wrong, he would go back to the classroom. If all went right, he would be boldly going where he never thought he would go before.

As they entered McGuffey Hall, Jacob and Murray noticed a sign blazoned with the words "Potential Principals Here." While ruminating on the fact that alliteration always had a place in the world, both men noticed a young lady, smartly dressed heading in their direction from the sign.

"Are you two here for the principal interview?" They nodded in affirmation. She continued, "Good. I am Emily Lohrey, Dean of the Educational Department here at Miami, Oxford. If you two men would scan your thumbprints on the tablet located on the desk behind me, you can proceed into the auditorium and await being called into the interview. The process shouldn't take too long today, there are only nine candidates and this represents only the preliminary screening process."

After this salutation, Murray began to feel a tad more sanguine concerning the process which had him unnerved on the ride over. He entered with Jacob, noticing that seven others already rested inside the auditorium; all seated up near the front. They proceeded upfront, took a couple of seats, and glanced around the room at the rather austere setting. They had no more than sat down when an official-looking, middle-aged woman crossed the stage and took over the podium.

"Greetings, potential principals, I am Kyle McDougal. I am the regional recruiter of education for the federal government. I want to stress that I am not here to preach to you about doctrine, orthodoxy or political dogma." She expressed this list as if they were sacrosanct topics. "I want to welcome you and remind you that today you will be interviewed by a panel of specialists who represent a rather eclectic gathering of government officials. I can not stress enough, relax, answer the questions honestly and what will be, will be."

While opining away in his seat, Murray fidgeted back and forth, then decided that the speaker, Kyle McDougal must be correct. Nothing to worry about. Just answer the questions. She had stressed that all of the questions asked reflected an extensive researching of each potential principal and to relax and enjoy this auspicious occasion. Jacob glanced at Murray with that look of "relax" and Murray did just that. When Murray finally heard his name to be interviewed, he casually moved into the room and faced a panel of three. All rose to greet and shake hands.

"Good morning Mr. Moore. I am Colonel Elizabeth Nutt of the Federal Government's Pedagogical Research Department. I am career military with a specialist's degree in psychological operations. With me today are Dr. Lauren Hauer, with expertise in the field of secondary education and Jennifer Alliston who represents the Principals' Guild of the United States. We will be asking you a few questions and expecting completely honest responses. I cannot stress enough the imperative nature of honesty in this and every step of the principal process. Do you have any questions?" finished Colonel Nutt.

"No."

"Mr. Moore," interjected Dr. Hauer, "we have studied your resume, transcripts, and work history. What we need now from you will elucidate upon your personal dogma. Please, answer succinctly and honestly."

"Remember," interrupted the Alliston woman, "do not over-think the questions. Just answer."

"I am ready."

"Okay," stated Colonel Nutt, "We have read in your records that you are familiar with Jonathan Swift's *A Modest Proposal.*"

"Yes, I adore Swift. Don't we all?" If Moore hoped for levity, the hope died. Three stoic faces stared back at him.

"Mr. Murray, please validate the logos used by Jonathan Swift in his pamphlet *A Modest Proposal.*" Murray initially felt a degree of perplexity, for addressing literature seemed a strange approach to vetting a principal. Murray felt incredulous when contemplating the advice he received to answer from the heart. In the presence of students, his level of verbosity hit high levels; here, though, Murray's initial inclination would have been to remain laconic. Seeing his façade of assuredness fade, Dr. Hauer interjected a comment attempting to assuage Murray's apprehension, "Please, let your answer be your feelings."

"Well," Murray, feeling the question innocuous enough, decided to take the advice he had received by more than one person, be resolute and state your core values. This compellingly simple advice would prove easy to follow, for Murray possessed a proclivity for honesty, even if that honesty could be hurtful; therefore, he continued, "I believe the logos used by Jonathan Swift represents an egregious error in being overly Spockian. Though the pamphlet enumerates the copious reasons for the infanticide and cannibalism, the logos collapses in on itself for its misapplication."

"Please," added Alliston, "continue."

"Well, logically speaking, the children never had a chance to grow, blossom, and thus prove themselves and their individual worth to society. If any creature should be cannibalized for the good of society, it should be those who are a persistent burden upon society. Eat the convicts. Eat the lethargic. Eat the deadbeat dropouts. Eat the people who care more to destroy the system of government and society and spare the children who may grow up and build the better computer or application. Aside from the issues of ethos, along with pathos, being expunged, this idea has multiple flaws, though I must add, reflects a particular level of brilliance in the laying out of the argument." Murray scoured his brain and felt his response honest, even to a fault.

"A quick follow up, Mr. Moore," inserted Dr. Hauer, "Would you advocate eating the prisoners on the United States Federal Penal System Island?"

"Absolutely, if only logos served as the basis of our system of thought. When ethos and pathos are included, the argument disappears immediately.

"Good. Second question then, please," continued Colonel Nutt.

"I am ready."

"Second question then. Another literary question, explain why the end of *Of Mice and Men* reflects a moral injustice."

"I hate to insinuate that your questions are tragically flawed, but they are." Murray daringly stated.

"Explain please," this time Alliston added again.

"Well, for instance the postulate leaves something to be desired. In our current world, this type of mercy killing would reflect outright murder, for modern America has developed a social safety net to keep a man like Lennie from hurting himself or others. Now if we view the same scenario through the prism of America during the 1930s, the act exhibits justification, not to mention a sense of compassion. Lennie had no place in that society, for our society's tolerance of the helpless, sick, and unstable had yet to develop. Remember, old Candy wished he had, and young Travis actually did, shoot their respective dogs. Unfortunately, the business of mercy killing evokes the pathos and makes a muddle of ethos, but logically it can be deemed nothing less than a necessity."

Murray's confidence waned, for oftentimes people take umbrage regarding the topic of mercy killing, for did not these two questions cross that line? Moore began to surmise that the panel sat in disbelief for his answers did reflect the impingement of his country's national morals. However, he had been instructed to deliver verity; and truth proved to be the response that he gave to the questions—no prevarication. Throughout his life, Murray had been praised and demonized at times for his unwillingness to engage in circumlocution, especially when touching upon an issue of national importance. The panel had asked numerous questions, some ambiguous, some evoking ambivalence, but finally ending with, "As a science fiction teacher, along with your use of the adjective 'Spockian,' please answer the following." Clearly the question had been concocted during the interview, "In the 20th century classic film *Star Trek: the Wrath of Khan*, Mr. Spock selflessly sacrifices himself for the ship stating that 'the needs of the many outweigh the needs of the few.' If you found yourself in Captain Kirk's position, but without a Spock, what would you do knowing that you yourself could not enter the chamber being the captain of the ship?"

These questions seemed all too facile for a principal preliminary examination, for the answers and responses—at least in Murray's mind—were incontrovertible. The logos applied by Mr. Spock to Murray reflected an axiomatic response, not critical thinking. Though he felt he may be viewed as vicious, he did not vacillate with his response. "If in the same scenario as Captain Kirk, and unable to enter the chamber myself, I would send in a volunteer either by request or gunpoint."

"Why?" Countered Dr. Hauer.

"Simple. Spock stated the verity of the matter succinctly."

"How would you feel sending someone to their death?" this time Colonel Nutt.

"Being a weak-kneed leader here would result in the death of all with a clear conscience. As a leader, you must make bold decisions and face the consequences later. If I had to force a crew member in, I would personally mourn the loss; however, I would focus upon all that survive. I would view it as sending a ship of people to their life. Sorry if my response seems callous." It did not. The interview ended shortly thereafter, and then they were dismissed. Meeting in the parking lot later after their separate interviews, neither Jacob nor Murray felt assured as to their individual performance; and indeed, the queries had been modified, especially the field questions. Jacob answered similar scenarios but concerning historical events. Murray inquired, "Can you remember them?"

"Of course," responded Wilde, "First, explain why Winston Churchill should have warned Coventry that the Germans would bomb it. Second, why William Tecumseh Sherman should have been hanged for war crimes, and third, during the last war on terrorism, defend America's 'enhanced interrogation' even though the world clearly decried 'torture' and did nothing in response."

"How did you answer?"

"Brilliantly easily," continued Jacob, "Churchill had to sacrifice a town to win the war. Next, total war unfortunately requires nastiness to civilians as well as soldiers. War cannot play nice with anyone; only a muttonhead could construct rules for warfare. And on the last one, enhanced interrogation, who cares? Honestly, these international criminals received three hots and a cot; however, if we give them a free shower via water boarding on a tropical island, Cuba then, or Guam now, who cares? The terrorists of this century categorically rejected civilization, flushing toilets, women's rights, gay marriage, and modernity. They got what they deserved. Kill 'em all, let God sort them out." Wilde had always been far more resolute on the political issues than Murray had ever dreamed of being.

CHAPTER SEVEN

"I went to the woods because I wished to live deliberately, to front only the essential facts of life, and see if I could not learn what it had to teach, and not, when I came to die, discover that I had not lived."

HENRY DAVID THOREAU *WALDEN* – **1854**

A week later, Murray Moore sat at his desk, feet up, sipping coffee, reading his email off his hand-held tablet. As he perused his email, he caught a glimpse of one sent from Principal Feinauer labeled urgent and composed tersely, "Results in, report to my office after school." Since the interviews at Miami, both Jacob and Murray anxiously awaited some feedback. Many were nominated, but few were selected to move forward. Statistics revealed that only about 10% made it through to the end, which fascinated Moore. Scanning the email, he saw that Feinauer sent it after Wilde's planning period, and knowing Jacob's tendency to only check email before and after school, it seemed apropos to amble down to Wilde's room to inform him about the long awaited news. Plus, who knew what topic of discussion would be afoot in Wilde's room? Murray tucked his computer tablet under his arm, grabbed his coffee cup, then bolted down the hall.

"Mr. Moore! Good morning." Looking up from their mural work, two of Moore's students, Ben Forsyth and Erik Hoffman, greeted him blistering down the hall. Murray had a penchant for obliviously cruising the halls lost in thought until his students broke his reverie with either questions, comments, or general salutations.

"Looking good boys! I would know that disgruntled employee anywhere, especially in the shadow of Trinity Church." The boys had been assiduously painting in one of the free panels of masonry left in the Language Arts hallway. Nearly every available nook and cranny of the hall, offices, and classrooms had been painted with literary characters, quotations, and scenes. Inspired by a nearly 100-year-old painting of the whale Moby Dick, the custom blossomed nearly seventy years prior, by the then English teacher Jared Soergel who commissioned the painting of Big Brother utilizing George Orwell's visage. Upon his retirement, he requested that the hall be finished, then the classrooms. More compelling to the cause, on Soergel's death bed, for he died the death of a teacher, surrounded by colleagues and students past and present, he reiterated that request, which then department chair Vicki Tate, a lover of art, vowed to continue the tradition until completed. Every succeeding chair subsequently continued and all students and faculty knew their names for somewhere in each mural, the name of the student artist and department chair appears. From 2008 through Murray's present day the names of past leaders: John Luzader, Mike Jasper, David Phillips and Bonnie Sheehy, manifested themselves throughout the wing. A quote on the wall near the top of the hallway reads, "I, Jared Soergel, hereby commission the Sistine Chapel of Mayfield High School." The art represented the envy of the Midwestern section of the American Public School system; the tradition had imitators around the nation.

"Bartleby looking rather svelte lads."

"Thanks Mr. Moore," responded Forsyth.

"Which would be better," queried Hoffman, "to have him hold the parchment or let it flutter toward the ground in disgust?"

"Artistic license boys! Do it your way. I just want the painting."

"Yes, but we want you to give us your opinion."

"I would 'prefer' not to," Murray grinned perfunctorily, then walked on down the hall with the boys laughing and adding, "Good one!"

Traipsing through the hall, Murray detoured into the teachers' workroom to commandeer some more coffee, sauntered through the library, strolled by and patted the one hundred-plus-year-old, fully bound Oxford English Dictionary, then waltzed down to Wilde's door to reconnoiter before entering.

"You two never grow up," Murray heard at his back, as he spied through the window of Wilde's classroom door, snickering to himself. He turned to find a colleague, Liz Gladish wryly smiling and shaking her head.

"Buenos Dias, me favorito teacher-o of la esquela."

"Nice, I see your Spanish remains as weak as ever," scolded Gladish.

"Gracias! Perdone. Vaya con Wild-o!" Though Murray knew Spanish, he loved to butcher it for the comedic relief and to the great annoyance of the Spanish teachers.

"Wrong conjugation. Yo voy!" Gladish hollered back over her shoulder heading in the other direction. Murray chuckled to himself, then burst into Jacob Wilde's class while he attempted to lecture.

"Well, well, well, Mr. Murray. What brings you to our discussion on the Mount LeConte Summit?" Moore hit the jackpot of political discussions; the Mount LeConte Summit offered one of the best chances to work with students over the flaws of partisan politics.

"Just stopping by, I will wait until after the lecture to chat with you. By all means continue." The Mount LeConte Summit proved to be the fulcrum of the Great Compromise of 2025. With the economic collapse of Europe following a decade and a half of financial deficits, malfeasance, and overspending, the hoard of rioters all but destroyed even the strongest economic countries. Whether deemed a civil war, revolutionary war, whatever, Europe plunged into economic chaos, social unrest, and neo-fascism as immigrants had to be protected by the faltering governments while the out of work and hungry masses engaged in a vigilante warpath. America, long following in Europe's economic footsteps on deficit spending, found itself lurching over a precipice due to political in-fighting, a morass of legislative gridlock, querulous partisan political opponents and a fastidious constituency. Wilde loved to lecture on LeConte; Moore loved to hear of it.

"What Senator does history credit for starting the Great Compromise?" questioned Wilde as he scanned the class for answers. "Yes, proceed," pointing a finger toward an eager student.

"Senator Johannes Schmitt of Tennessee," replied Cavalaris from the back of the room.

"Excellent, Jordan. According to your class BLOG and website, I requested to know the full eclectic group assembled on this now infamously tragic, yet politically expedient excursion to the top of Mount LeConte. Kristen, if you please." Wilde, forever the iconoclast, refused to quit lecturing on a consistent basis for the pedagogical community had forever labeled the practice an anathema. Wilde, along with Murray, always addressed this so called abomination with particular scorn and deemed it a spurious claim. There are those who can lecture, and those who cannot.

"Uh," continued Kristen Bevins, "Besides Senator Schmitt, liberal Congressman Adam Reed of Ohio, Independent Congressman Mahatma Belarski of Pennsylvania, Evangelical Congressman Douglass Lopina from Kansas, Mormon Congresswoman Emma Bowers from Utah, Conservative Senator Kim Young of New York, and Liberal Senator Colin Reusch of California."

"Well done, Kristen." Wilde paused and glared around the room to locate the snickering student, "Ray Kuertz, what do you find so humorous?" Kuertz quickly quieted himself and looked around the room for mischievous support, receiving none. Ray had been discussed ad infinitum between Wilde and Murray as another potential for the "Wall of Shame." Putting more effort in frivolity than serious students, though not quite a pariah yet, Kuertz often found himself scolded by faculty and peers alike. Ray gulped and responded.

"I am laughing because the idiot liberal from California fell off the top of the mountain."

"Mr. Kuertz, I hardly find the death of Senator Colin Reusch a cause for jocularity."

"Yeah, but," he paused, "Mr. Wilde, who falls off a mountain in Tennessee?" Murray drifted off momentarily; he flashbacked to his own civics class in college where he learned of the Mount LeConte Summit, not truly embracing it at the time, but more so as he continued to teach.

"Well, what happened? Who would like to share? Yes, Ms. Toensmeyer, please enlighten our young Neanderthal, Ray here, who wallows in human tragedy much like a pig in slop." Katie astutely edged up in her seat going from straight to straighter.

"He fell off an edge as they were leaving from the spot watching the sunset, right?"

"Exactly, Senator Reusch and the lawmakers were viewing the sunset on the Cliff Tops behind the Mount LeConte Lodge. As they turned to go, Senator Reusch misjudged his step and over he went a good hundred feet down. He didn't survive the impact with the rocks below. Naturally, that ended the summit, though only a day remained anyway." Wilde needed to change the conversation, for the results of the summit directly led to the Great Compromise; furthermore, he needed to adhere to the lesson that reflected the information the students needed to comprehend.

After further questioning the students upon the research of the weekend, Wilde ascertained that the rote facts had been memorized, but the political rationale, along with stagnated quagmire into which D.C. deleteriously descended, proved to be a nebulous enigma to this generation since political parties and partisanship had faded into the annals of time. It made perfect sense to the class for Schmitt to embark on this mountain seminar and return—regardless of the accident—with a gang of six called the Inklings. With the college preparatory curriculum being based upon interactive group and solo research based on-line inquiries, American students long embraced that now cliché, "United We Stand, Divided

We Fall" mantra that long found itself etched on coin, currency, and edifices throughout the land.

"Let me get this straight, Mr. Wilde," questioned Anna Braam—another immigration victory—wearing a rather dubious expression upon her face, "Politicians picked sides, then disdainfully attacked the others?"

"Exactly!"

"To what end? Why?" Anna continued, "How did anything ever get accomplished? And, can that happen again?"

"Let me assuage your fears Anna. Since the Inklings came down from Mount LeConte this coterie of politicians, this gang of six reeled in another six senators and fifty or so congressmen and congresswomen. Be it remembered, that Senator Reusch at the time of his death served as Minority leader in the Senate while Johannes Schmitt served as Senate Majority leader. Congressman Lopina served as Speaker of the House and his power in the South proved unparalleled. When Senator Schmitt and Congressman Lopina brought in the Independents with Congressman Belarski and the Mormons with Congresswoman Bowers from Utah, the Inklings moved into phase two. The numbers they drew in amounted to enough votes in both chambers to control all legislation; thus, they declared themselves the 'Fighting Moderates.' Questions? Yes, Whitney Jo."

"I thought these politicians fervently fought about everything. Since Schmitt's Fighting Moderates did not have a majority, let alone a super majority, how did he get laws passed?"

"Great question Whitney," interjected Jacob, "Simple. When Senator Schmitt stole a nearly equal amount of Democrats and Republicans from each side, closet Independents began to join his ranks, along with other maverick politicians. His numbers swelled. When partisan items were brought forward, Schmitt and Lopina not only eschewed the politician publicly, they harangued them on the Senate and House floors. When bills came into law through the bi-partisan workmanship of the Fighting Moderates, the hard line party members attempted to avenge their public defeats; they first attempted to bring acrimony back into the hall of Congress with more fighting and arguing. Through a series of spurious charges and inimical innuendo, a pair of Senators, Cate Adams from Maine and Congressman Jonathan Stupak of Massachusetts, brought numerous claims against both Senator Schmitt and Congressman Lopina. All charges fizzled. Now, I can tell by your eyes, those names are ringing a bell."

"Weren't they killed in a terrorist attack?"

"Very good, Eric." Jacob Wilde had successfully instigated the type of historical and political discussion he felt most comfortable delivering. "Explain the significance, Mr. Lee." Wilde continued.

"The terrorist attack on Washington D.C. in July of 2025 represented the first time since the attacks of September 11, 2001, that Americans had been attacked on their own soil."

"And the last, Eric," added Anna Braam. Eric glared at Anna momentarily, then decided it best not to respond. Murray Moore internally chuckled to himself for he understood the basis of their animosity towards each other stemmed from their competition to finish first in their class. Eric continued to look up front, Anna in a most haughty fashion, disappointedly gazed at Eric, wanting satisfaction that Eric refused to grant.

"Well class, look at the time!" Wilde realized that the time allotted for class had quickly dwindled to nothing and judging by the students' faces, they concurred. So much for the imbeciles who preach against lecturing. Intellectuals crave knowledge from those who can supply it. "Tonight, I want you to research the topics investigated. Judging by your facial expressions, you were shocked at the names killed in the Congressional Massacre of '25. I know you all knew about it, the when, where, why; now you understand the who and the significance. Tonight look into the policies of those lawmakers killed in the attacks; furthermore, peruse the main points of the big three in the Great Compromise. This will set the stage for America's transformation from political parties to independent lawmakers." He glanced up at the clock and saw Murray Moore rising from the back desk, "I see I have gone over time again; you are released."

As the students filed out, Jacob inquisitively looked at Murray and without explanation, knew that the news from the Principal Screening had arrived. Murray did not bother to show him the email on his computer tablet, he just stated, "See you in Feinauer's office after school."

With that, Murray Moore bustled down toward his classroom for the change meant he now had a class coming in; likewise, Jacob Wilde, too, had as many entering the classroom as leaving.

CHAPTER EIGHT

"However, [political parties] may now and then answer popular ends, they are likely in the course of time and things, to become potent engines, by which cunning, ambitious, and unprincipled men will be enabled to subvert the power of the people and to usurp for themselves the reins of government, destroying afterwards the very engines which have lifted them to unjust dominion."

GEORGE WASHINGTON
FAREWELL ADDRESS SEPTEMBER 17, 1796

After school, preparing to see Bobby Feinauer, Murray Moore waited anxiously for Jacob Wilde beneath the "Wall of Shame" mural. The cacophony of noise began to die as the students began clearing the hall, minus the small groups of students still cavorting around the locker bay. He glanced up at the wall filled with the lethargic, hedonistic, and degenerate. He chuckled at a couple of names listed in the paint of infamy: Alex Pettit, who attended until three years ago, along with Aaron Lawson of the same year. Murray spent a school year attempting to discern the depths of Alex Pettit's lassitude, so when his homeless body turned up under a bridge over the Little Miami River, he had to admit that surprise did not cross his mind. Behind his name read "death from vagrancy." The atypical entry upon the wall fell to his friend Lawson, who wound up in L.O.F.I. much to the consternation of many of his instructors. Moore's excitement began to atrophy standing under the "Wall of Shame."

He found himself beginning to chronicle the names which had passed his classroom threshold. One of the more troubling upon the list above confounded him; Travis Ritzie had exhibited so much promise. Three or four years ago, they all began to amalgamate after a while, Murray remembered teaching capitalism in conjunction with H.G. Wells' *The Time Machine,* when a promising young upstart name Travis Ritzie interjected upon the glories of the American economic system, since he apparently took umbrage with the anti-capitalistic tone of England's proud Fabian. Murray generally ambivalent towards those making the "Wall of Shame," felt a particular sting with this social miscreant for Moore wrote Ritzie a letter of recommendation that landed him in the business school at Ohio State, then he subsequently moved right into Morgan Stanley and international business. The last Murray saw Ritzie, police led him fettered from the federal courthouse into a van bound for L.O.F.I. for six felonies that included embezzlement, fraud, perjury and extortion in multiple forms. So much promise destroyed by capitalistic avarice.

Moore turned away from the mural for that steady shuffle of feet that served as the antecedent of Wilde's advent could be heard long before Jacob arrived. Without a word, the two men started down the hall under the ubiquitous eyes of all the literary and historical figures gazing upon them. The sullen mood brought on by the reflective perusal of the wall, quickly melted and transcended to sublimity as the two headed for the office of Principal Feinauer. Murray could not fathom at that particular moment the extent of his fickle feelings; first melancholy at the wall, then elation coming down the hall, now foreboding entering the office, all the while

Jacob Wilde manifested an air of aplomb and equanimity. Murray took a surreptitious glance at Jacob who provided him a look of empathy, on one hand, for Murray's nervousness; yet, a degree of confidence as a mountaineer approaches the base of a mountain. Wilde had no reservations.

"Gentleman, come in. Relax." Principal Feinauer shook their hands and indicated to them both to sit. "Thanks for your promptness." Neither man spoke. "Well, as you know, I did receive official reports on two of my top educators. Needless to say, I am proud to gloat that not only one, but both of you have passed the selection process. You will both begin phase two of the principal training program."

Murray, cognizant that nothing came to mind to say, relied on Jacob to carry the conversation. Feinauer's candid nature in the matter seemed a tad surreal, but Jacob, adroit in matters of elocution, inquired, "How did we score? I mean, if they do score. Plus, I am sure the next step will be soon on the horizon."

"Actually, a score for the interview does not exist. You either pass or fail. Of the scores of nominees interviewed at Miami and the scores throughout the states that day, only four from this Midwestern region made it through to the next level. Think about it boys, around a hundred nominated from this region of states, only four make it through the screening and testing. And you two are from the same building! I assure you, that represents an unprecedented event. You two should be proud."

"What next level, boss?" inquired Jacob.

"Before we get to that point, I need to expound upon some items of the gravest importance. First, you two have been awarded quite a commendation. The myriad questions you answered at Miami were designed to probe your ethos, logos, and pathos. Never contemplate how you should respond. Speak the truth. At the end of your training, an aggregate of responses to physical, mental, and intellectual stress will be compiled and analyzed. At any point, a candidate who exhibits qualities not compatible with the corps will be removed and sent home. Boys, if you make it to the end, you are no longer educators; you are principals. Your lives will be irrevocably changed from that moment on. I believe you two have what it takes. I have been the O'Brien for both of you. In a couple of weeks, a few representatives from the Academy of Principals will be here to conduct a polygraph test upon the two of you, then conduct a preliminary swearing in. Jacob, Murray, you understand?"

To Moore this type of talk resulted in a harrowing effect upon him. All seemed daunting after hearing his speech. Consequently, he felt a strange exuberance for what lie ahead. "Mr. Feinauer?"

"Please Murray, call me Bobby."

"Okay, Bobby. Where do we head next?" timidly inquired Moore.

"Well boys, you will be attending the national conference of principals-in-training." After his answer, Feinauer bore a grin that seemed devilish at best.

"Where?" Jacob boldy asked.

"You will be attending a team building and educational summit at the Grand Canyon in Arizona. Excited?" If Murray had been fraught with angst and Jacob bursting with chutzpah, both evinced an air of boys who found presents under the Christmas tree. "I thought you two would be pleased."

Heading back through the hall up towards their rooms, the two educators—one filled with apprehension, the other anticipation—walked silently until they reached the closed classroom of Murray Moore. No matter Moore's mood—aggravation, ennui, melancholy—nothing turned him from dour to elation quicker than his students. Murray could be nothing but felicitous when his "disciples" called upon him to divulge some nugget of knowledge. He could jump from quiescent to garrulous instantly, and now, gathered in front of his door stood a group of students.

"Look out, Mr. Wilde! Call for assistance. The Mormons are on the prowl!" A hardy laugh erupted from the group of students. Murray, recognizing one of his favored religious group, hailed them. In all of his years of teaching, Mormons proved to be the only domestic group he taught which rivaled the intellectual prowess exuded by the Indians and Orientals. The Mormons, with their indefatigable work ethic, coupled with their impeccable character, made it difficult not to admire them. "What can I do for you guys?" Not prone to heap adulation upon students, Murray, preferring to engage in irreverent humor, glanced over the crew consisting of Brittany Simpson, the DeGraw clan: Jeffrey, Curtis, and Sarah, along with two or three he didn't recognize for they were too young to have been in his class yet.

"We came to congratulate you on your appointment to the Academy of Principals."

"Well, Brittany. I didn't tell anyone yet; how do you know?"

"Mr. Moore," Brittany dragged her voice out in a playful and childish manner, "You know, we Mormons stay in contact."

"How well I know that; your group's ability to disseminate information has never ceased to amaze me." Jacob looked incredulously at Murray who continued, "My question would be this, why on Earth would you know that information already?"

"Mr. Moore," Sarah, stepping forward, flaming red hair symbolically reflecting her current disdain for her instructor's memory lapse, "Don't you remember who founded the Academy of Principals?"

Murray diligently racked his brain trying to comb his historical knowledge, but the tumultuous pace of the last few days had rendered him mentally exhausted. Quickly stepping forward, Curtis cordially responded, "Senator Emma Bowers of Utah from the Inklings."

"Emma Bowers belonged to the Mormon faith," finalized Jeffrey. "Our faith, LDS, proudly supports the Academy of Principals and the educational institutions of which it supervises." Murray felt languid and apologetic.

"I am sorry that I forgot that. However, that still doesn't answer my question, how did you guys all find out?" With that question, the normally quiet group became fidgety and loquacious.

"Well, Mr. Moore, we have to go to our religious studies," stated Brittany attempting to efface the enigma of their knowing about his appointment. Moore knew better than to try to nail the group down for an answer. The Mormons moved out quickly chatting and waving back. Murray smiled at Jacob, and they decided to call it a day.

The following day, Murray found himself in the classroom of Jacob again during his plan period—this time at the beginning of the class. Remembering that Jacob had assigned research on the terrorist attack on Congress in 2025, along with historical investigation of the Great Compromise and wanting to brush up on all of his history, Murray figured he would kill two birds with one stone—review and enjoy. Being colleagues, friends and intellectual equals, they enjoyed listening to the other lecture. Wilde frequently sat in awe as Moore directed and guided students through various novels, deconstructed their geo-political themes, and then conducted class-based inquiry research on them, having the kids climb right up the ladder of Bloom's taxonomy in developing their intellect. Moore often would chuckle at Wilde when he would concede that Moore indeed got credit for being the superior teacher because Moore diligently worked to master Wilde's subject matter, but as to the other, Wilde had no interest in reading the literature. "I give you props; you are superior, because I am not reading *Brave New World*, *Fahrenheit 451* or *1984*. I read the Orwell book with animals though. I would rather just study politics." Murray would argue that the books were a study of politics, but he would invariably fall into delight touching upon literary techniques, characterization, thematic implications, and so on. Wilde would toss his hands in the air.

Here today, Murray would be the pupil and Wilde the instructor. Since they shared many of the same students, both enjoyed watching them engaged in other classes, not to mention it offered them an abundance of collaborative tactics to employ with their students.

"Mr. Murray, what are you doing here again?"

"Well, good morning to you too, Ms. Fowee."

"You know I don't mean anything by it"

"Just kidding, Allie. I came to see how you did on your research, and how I can tie it in to the final research projects being presented in my room down the home stretch of the term." The time for class had started and Jacob Wilde stormed into class at his usual brisk pace. He went straight for the front of the class, dishing out his usual one-liners and zingers along the way. Before he could begin class, a rather impatient young lady waved her hand then spat out without acknowledgement.

"Mr. Wilde and Mr. Moore. Mr. Wilde and Mr. Moore!"

"Yes ma'am," spouted Jacob with a look of trepidation upon his face, for Katie Reece, whom both men taught, had an uncanny ability to derail a class faster than anyone the two collectively could think of.

"Oh…Mr. Wilde. Mr. Moore. Did you hear about Cody Rosenbaum?"

"No," stated Wilde. Moore appeared apprehensive.

"Remember Cody, Mr. Moore? Do ya? You once said Cody, 'you are a disgusting human being and a waste of flesh,' remember?"

"I do," Moore admitted. Rosenbaum served as a proof that the public school system, though infallible, did not exhibit perfection; Cody slipped through. He passed the high school entrance test and then proceeded to be a completely uninspired student.

"Well, it just came through on my tablet that a car hit him and killed him when he left work." Moore had great difficulty coming to grips with this sudden bit of information. He felt that he should experience some form of remorse, but his stolid nature on such matters rendered him stoic.

"Thanks for bringing us all down, Katie. Hopefully, the instant message you received turns out erroneous." Jacob stepped in to deflect the attention from Moore, because he remembered discussing the aforesaid student with Murray last year. Jacob also remembered Murray saying that it would have been better if the Rosenbaum kid had never been born. Though he often told students that personally as scathing banter which rolled off of most young people, when he would make such proclamations in the safe confines of the work-room, the dorm, or "Little Britain," he meant it.

"Let us begin class," Wilde appeared frustrated; for the year, quickly waning, would become more and more difficult to teach as the students sniffed that summer air, and he and Murray prepared to jet off to the Grand Canyon. "What did we learn last night about the Congressional Massacre of 2025?"

It took a minute for the students to transition from the reported loss of a former student to the material at hand, but the commonality of deaths in the community due to accidents, murder, suicide, and so on happened enough for the matter to not be overly shocking.

"Mr. Wilde, I am ready."

"Anna Braam, what did you discover?" Wilde instructed, while her rival Eric Lee looked scornfully her way.

"Well, a three-pronged attack against lawmakers on multiple targets took place simultaneously on July 18, 2025. Over 100 people were killed, many were Senators and Congressman," Anna stated concisely.

"Good," Jacob scanned the room for an eager countenance finding one in the back, "Becky Taylor! Who attacked and why?"

"Weren't the terrorists from Yemen and Pakistan?"

"They were. Go on."

"I think they," Taylor looked around apprehensively, "attacked in some buildings and even the Congressional Building, didn't they?"

"They did," Wilde scanned the room to find Murray twitching his head in the direction of two gentlemen who perpetually needed a foot in their respected backsides. "Alec Waldeck and Arlie Turner, which of you can inform the class of some of the casualties?"

"Senator Adams of Maine and Congressman Stupak of Massachusetts," offered Arlie with an air of confidence.

"And you Alec," pressed on Wilde.

"I don't know what party they belonged to, but I have on my tablet here Senator Greg Dodge of Michigan, a Congressman Charlie Gray of Oregon, and Anthony Flick a congressman, no, I mean a Senator from Florida," added Waldeck.

"Yeah, don't forget that radical feminist congresswoman from California," added an up until now quiet Eric Lee, "Julie DiNuoscio."

"Very good. How did they attack?" Jacob knew who would revel in this answer; Rory Lloyd, Mayfield's resident intellectual fighting machine. With a black belt in judo and jiujutsu, a grasp of ancient warfare which would intimidate a college professor, and a career goal of military Special Forces, the class expected a profound answer from Rory.

"The attack itself," started Rory, "manifests a brilliant yet lethal plan, untrained for by the secret service. The terrorists drove truck bombs over the underground tunnels leading from the Capitol Building to the Hart Senate Building and Longworth House Building. The trucks were lined and shielded to force the blasts downward using powerful high grade explosives, probably obtained or stolen from the Russians. Then, follow up vans went to each crater and dropped suicide attackers in each using the tunnels as a conduit into the offices and the Capital. Ten senators and thirty-seven representatives killed along with a slew of staffers, Capital police, civilians, etc." Rory leaned back in his chair and finished, "Brilliantly executed; if I may say so."

"Well done, as usual Mr. Lloyd." Wilde continued, "Now the importance lies here; the Mount LeConte Summit had wrapped up at the beginning of the month and Congress had set itself up to vote in August on these enormous matters. Much contention began to brew. Some Senators began to upbraid Senator Schmitt for his power grab; however, much of this clamor died down in the wake of the events, plus a few of the most vocal antagonists of Senator Schmitt were killed in the terrorist attack. The special election waited until November; for obviously in the wake of the attack, American retaliation came into the forefront along with protecting Washington. With the public demanding change and vengeance, Senator Schmitt and his Inklings gathered enough Fighting Moderates and great change came to America." All of this type of information reflected the very minutiae that Murray often ignored, thus inspiring him to brush up in Wilde's class prior to departure.

"Now," Jacob continued, "Who can give me one of the signature bills passed because of the Great Compromise of 2025?"

"I can," added Anna Braam after a nod of the head acknowledgement by Wilde. "First, the Benevolent/Malevolent Act which guaranteed 'cradle to grave' health care for every good standing American."

"Good, Anna. How did this Act get funded?" Wilde prodded.

"The hard line right Conservatives promised the health care that the venerable Liberals on the left pushed. The compromise shut down all maximum security prisons and sent all inmates serving life sentences or facing the death penalty to the island of Guam.

Then with the elimination of welfare and the work-to-eat program set up by the right, the left attained one of their signature causes—universal health care."

"Well done, on your part and theirs. America saved money with a little simple logic. These violent animals did not want to be a productive part of society; therefore, banishment became their fate. Productive Americans were now healthy as well. Eric Lee, I see a hand."

"The second act. I can explain."

"Proceed," Wilde added in a Churchillian manner.

"The Immigration for Malcontents Act where every miscreant sent to L.O.F.I.," Eric Lee saw the admonishing eye, "I mean the United States Federal Penal System on Guam. Every time we sent a prisoner to Guam, we admitted an extra immigrant."

"Good," affirmed Wilde, "the compromise?" He acknowledged Taylor.

"Yes," Becky continued, "All illegal immigrants in 2025 were given a path to citizenship in return that after this date all subsequent illegals would be deemed as 'enemy combatants' housed in GITMO, I mean Guantanamo Bay, until deported or exiled to Guam."

"Very good. Class you must understand that it took some wily politicians to pull this off. They mollified numerous radical elements in the American political spectrum in order to transmute the partisan gridlock into commonsensical legislation." Wilde glancing up at the clock, realizing time quickly moving towards the end of class, pushed on to finish. "Allie Fowee, the last one please."

"The Life, Liberty, and Pursuit of Happiness Act."

"Very good, I picture a rather unctuous arbiter settling this hot button issue," smiled Wilde, "Explain Allie."

"Right-to-life groups finally got their wish. Abortion became illegal, deemed murder even, in all fifty states, so that gays could get married," Fowee's tone manifested to all that she indeed finished her response. Wilde sensed this also, plus he needed to correct her and finish the topic so class could move on.

"Hold on a second," Wilde chuckled a bit. "Same sex marriage did not occur because of the abortion issue exclusively. We want to make sure the argument and rationale are clear here. Senator Schmitt, during the Great Compromise, brought all of the lawmakers in who represented various social appeals. Since the church had been clamoring for decades to end abortion, Schmitt orchestrated a masterful compromise on the banning of abortions, but assured reproductive control for women. In some sort of smoky, backroom deal, same-sex marriage found its way tossed into the compromise. Many conjecture that the Christian church's waning influence in America held in juxtaposition with radical religious extremism found on a global scale helped tilt the issue for the gay community. Be it remembered class, Europe nearly had a holy war. As their socialistic economies crumbled in the second decade of the twenty-first century, radicalized Muslim factions became violent when the shortage of jobs caused the native Europeans to attempt to push the immigrant population out. The Church, not wanting to appear extremist and out-of-date, capitulated."

"That makes more sense, Mr. Wilde." Allie finished.

"Remember class, the title signifies it all—Life, Liberty and Pursuit of Happiness. The Church got its wish, abortion illegal, thus 'Life'; however, you forgot Allie the 'Liberty' enforced—that being all women had every form of birth control available to them free of charge, courtesy of the universal health care. God knows in countries without birth control, women have no rights, hence no liberty. Not a tough sell on the Great Compromise since all of the terrorists came from countries where women had no reproductive rights. I surmise that the Church felt that to stand opposed to women's reproductive rights futile; furthermore, abortion had haunted the religious for decades. A sensible argument could be made to eliminate the practice for only a blind man could fool himself into thinking abortion not murder. Finally, the 'Pursuit of Happiness'—gays could get married. The Church ostensibly had to bite its lip; after all, the unborn babies were granted the right to life, should not same sex couples be granted the same shot at liberty? Remember, part of America's founding doctrine requires its citizens to tolerate their neighbors so long as their neighbors do not attempt to infringe upon their own rights. The government needs to protect that guiding principal. Let's face it; the tolerant nature of our country has often been preserved when big government stepped in the way. Whether 'big government' invaded the South to prevent the disintegration of the Union in the 1860s, sent paratroopers to Arkansas to take the 'Little Rock Nine' to class or impose and enforce Affirmative Action after the Civil Rights Act, times manifest themselves when the Federal Government's push for civility enhances all of our lives. Gays received equal opportunity protection, and the churches were guaranteed that they would never be forced, let alone asked, to marry gays inside a church, mosque, or synagogue—like some religious had feared. The hard line religious groups agreed to quit preaching that gays were going to Hell, and the gays agreed to quit trying to push that their lifestyle be viewed acceptable in the religious world—unless invited of course. Live and let live." Jacob looked up at the clock, glanced at Murray, grinned, then said, "Class dismissed."

CHAPTER NINE

"We have an unknown distance yet to run, an unknown river to explore. What falls there are, we know not; what rocks beset the channel, we know not, what walls ride over the river, we know not. Ah, well! We may conjecture many things."

JOHN WESELY POWELL **1869**
FIRST EXPEDITION GRAND CANYON

A bright, warm day in May, and the clocks were striking three. Murray Moore reluctantly walked down the Language Arts hall heading for a swearing in to the Academy of Principals, along with a lecture that would delineate the events on the horizon at the beginning of the summer hiatus, which would not be a break for Wilde and Moore who would be heading toward the wilds of the Grand Canyon. The weeks since the announcement had been divulged of their training in the Academy had the school in a buzz—a veritable hullabaloo. The building, which normally lacked any modicum of docility in May, now bloomed into an effervescent hubbub of noise fulminating about its two sons about to go off in hopes of returning full-fledged principals.

It had been difficult for Moore to remain didactic in class, for his students habitually wanted to inquire into the subject of his appointment; unfortunately, his knowledge had been nebulous. Even in class, as the students presented their end of the course speeches and presentations, questions invariably went from the topic of the class to the topic of the school. Murray frequently had to repulse questions about that which he did not truly comprehend. Now Moore found himself entering the Community Room, where representatives from the Academy of Principals would swear Wilde and Moore in; this would be followed by a polygraph test for each.

As he entered the door, Principal Feinauer stood shoulder to shoulder with a well-dressed man holding a computer tablet. As soon as their eyes met, the man held out his hand for a shake and introduced himself as Dr. Mathew Larson, PhD psychology. After the initial salutations, Murray made it all the way into the Community Room which had been arranged with a podium up front across from a table with two chairs. Off to the side of the podium and table, ten chairs were arranged. In the back of the Community Room, a couch, next to a table containing a portable computer with a gratuitous amount of wires, sat with a rather cantankerous young looking computer technician.

"Hell's bells! Whoever created this ridiculous polygraph system and its overly complicated set up may they have their heart boiled in their own pudding with a stake of holly shoved through it!" Murray chuckled. He admired anyone who engaged in literary tirades. The technician continued, "What disreputable scallywag would have constructed this pernicious piece of human waste?"

"John, relax," soothed a voice from a female Murray had not noticed, for all of his attention had been turned to the enraged man.

"Mr. Moore. Mr. Wilde," interjected Dr. Larson, "Before you we have Jonathan Erdman, computer technician, along with his assistant and sometime 'keeper' Sarah Wesley. I assure you, despite his petulant behavior at the moment, his computer expertise…well, trust me. He will be fine."

"He gets like this," Sarah stated walking away from Jonathan and heading toward the men. "There are times when he finds the love of his life the bane of his existence."

At that moment, the group had their attention turned to the back of the room by an appalling yelp as Jonathan jumped up to the tips of his toes, holding what appeared to be the last cord needing to be hooked up and spouted out, "From Hell's heart I stab at thee; for hate's sake I spit my last breath at thee." Then the idiosyncratic fellow plugged in the cord, which had caused so much duress and sat placidly in the chair awaiting instruction. Murray thought, *what a strange man.*

By this time, the ten chairs had been filled by the Principal, Assistant Principal, Superintendent, and other school officials. It became completely obvious to Murray and Wilde that their presence up front took precedent over the raging computer technician and his affable assistant. Murray and Wilde took the two seats at the table across from the podium where Dr. Matthew Larson stood waiting. Now that Erdman had become quiescent, Larson began, "First gentleman, we would like you each to submit to a polygraph test. If you successfully are moved on, we will then administer the oath."

Murray volunteered to be tested first. He felt more anguish dealing with this erratic technician than he did about the questions he would be asked. He sat down and the Erdman fellow rather slapdashedly placed electronic monitoring devices on his chest, his head, and his finger. The Wesley woman then would soothingly follow Erdman's work to ensure that it had a comfortable placement upon Murray. Within minutes, Dr. Larson sat down beside Moore and stated, "I have some questions for you. I know that you have heard this before, but I am informing you again, you must answer truthfully. Any questions?" Murray had none. The polygraph test began with a series of baseline questions, but after a dozen or so, Murray began to receive more intriguing ones.

"Alright, baselines over, question one. Once admitted to the Academy of Principals you will be a part of an elite group of former educators. Will you be okay with this?"

"Yes," Murray answered calmly, for in his mind it offered a level of excitement, though he did not comprehend what it meant to be a "former educator."

"Good," Dr. Larson stated looking at the computer data. "Now, as a principal, your colleagues may begin to view you as an officious sell-out working for the government—a pedagogical Uncle Tom mind you. Will you be okay with this?"

"Yes," Murray answered again without the slightest reservation, for his antipathy towards most teachers anyway, provided him with a feeling of superiority which made currying their favor superfluous.

A few more questions interspersed seemed to tie back to the baseline questions. Then Dr. Larson continued, "Question three. Teachers who do not complete the Academy of Principals training find themselves in a quandary, for information divulged at the academy must remain there even if you go back to the classroom. Will you be okay with this?"

"Yes," again Murray had no trouble with this response for he believed that the public did not need to be inundated daily with every piece of information. There are times when discretion in the divulgence of sensitive information becomes tantamount to preserving peace and harmony, in a school, workplace, and home or national security on a global scale. Murray never possessed the bug that made him overly inquisitive.

"Let us move on. Secret Societies represent evil in the world." A pause.

"No." Murray, not hesitating much, thought the questions all odd. He could think of copious secret societies filled with philanthropists acting as benefactors for the community, country, and even the world. Heck, some of the worst societies overtly displayed their collective loathing for man. Skinheads and Nazis represented two malignancies of the world that openly attacked and slaughtered people. On the other hand, the Freemasons, a secret society, helped found America and provided the country with the likes of George Washington, along with a host of other Presidents. Numerous groups work under the radar for the benefit of man and society. A few other seemingly innocuous questions covered topics on authority, duty and loyalty, along with a few concerning leaving the classroom permanently and making decisions affecting the lives of teachers and students. Murray continued to relax and do what he had been instructed to do: answer truthfully. Finally, he finished, rose and walked off, allowing Jacob Wilde to have his test.

Moore had a space of time to nervously sit and ruminate upon the rapidly advancing events changing his life so dynamically. For years, Moore and Wilde enjoyed each other's company, the teaching of students and the challenge of each other's intellect with relative anonymity. All of that could end soon, he thought. Upon Wilde's completion, the pair, then invited to the table for the swearing in, sat cautiously down. Dr. Larson took the podium as Erdman and Wesley stood at attention in the back of the room. The guests, the principal, superintendent, and some with whom Murray and Jacob would later become acquainted, also stood at attention. Dr. Larson spoke.

"Congratulations gentleman, having been proudly nominated by your principal, successfully screened at Miami University, and sufficiently questioned on the polygraph, I, as a representative of the Academy of Principals, would like to swear you two in and begin the process of your conversion. I would like you to repeat after me the oath of the Academy of Principals." Larson read a line, Murray and Wilde repeated. *And so it goes* they both thought.

"I, Murray Mallory Moore, swear by the Almighty that I will be faithful and bear true allegiance to the Academy of Principals, its predecessors and successors, and that I will, as in duty bound, honestly and faithfully defend the Academy of Principals, its predecessors and successors, in person, in principle, and with dignity against all enemies of pedagogy and will observe and obey the dictates of the Academy of Principals, as set forth by predecessors and followed by successors, and the superintendents and other government officials set over me."

Larson smiled, then he began a mild applause followed by the guests. Both were presented with packets of information, travel plans, and tickets to head to the Academy of Principals training held in Grand Canyon National Park that summer. Again, Murray reflected upon the bizarre place to transform an educator into a principal, but, since the process had been successful for nearly fifty years, he felt the best plan of action would be to acquiesce.

"Mr. Moore. Mr. Wilde. From Mr. Erdman and Ms. Wesley in the back and the dignitaries here and some that you will formally meet later, we wish to once again congratulate you and wish you safe travels." He paused, dropped the official tone, then added as a post script, "Oh, and have fun."

Murray and Jacob headed out of the Community Room toward the cafeteria which served at this time of the day as "homework" central. Students awaiting rides, doing group work, looking for tutoring assistance, or just wanting to finish his or her homework prior to heading home, had a window of a few hours after school to finish work and study. Both educators, relieved to be finished with the polygraph and oath, decided to head through the cafeteria toward the dorm for a break and to prepare for dinner. Furthermore, knowing the pitfalls of walking through the cafeteria, both were ready to be whisked off to a table of students struggling with some issue in their respective subject matter. Sure enough, today would be no exception.

"Mr. Moore!" A hand waved erratically back and forth. Murray, not only ready but eager to assist, told Wilde he would catch up later. Heading toward the table, he recognized two of his more outstanding young Alphas, Aly Yorio and Ashley Boomer. Yorio, another assimilated and shining example of the successfulness of the American immigrant recruitment policy and Ashley Boomer, an upstanding minority white student bound for the military to serve on America's pride and joy drone-carriers, patiently and eagerly awaited Murray's arrival at their table. Boomer's future with the drone-carriers intrigued him. These miniaturized versions of the past's goliath aircraft carriers, carried a small crew of sailors, a robust crew of UAV pilots, and a plethora of predator drones, sporting a cornucopia of weapons. These drone-carriers patrolled the world oppressing America's enemies by the invisible hand of technology. Ashley had already made sufficient marks in high school to join this elite training crew. For the last fifty years, the United

States had minimized its force and budget but radically increased its power, scope, and dominance over the world.

"Yes ladies, how can I help?" Moore offered.

"We are working on the end of our project. Remember, we are analyzing H.G. Wells and the evils of capitalism," reminded Ashley. This novel, *The Time Machine*, embodied why Moore chose literature to teach, and not history. Here, Wells implicated capitalism as the downfall of humanity in his hypothetical time traveling tale where man devolved into animals basically due to the rich/poor divide. Moore utilized novels such as this to enumerate the number of mistakes made or changes implemented since the publication.

"I remember. What question do you have?"

"How could Wells be so wrong? Our society, though not perfect, seems to run extremely well on Capitalism," offered Aly.

"Good question, ladies. Remember, Wells' hypothetical novel works on the premise that the divide between rich and poor would continue unfettered as late Victorian England reflected. Your instincts are correct. Capitalism should be proudly credited for its victories and chided for its failures. This, however, reflects a topic paramount to your comprehension; the nations that are Capitalistic have the highest standard of living on this earth. Sure, in Wells' world, the rich, unencumbered, may have well destroyed civilization, but that world dissolved. Great changes occurred since 1900." Moore continued, "World War I, the Great Depression, and World War II forced the first world countries to recognize all levels of society—not only the rich and powerful. Following those tumultuous times, the era of social upheaval occurred—its zenith the 1960s—civil rights, women's rights and on down the line. The 20th century manifested a level of destructive chaos unmatched in history and that spilled over into the early part of our century. The Great Compromise changed it all."

"Now, I know why we were miffed," continued Ashley. "All the data Aly and I have read suggests our system works."

"Right. Like what?" Murray prompted.

"America has had a 3%-4% unemployment rate for nearly fifty years. The national debt went from 19 trillion in 2020 to nearly nothing in forty years. All citizens have health insurance and the aged receive Social Security," offered Ashley.

"Okay, your question?"

"How could Wells be so wrong?" interjected Aly.

"Simple, ladies," Murray offered, "His futuristic scenario offered no compromise."

CHAPTER TEN

The term had ended. The building lay docile. The dust began to settle. Murray Moore reclined in his Union Jack chair ensconced in "Little Britain." Summer exuded the best of times; summer exuded the worst of times; a time for reflection, a time for rumination; a time of liberty, a time of isolation. Many teachers in the summer spent time with their own children, frolicking about the pool or exploring the local library. Murray chose to monk it. Moore loathed summer; he wanted to teach. In moments of extreme rage, anxiety, or melancholy, Murray frequented "Little Britain"—an oasis from the tumult of life. At times when the world beat at Murray from every direction, he would retreat into his mini-redoubt and spurn the world by immersing himself in his less than Jeffersonian library. He felt an intellectual link to the former president and other Age of Enlightenment characters such as Benjamin Franklin and Samuel Johnson. He often found himself hopping from one topic or subject to another, though his passion for science extended no further than the National Geographic Magazine—the last paper periodical publication left in America. However, as he scanned the wall of his scriptorium/library, he laid eyes on the men who sparked his imagination, drove his ambition, and subsequently ruined his one chance at marriage. Tomorrow, the Grand Canyon called; but tonight a full analysis of his life's decision seemed mandatory.

Murray suffered great anticipation, seeing the Grand Canyon, much like the Star of David, hung in front of him; he had wanted to see it, hike it, climb it, sweat in it. In his life, he had made no less than three efforts to make it to Arizona, but Colorado always hindered him with the siren song of the Rocky Mountains. Murray would think when driving across country, "Now I can see Colorado looming ahead of me like the Promised Land." Standing, snatching, then sinking back into his chair, Moore opened one of his prized books—*Last Climb*, a history of Sir George Mallory, a man that exuded all Moore wished to embody, so much so, that he changed his alliterative birth name of Murray Michael Moore to that of Murray Mallory Moore—much to his mother's chagrin. Murray looked around for his mug, hoping for tea—Earl Grey—only to remember he had depleted his box of tea last week. "Blast," his audible disgust. Mallory did not stand alone on the wall; Shackleton occupied spaces adjacent to Sir George. Murray admired them, for both men engaged in arduous, near hopeless quests for king and country, but most of all, because the Antarctic for Sir Ernest and Everest for Sir George infected their souls, rendering them perpetually restless. These represented to Murray, two of the last real men, true explorers, in every sense of the word—unlike the pretty boys of the mid 20th century who rode to the moon in a tin can to hop out and play golf. Willy Loman and Neil Armstrong were a "dime a dozen." Britain's heroic explorers endured endless suffering all for a fleeting moment of bliss—a fleeting moment only the mind of Keats could articulate into words. Moore took up the hobby of mountain climbing—on a novice level of course—and suffered numerous sleepless nights, altitude sickness, brain-busting oxygen deprived headaches, always swearing this time would be the last. However, once home, back in the same routine of school, a mere glimpse of a mountain or a glacier sent his heart racing and his mind concocting places to challenge.

His fickle temperament and rambling desires failed to keep him focused on any one item too long. Teaching served as his anchor, but only in as much as a place to divulge his insatiable appetite for adventure. For Murray agreed with Mr. Tennessee Williams: man naturally must pursue his instincts of lover, hunter, and fighter. Though he wished to emulate the Brits from the Age of Heroism, he surely would not carry it so far as to attempt Everest, but maybe an excursion to Kilimanjaro; he would never walk to the South Pole, but would kill a man for the chance to shed a tear on the grave of Sir Ernest Shackleton. Murray reflected upon the night that he and Jacob found themselves rain soaked on the side of a Colorado 14er with only his sleeping bag dry. Murray reveled in the survival moment offering to spoon with Wilde; Wilde threatened to kill him, then walked off the mountain in the dark, cursing Murray all the way down to keep himself warm. Murray loved the fight, but adored the hunt. He continued to scan across his anthologies of explorers, the journal of Robert Falcon Scott, and he began to dispel his depressive state. He glanced up on the shelf and read the framed advertisement:

MEN WANTED for hazardous journey, small wages, bitter cold, long months of complete darkness, constant danger, safe return doubtful, honor and recognition in case of success— Ernest Shackleton.

Though the quote animated his soul, it likewise brought about anguish as well, for these dead bombastic explorers' exploits, along with the ardor he possessed for them, served as the sole reason he chose the monk life of education and not marriage.

He had come close to marriage once and only once. He erroneously thought that Tennessee the playwright surely felt the instinct of love meant human companionship. After the debacle of an attempted marriage, Murray discovered that love did not restrict itself to humans. To love an ideal or belief proved far less fickle than that of a woman, but he tried. The courtship proved lengthy, the breakup brusque. At the start of college, he met a young redhead named Margaret. While dating, both in their youth, they dreamt of large families, buying houses, raising children and all the other romantic flapdoodle that went with the domiciliary lifestyle. Murray contented himself with these thoughts then would be overcome with songs of the open road. Something would always pull him away from Margaret. Early in their relationship, the thrill of traveling, studying in Europe and the adventure of firefighting instilled a burning in his soul. These whimsies were soon followed by the captivation of literature, of adventure, of philosophy, of politics and again, of travel. And then Murray hiked. Red River Gorge in central Kentucky proved the tipping of the fulcrum to the negative side for their relationship, though neither at the time understood it. The coup de grace proved to be Mount Elbert in Colorado, a 14,433 foot behemoth which Murray, the flatlander, felt for sure would kill him. He stumbled up it, fell up it, crawled up it—totally unaccustomed to the altitude—however, when he reached the top, much to the shock of the locals who left him for dead, he looked out over the endless snowcapped peaks and felt the brace of cold air in his face, and he knew he found his love, his passion. That which followed consumed him day and night. Though he had proposed shortly prior to the Elbert expedition, the ephemeral bliss of that engagement proved fleeting. As Margaret planned the wedding a full year away, Murray, fraught with the burning desire to leave and explore, found himself hesitantly contemplating his future. This burning became exacerbated by the lives of dead British explorers and further adventures in the Colorado Rockies. The mountains became more enthrallingly dangerous and on Capital Peak's Knife's Edge he swore—as his legs straddled a 2,000 foot drop on either side—that if he lived and made it home, he would never leave her or home again. Unfortunately, Murray found himself home only a couple of weeks dreaming and planning his next adventure—the women of Scott, Mallory, and Shackleton must have been patient to endure the restless wanderlust of their husbands.

Margaret attempted to forestall Murray's adventures until after the wedding—maybe she hoped a child would calm his burning desire. Margaret, sagacious as Murray, also began to read up on these very explorers that she found Murray studying during family functions. It would be nothing at Christmas to find him hiding in a corner reading the death letters of Robert Falcon Scott and have to pry them out of his hands for dinner. Margaret saw the women of these men, the emptiness and hollowness of their relationship. As Murray became more insular, Margaret understood the indomitable nature of this calling of the mountain and the wild. She refused to play mistress to this lifestyle; a lifestyle of broken promises, men away from home, and widows and orphans a plenty. One month prior to the wedding, Margaret returned the ring that Murray gave her in possibly one of the most unromantic proposals in the history of romance.

"What are you doing?" Murray looked up from a book while at Margaret's parents' house.

"I am returning what you shouldn't have given, and I shouldn't have taken," Margaret responded bitterly.

"What do you mean? I want to marry you."

"Why? You spend every free moment you have coming up with reasons to leave," continued Margaret.

"Yes, but I always come back."

"Hmm," Margaret grunted, "we have dated for four years and have been engaged for nearly one year, and I can tell you that I will not spend my life as your base camp for some next adventure."

"But," retorted Murray; however, there did not appear to be anything else to say.

"I don't know if you are a selfish bastard or just an unfeeling Scrooge, but I can tell you this, I won't be sitting around here like a complete dipshit while you gallivant about the world." Murray could not find words. "You are a hypocrite. You say you love me, but your true love pulls you away."

"Hmmm," he paused with a transcendental thought upon the pallet of his mind, "I contradict myself?"

"Yes."

"Very well then, I contradict myself. I am large; I contain multitudes." The conversation became futile; he knew it, and Margaret proved correct. He had no business being married, and he began to feel remorseful for the five years of Margaret's life that he had wasted. With marriage came children, and what a distracted father he would have been. They would interfere with his endless dreams; children seemed an unbearable nuisance. Shooting the albatross without provocation, having it hung about his neck like a millstone then drowned at sea made more logical sense than producing children. He would have ruined Margaret. Though, he felt sure that he loved her, but he could not control the quandary that existed in his soul, the need to move. He always felt the need to attempt to find in motion what had been lost in space. He blew out Margaret's proverbial candle. Moved on. Reflected. He realized that of the few girlfriends that he had in life, he had made all of them miserable. Eventually, they all cried and loathed him. Perhaps the only girl not disgusted with him in his life would be Melissa Thacker, the girl he kissed under her grandma's porch at the age of seven. Somehow, this did not quell the inner angst in his soul. Thus, his monk life seemed seared into his future. Murray came to grips with his perpetual discontent with life—finding solace in teaching, passion in reading and happiness in fleeting moments like that of an appearance of a rainbow following a violent storm. His destiny seemed foreboding. He suddenly felt like the poor player strutting and fretting his hour on the stage. Though life may be a tale told by an idiot signifying nothing, this overwhelming air of Weltschmerz lifted for he would leave for the Grand Canyon tomorrow, tomorrow, and tomorrow.

CHAPTER ELEVEN

"We had seen God in His splendors, heard the text that Nature renders. We had reached the naked soul of man."

SIR ERNEST SHACKLETON ON SEEING ANTARCTICA

Jacob Wilde and Murray Moore sat in their respective seats for their transcontinental flight from Dayton, Ohio to just north of Flagstaff, Arizona along with a host of other educators nominated for the Academy of Principals. Wilde sat coolly and confidently nestled in his seat, while Moore incessantly tapped his feet, drummed his fingers, and squirmed in his chair. The previous night had been a restless sleep; Murray loathed flying. The abhorrence for air travel boiled down to one ingredient, fear. His palpable trepidation could be seen by all around him. He trusted no aircraft big or small. The fifty-passenger Bombardier only saw half of its seats filled when the female flight attendant closed the outside door. As she walked back down the walkway toward the front of the jet, out strode the captain.

"Good morning, y'all. I am Captain Richard Newberry from the great state of Oklahoma. I will be jockeying this here tin can across what the elitist snobs of America call "fly-over" country. We Okies don't take too kindly to that claptrap. So, you best behave yourselves or I will land this two winged coffin in a corn field, take out the keys and leave you stranded in some casino town like Weatherford with nothing to do but listen to some old washed up singer belting out ancient Eddie Money songs!" Newberry looked around and smiled, "Heck, just kidding. Welcome aboard. We will be flying non-stop to Grand Canyon National Airport north of Flagstaff, Arizona where you all will be transferred to the shuttle bound for the South Rim! If you got any questions, ask the flight attendant. This non-commercial flight comes to you courtesy of Uncle Sam, so have all the peanuts you want." He waved, turned, and swaggered into the cockpit, to be immediately followed by the flight attendant who felt it necessary to rant about float devices and cushions—even though the only water they would see would be coming out of a sprinkler growing corn. Jacob and Murray tuned out, lost in thought. After the droning of the flight attendant and an uneventful take-off, Wilde, sensing Moore's uncomfortable nervousness, began to speak.

"Murray," began Jacob.

"Yeah," Murray stated in a clearly uncomfortable nervousness.

"Did you catch the news today?"

"Hey, if you think jabber-jawing will keep my mind off this obsolete rust bucket and our chances of survival, you are nuts," Murray frantically stated looking nervously around.

"Relax. NPR did an entire show today titled 'Unemployment: 50 years of 4% and under.' Did you catch that?"

"I didn't hear it."

"Want to pull it up on your tablet?"

"I can't read on a plane; you know that. This thing could go down!"

"Relax."

"I can't, but I will try." Murray looked around at the over abundance of aplomb throughout the cabin. "I think you have a great idea; let's talk about the news. Maybe it will keep my mind off of the flying," Murray willingly surrendered.

"Well, pull up NPR on your tablet. You know we hit Iran again today."

"We did! Why?"

"Man, you have to pay attention to the news more," Wilde scolded.

"Jacob, summertime," he drew out the word. "I need a break," as Wilde explained with his normal sobriety while Murray pulled up the video on his tablet.

"The Obama hit Tehran, along with oil refineries." The Obama represented the original in Drone Aircraft Carriers. After the Great Compromise, America curtailed its military, not out of parsimony, but logistics. The world developed into an economically linked global economy; America could inflict more damage with pen over the sword. Freezing accounts, trade embargos, and boycotts all served better than a standing army. By 2035, the United States had cut its military numbers in half. The global economy rendered invasion untenable for even America. By slashing the troops and making the full time soldiers as much of a Special Forces unit and purely a defensive force, America cut the budget by close to half and turned its Navy into a paucity of submarines and a plethora of drone carriers. When a belligerent rogue country, such as Iran, began to mess with national security, i.e. the economy, one of these drone carriers engaged and inflicted economic damage upon the enemy. No more going in and winning hearts and minds. America could not care less about hearts and minds. The world beat a path to America for trade, and the citizens of the world moved Heaven and Earth to get in. When an Iran or Yemen caused trouble, drones flew in and reminded the little dictatorships which country still retained the title of "boss."

"Oh yeah, I like to hear that. I can't believe the Obama still sails."

"Still works! Effectively at that. We apparently nailed a couple of refineries, so Saudi Arabia dropped the price of crude for us. A pittance really, but we don't ever want the Iranians to forget their place."

"Hey, I found one." Murray, forgetting momentarily the flight continued, "American economy expected to grow by 3%-3.5% this calendar year. Not great."

"What are you talking about? Russia down 1% this year; China off 1.5%. Brazil the only economically growing country persistently beside us." Wilde, due to his civics and financial teaching requirements, constantly kept up on global economics and civil injustices in the United States. Oddly enough, his partner in crime, Murray, believed that civil injustice did not occur within the American boundaries. If anyone pointed out an American hardship, he would relate a tale from National Geographic shaming the original gripe. He possessed the miasma of a Catholic nun when Americans tended to complain. If a student complained of thirst, he reminded them of the African nations where the poor spent the entire day looking for fresh water. If they complained of hardships, he would flash pictures of Yemen. Women's rights, here comes Saudi Arabia. Gay rights, pictures from Iran. The civilized world consisting of the Americas, Europe and Asia basked daily in the glow of global capitalism and trade—America at the top of course. Jacob continued, "Our economy has grown at such a steady 3% clip most analysts question the verity of it."

"What do you mean?"

"Some think the whole economic game has been rigged."

"By whom?" Now Murray found himself curious. As a teacher of dystopian societies, he quickly became enthralled when speaking of worlds that proved the antithesis of his own. Some instructors dabbled in tales of love, feelings and all that general rotgut; Murray would dose it with kerosene and call for Montag. He did have a proclivity to bring in books where the main character found that society had an inexorable grip around his or her proverbial neck and would squeeze till the end. Those tragedies never lost their zeal. However, if Murray found himself forced to pigeonhole himself into one genre and one genre only, it would be the realm of dystopias. His favorite aphorism to say to his classes, "there but for the grace of the constitution go we, remember that kids."

Murray found the flight tolerable due to his political bantering with Wilde.

Before he knew it, the seductive, blonde flight attendant with Smith upon her lapel leaned over him and spoke, "Gentleman, we will be landing soon. Please make sure everything loose has been secured."

"Thanks Kathy," spoke Jacob. "Too late for a cocktail?"

"Uh, yes. Happy landings." Smith moved down the aisle completing her rounds.

"How did you know her name happened to be Kathy?" Murray inquired.

"Unlike you, I pay attention when people tell me their names. She introduced herself after the pilot spoke. You probably were praying!" Murray chuckled, for Wilde proved correct, he never did really listen when people told him their names. It always proved annoying, for Murray constantly walked the world looking at nameless, yet familiar, faces.

Upon landing north of Flagstaff at the John McCain Grand Canyon National Airport, the principal candidates found themselves ushered into a shuttle and whisked up U.S. 180 highway for the remainder of the trip to Grand Canyon Village. Murray still pondered the rationale of principal training in the world's biggest hole in the ground, but mainly he did not care; as a spot he often dreamt of seeing and hiking, he would relish a free trip to the South Rim. Who knew, maybe they would be granted furlough and be able to ramble alone a bit into the canyon. Being that the airport sat close to the Grand Canyon Village, the shuttle pulled up to the El Tovar Lodge after a short drive on the plateau.

Jacob and Murray grabbed their gear from the shuttle and ascended the stairs of the El Tovar—an amazing edifice of wood nearly 200 years old. The commodious porch, the searing heat, and the enormous canyon all hit both men in a surreal tidal wave. Here, preparing to train as principals, they sat at the edge of hikers' paradise. Strolling through the front door into the air conditioning, the temperature dropped twenty degrees, while they observed the dimly lit, ornately adorned black wooden lodge. The ubiquity of mounted wildlife upon the walls seemed daunting—moose, deer, elk, buffalo, all amazing.

"Welcome! The shuttle from District Four has arrived." Murray turned, appalled, to be referred to as a resident of some fictitiously lame children's dystopia. He saw that the announcement came from a familiar voice. He recognized the woman from Miami University, but of course, he couldn't remember her name. "Greetings, our candidates from the Mid West Region," she walked toward Murray's and Jacob's group, "maybe you remember me, I am Jennifer Alliston, and I represent the Principals' Guild. We met in Miami. Welcome to the Grand Canyon, I hope you enjoy your team building session."

"Thanks," joined Jacob. Murray found himself myopically fixated upon the District Four distraction. He attempted to discount it as a mere capricious statement for surely this woman didn't read that century old juvenile tommyrot.

"We have been waiting for your group. All of the principal candidates are here mingling in the dining room, having hors d' oeuvres. Please, give your gear to the porters and go in. We are ready to begin." Jacob immediately handed his gear to a porter heading his way; Murray hesitated, discounted the District Four comment, then handed off his gear. As he crossed the threshold of the El Tovar dining room, his petty fixation with rubbish-filled adolescent books turned to a different type of hunger games as he took in the awe inspiring sight of the dining hall with its view of the Grand Canyon. Murray had hungered for years to get a shot at this hiking challenge; now, it would prove two-fold—physical and mental. Elated, he took a seat and scanned the room, surprised that only around forty candidates presented themselves for the Academy of Principals. Surely, more wanted the job. Murray perused the candidates, but found he could draw no judgments, and then another woman he recognized walked in the hall with a quick, military gait. The room hushed.

"Greetings. I am Colonel Elizabeth Nutt of the Federal Government's Pedagogical Research Department. You may remember me; I met each and every one of you at your various screenings across the country. Also with me, Jennifer Alliston of the Principals'

Guild and Dr. Lauren Hauer who holds a PhD. in secondary education." The Colonel evinced an air of Patton standing there in her
pressed dress greens, hair pulled tightly down. "Firstly, congratulations. Your selection here reflects more than you know. You have
been observed by your principals, you have been tapped, you have
been scrutinized, you have been vetted, you have undergone mild
interrogation, and you have been polygraphed. Hundreds began
the process nationally, only thirty-seven remain. With that, I welcome you to the Academy of Principals team building exercise here
at the Grand Canyon. If you successfully survive this portion of the
training, you will be on your way to the United States Federal Penal
Colony on the Island of Guam where you will complete the last
phase of your training."

No one spoke; no one moved. Jacob Wilde appeared to be a
kid in a candy store; Murray Moore could not discern it all—flummoxed by the lack of numbers considering the girth of the United
States. Colonel Nutt continued.

"This team building exists in two phases. First, beginning tomorrow morning, you will begin a trek down to the bottom of the Grand
Canyon where you will spend two nights at Phantom Ranch. On the
way down, you will experience extreme heat, discomfort, and awe-
inspiring beauty. I suppose now you know why you had a physical
exam. You must be healthy to serve your term as principal. As you
already know, you must lead a monk lifestyle. You will need both to
endure the twenty-five to thirty years of service you will perform—
though most serve, like a Supreme Court Justice, for the remainder
of their lives. The challenge of the Grand Canyon, along with the
camaraderie that you will build, along with the seminars at the bottom, will propel you to the next and last phase. We are to the 'all
in' stage of the training folks. If any part of this training negatively
affects you, see me, Dr. Hauer, or Jennifer Alliston, and I mean any
part. I will now turn it over to Dr. Hauer."

Dr. Hauer exuded all the qualities of a doctor of education.
She looked the part. Maybe even that of a librarian; she appeared
to be a meek librarian, but spoke with force and bravado. "Good
afternoon and welcome. Tomorrow will be an exciting day. When
you get to your room, you will have a note on your door informing

you of your team tomorrow. One third will march down the Bright Angel Trail, and at dawn the second third will proceed down the South Kaibab Trail to Phantom Ranch, followed by the last third two hours later. Remember, this hike represents a physiological, psychological, sociological, and somewhat pedagogical test. Every aspect of your trip will be assessed. In your instructions, you were informed to dress for the heat and have gear for carrying water. Your food will be provided." She glanced around the room; all look enthralled. "I would like to reiterate the words of Colonel Nutt; if at any point from here to the bottom of the Grand Canyon, you feel this honor may not be for you, please inform us. You will be promptly returned home. And with that, dinner will be here at 5:00 p.m.; you have until this evening to get ready for your hike, and then we will see all of you on the front porch of the El Tovar here at 5:00 a.m. tomorrow morning. Ms. Alliston, Colonel Nutt, and myself will be available for the rest of the afternoon in the dining hall here. Any questions?" There were none.

CHAPTER TWELVE

---

*"And now 'you' understand. Anything goes wrong, anything at all...
your fault, my fault, nobody's fault... it won't matter – I'm gonna blow
your head off. No matter what else happens, no matter who gets killed, I'm
gonna blow your head off."*

JOHN WAYNE – *BIG JAKE* – *1971*

With unmitigated enthusiasm, Jacob and Murray lay their gear
on the wall overlooking the edge of eternity. The view defied
expressions like 'expansive' or 'gorgeous' or 'magnificent.'
Only the word 'ridiculous' seemed to convey, in a palpable sense,
the magnitude of not only the enormity of the Grand Canyon, but
also the complete degree to which the viewer had been rendered
insignificant in the grand scheme of the universe. The dwindling
sense of importance Forster's cave in *A Passage to India* thrust
upon Mrs. Moore had now been pressed upon Murray. Whereas,

the character in the novel found herself ruined—for her own sense of self-importance provided her with the driving force in life—that same "boum" of the universe now put Murray at the complete antipode on the globe of reality. He had always sensed insignificance; now confirmation bloomed.

Gazing down into the abyss, Murray followed the Bright Angel Trail down the switchbacks, out to Indian Gardens, and off to Plateau Point. There amongst the scrub and dirt, the rock strewn carpet of the canyon offered the viewer a bleak reality of survival in such a waterless and dry desert. And, as his eyes scanned the 180 degrees of hole and heat and desolately apocalyptic beauty, Murray could discern not only the trail cutting through the wasteland, but a sole solitary blip moving upon it—a man, or woman, walking, strolling, trudging, living or dying, so far out there that from this distance nothing the hiker could say or do could be transmitted to Murray and vice a versa. Both were solitary entities in the universe at that moment. He could not help, nor hurt, the speck of a hiker miles off in the distance. The solitary traveler must walk that path alone: fight the heat alone, climb out of that crevasse of rock alone, fight through life alone, all, all alone. Alone on a wide, wide sea. Murray immediately became invigorated to a level of bliss so overwhelming he could have leapt into the expanse of air in front of him. Glory! The Glory!

Moore's silent reverie broke with the emergence of a fidgety squirrel, zipping along the rock wall back and forth desperately looking for something to scavenge from the hoards of hikers, gawkers, and unmotivated slobs that rolled out of their cars and sweated their way to the edge to take a picture with a donut in one hand, coffee in the other. Murray pushed the non-living out of his mind and focused upon his new friend, the squirrel. He, assumingly he, had skittered down off the wall, snagged a dropped peanut from someone's trail mix, and perched back up in the same spot. Chomping vigorously upon that peanut, twitching left and right, left and right, left and right, the squirrel filled his gullet, all the while watching for the next opportunity to land in his view. Fascinating, with the canyon making an I-max sized backdrop, that squirrel, in all of his simplistic energy, eked out his existence in what appeared a most quiescent manner upon the pittance of the people. In this inhospitable, arid, beautiful desert, he fought, he survived, he squirreled.

Murray could have died at that moment and been content. How many feel that way at their demise—content, sublime, ready? Murray feared few. A noise shattered his meditative soliloquy; Jacob had dropped his knife rattling Murray back to reality. Jacob had nearly finished his packing oblivious to the fact that Murray had lost himself in the moment, and his gear laid spread out in the same disheveled heap it had been when they arrived. It mattered not, Murray's bag would be ready; he would be ready. As the sun began its race to the edge of eternity on the opposite side of the canyon, Murray knew he would be ready. Murray only hoped he could sleep a little for he felt tomorrow would begin the first day of the rest of his life.

A knock on the door at 4:30 a.m. startled Murray and Jacob, but both would swear they were not sleeping. Murray felt sure he hadn't succumbed to slumber, though he felt rested, energized and motivated. The group of teachers had been scheduled to meet at the top of the Bright Angel Trailhead at 5:00 a.m., fed, dressed and ready. Murray and Jacob had hiked long enough to know that going into a long haul, they preferred to snack all the way to the destination, and then have a full meal. Since they had slept in their clothes, packs ready and leaning on the wall, a simple exercise of putting on and tying the boots seemed to be the only effort needed to be ready to head out the door.

With packs on, hiking sticks in hands, and hats on heads, the pair exited the El Tovar, descended the steps, and headed down the Rim Trail passed the Bright Angel Lodge. Neither were surprised to find themselves the first at the gift house next to the trail. A couple of minutes later, a few more straggled in, all arriving by 5:00 a.m. All were noticeably nervous, more concerned with the next step than the fact that dawn began to break over the eastern edge of the canyon. As the tension arose, Murray noticed that only twelve principal candidates had shown, last night thirty-seven had attended the conference. He thought of asking Jacob, then he remembered the three groups discussed last night, when out of the gift shop door erupted a man not less than a day under fifty, who manifested an energy level immediately of one half of his age exploding with, "Good morning girls!" Murray and Jacob glanced at each other, for this seemed a crass greeting since over half of the party were women and likely to take offense. "And ladies, good morning to you all."

While some of the men looked a tad put out by his acerbic tone addressing the men as girls, Murray found it tantalizingly humorous. He possessed the swagger and look of Clint Eastwood and a gait to rival the Duke. Donning an Aussie full brimmed bush hat, a "Go Hike the Canyon" tee-shirt, stereotypical hiking shorts and boots with some not-so-typical colored socks, he skulked through the twelve candidates, looking at the men as if he would like to carve their livers and the women as if dinner and a bottle of wine would be possible with only a wink and a nod. After they had gone down the trail, all the men ranged between intimidated to agitated and the women interested; Murray just sat back eagerly awaiting the guide's next move. The first five minutes at the top of the trail by the gift shop and the first twenty down the trail surely were an interesting testimony to testosterone. This creature, carved out of Hollywood Westerns, caused all to look for cover and Murray for approbation.

"I am Edward Joseph. I will be escorting you ladies and taking the girls with you down to Phantom Ranch. I hope you are all prepared for 9.3 miles of searing heat. We will need to be making a good pace to get down by lunch. Just so you know, there will be restrooms in 1.5 miles, 3 miles, and 4.9 miles, then all canyon. If you are wondering where the rest of the candidates are, they will be following you later—one group on this trail and the third group on the South Kaibab. I'm not here to talk about education, my job requirement lies in the fact that I am to bring you in alive."

Edward continued, "I suggest you hydrate yourself all day, wear sunblock, don't get too close to an edge or do anything stupid. Either way, I get paid—whether you make it to Phantom Ranch, drop dead, or get flown out by the Rangers. I would advise death over the rescue; death would be cheaper. See you at the Mile-and-a-half Resthouse!" Edward turned and darted down the trail, stopped, turned and bellowed, "Oh yeah, if the mules come down, and they will, step off the trail, listen to the mule driver and don't move. Those brutes will kick you right in the head!" Then with all the force his bluster and bravado could exude, he bounded down the trail at a pace no one in that pack of educators could maintain for long.

Murray and Jacob separated themselves from the pack attempting to keep up with Edward Joseph but to no avail. Moving like a gazelle, Edward seemed to disappear down the switchbacks. "Well, what now?" Murray asked.

"All good. This trail only goes one way captain," remarked Jacob grinning.

"Well, we can't keep up with 'Steady Eddie,' but we have dusted the other candidates. If this turns out to be a race for placement, we may do alright." Both Murray and Jacob decided to mellow out and roll with it. With the herd behind and the boss out front, they decided to cruise down at their own pace and breathe in the glorious path in front of them. Within an hour, the two teachers had made it to an ancient little shack sporting three vents sitting right off the trail—clearly a pit toilet with fresh water. Edward Joseph seemed to be missing in action.

"Now what?" Murray inquired desperately from Jacob.

"Well, looks like the trail guide vamoosed on us."

"Do we stay and wait on the group or try and catch Wyatt Earp?" continued Murray.

"Definitely wait for the group. Since 'Steady Eddie' or 'Wyatt Earp' or whoever took off, and we are the second fastest—and obviously the most experienced—we need to wait and take charge." Before Jacob's words could register and Murray could agree, a horrendous sound erupted from the pit toilet area as a stall door had been flung open with such force and velocity that it slammed the wall, causing a ricochet of violent noise; it felt as if the entire canyon would collapse in on itself.

"Hell's bells boys! I thought you two were ignorant flatlanders. You may have a future out here ladies." Edward chuckled at them as he stood, legs spread, shorts down, boxers on—thank God they thought—arms akimbo with a pit toilet behind him.

"Hell, I didn't think half of ya would survive to Indian Gardens. All right girls! You wait here for the rest of that bunch, I'll meet up with you later!" This tirade exploded forth from Edward Joseph as his voice inundated the finger of the canyon all while he pulled up his shorts as he walked. Then, without another word, he stormed by them down the trail a bit, paused, reached behind a rock, grabbed his pack, then proceeded to bound down the trail again. Jacob and Murray stood, incredulous, awaiting the slower part of the group still working their way down the Bright Angel.

Within twenty minutes, the group had begun to catch up with Jacob and Murray, first by two young teachers who immediately went to the water, the other limping toward a rock. Jacob wasted no time trying to establish some normalcy out of a rather odd start to the excursion.

"What hurts? You are limping."

"My knee always hurts when going down hill. Old soccer injury."

"I am Jacob, Jacob Wilde. This here," hooking a thumb towards his partner cleaning the dust and dirt off his half mooned spectacles, "Well, introduce yourself."

"I am Murray Moore."

"Interesting name," the second girl responded.

"Murray Mallory Moore to be exact."

"Too weird," continued the brunette with the big smile. "I am Francesca Jarrett."

"And I am Beth Basara," chimed in the blonde sitting upon the stone. "Where do you guys teach?"

"Actually, we are both from Mayfield, Ohio."

"We have heard of you guys!" continued Francesca.

"Really, why?" continued Jacob.

"Well, you are only the first set of principal candidates to make it this far from the same school." Jacob and Murray thought they had heard that somewhere, but if they did, it did not register.

"Where are you two from then?" Murray inquired.

"Well," started Beth, "I teach in Maryland, and Francesca teaches in North Carolina."

"And I am," bellowed a voice from behind, "Matthew Klaber from the biggest high school in the Dallas-Fort Worth area in the great state of..." he couldn't finish.

"Texas!" simultaneously sang Francesca and Beth.

"Well, glad you ladies were paying attention," Klaber continued unfazed by the snide response of the ladies, "Now, where did that loud mouth dinosaur get off to? He sure exuded a petulant air didn't he?"

"Well," Jacob continued, "I wouldn't worry about him. Murray and I thought we would wait here, make sure everyone felt fine, had water, and had no issues, then we could push on together."

"Thank you gentleman, a grand plan," another voice contributed to the growing conversation from up the trail. As he strode in, he introduced himself, "Kyler Humphries. Miami, Florida. I am glad you waited. I am feeling the effects of a life living at sea level." After a total of thirty minutes, the full group had been joined together, adding Adam Bockhold of Missouri, Nick Kues of Kentucky, Jackie Mapes of New York, Aaron Hirst of Montana, Nathan Simon of Washington, and Erin Pierce of Louisiana. This motley crew spanned the country along with the educational spectrum: math, science, language arts, history, even theater.

Jacob explained to the group that he felt that Edward Joseph only intended to beguile the group into suspecting they were on their own. Murray followed with words of encouragement intimating that they should stick to the trail, keep drinking the water, always apply the sunscreen, and inform anyone if they began to feel ill. The group fell in line and began marching down. Jacob and Murray decided that since they brought with them the most experience in regards to hiking, Murray would take the point and Jacob would sweep the rear. In this way, the entire party made it to Indian Gardens. Though Moore attempted to stay focused upon the beauty of the scenescape, he had found himself drifting back to school on the final day.

"Mr. Moore, I think you are crazy," Kaminsky had said.

"Justine, everything I do seems crazy to you," he had replied.

"Yeah, but on this adventure you are crazy." Justine had continued.

"Well," Murray had attempted to assuage, "I think I can handle the Grand Canyon, I have hiked more times than I can count."

"No, not crazy because of that; crazy because you are leaving teaching. You belong in the classroom," Justine finished. Murray had not dwelt too long on this concept, though it may have been the truth. Once a principal, always a principal. He had always heard that the teacher-gone-principal begins to fade away from their former colleagues and rule "from afar."

"Yeah Mr. Moore! Who will teach us vocabulary words and capitalism?" another student, Elizabeth had joined the conversation. "Who thinks Mr. Moore should stay?" This had resulted in quite the hullabaloo in the classroom. (Sarvak possessed a benign cunning for turning the attention of the class in her direction—at times, he thought, she enjoyed being the center of the universe.)

"Alright, alright. Look gang. Facts are facts. How many times have you been taught in this school, in our society, that men and women are called by their country? Some fight, some support. Some preach, some nurse. Some follow, some lead. A man, who stops moving, stops living. I love teaching you guys, but you know as well as I do, a principal ranks up there with senator, mayor, or representative. Don't try and dissuade me, it only makes it more difficult. I attribute all my success to the fact that you are wonderful students. But guys and girls, I have lived the last ten years as a monk teacher, sleeping in this building, attending your performances— music or otherwise—and devoting my life to this profession. Now, larger and more powerful forces need me, want me, whatever you want to call it, to try and run a school, maybe more. I would be a hypocrite if I didn't answer the call of my country."

Murray had seen the fact that Elizabeth Sarvak had simmered down, and thus the rest of the class had done likewise. He quixotically desired to hold his post as teacher, but he felt the pressure of the conundrum; how could he continue to teach about responding to the public and a citizen fulfilling his or her civic duty, if he failed to do his civic duty? It occurred at that moment; Murray went from contemplative to devastated. A young man in the back, John Overwine, a student who rarely said anything, but read everything had stood, and sent this phrase—steeped in double entendre—Murray's way, "God bless, Mr. Moore!" Overwine then sat, lowered his head, and sulked.

Murray blinked, choking back blasted tears that attacked his eyes. The canyon blurred due to his temporarily aqueous vision. The verity of the matter dictated his dedication to the cause. He lamented the loss of his students, yet knew he owed it to his country to serve, if possible, as a principal. When faced with crisis, Murray always considered his heroes. Horatio Nelson stated as he sailed to his glorious death at Trafalgar, "England expects that every man will do his duty." The men performed; England triumphed. However, Moore thought simplicity, simplicity. Murray had a duty to country, and as usual, George Mallory's words to his wife on why he must attempt Mount Everest for the final and fatal time provided him guidance, "The Empire expects it!" Moore pushed back and shoved down the tears and feelings as he lightly stepped down the rocky trail; he refused to fail his idealistic and historic mentors. He would finish the task. He would strive and not yield.

CHAPTER THIRTEEN

"The boast of heraldry, the pomp of power,
And all that beauty, all that wealth e-er gave,
Awaits alike the inevitable hour
The paths of glory lead but to the grave."

THOMAS GREY **1751**
"ELEGY IN A COUNTRY CHUCHYARD"

As the cadre of educators wended their way down to Indian Garden, they suddenly became aware that they were being hunted. Hunted by a plodding, yet methodical beast which appeared to be barely moving but in essence, outran nearly every human on foot whose path they crossed—the mule. The mule train marched up and down the trails of the Grand Canyon in a most traditional manner, supplying food and provisions to Phantom Ranch located at the intersection of the Bright Angel Creek and the Colorado River. Jacob first noted the lumbering train and pointed it out to what could ostensibly be defined as his party. Since joining forces at Mile-and-a-half Resthouse, the party—clearly out of their respective elements—followed like mere sycophants. Aside from Murray and himself, the collective crew viewed hiking as having a poor parking spot at the shopping center and walking to the mall, though none were out of shape. The group had just made it to the Three Mile Resthouse, when it became quite clear that to start back onto the trail prior to letting the mule train pass would just represent foolhardiness and invite possible accident.

"We might as well rest ladies and gents," Murray offered, "and let the mules pass." Beth and Francesca seemed to have no problem with this chance at rest and dialogue. Murray did not know if they knew one another prior to this adventure, but they sure manifested the air of two college girls taking a cross-country trip and popping off to have a go at the big hole in the ground. It seemed to Murray at least that these two had spunk and vivacity to spare. This idea of watching the mules garnered a mixed reaction from Klaber stating that Texan mules were bigger, Bockhold giddily wanting to see one up close, Kues hoping to ride one, Simon asking if you could eat them, Hirst attempting to calculate their load, Humphries wisely remaining quiet and taking it all in, to Pierce wondering how fast they ran, and finally Mapes betting they would smell. As Basara and Jarrett seemed to have no interest either way, and Murray and Jacob became enamored, for their big, burly, mule riding cowboy, turned out to be a young cowgirl.

Though she had to be mid to late twenties due to her occupation as mule team leader, she possessed a youthful face—almost that of a late teen. Her youthfulness aside—real or perceived—she commanded her mule and subsequently those behind her with gravitas. Jacob could not resist the opportunity to greet her as she ambled up toward the group's position, for he, earlier in life, loved to ride horses. He would frequently speak of his days training and riding often times hitting jargon that zipped over Murray's head and around his interest.

"Good morning. You have them all in total control," Jacob floated her way.

"Yes. You the educators?" she inquired, slowing the mules.

"We are. How did you know?" Jacob returned.

"We were told to look out for you." She smiled wryly. While Jacob seemed fully enthralled with the beast, Murray caught sight of a saddlebag that had its lid latched and bunched up with a copy of what appeared *The Complete Works of Shakespeare* in not only book form, but also apparently an ancient copy, maybe a hundred plus years old.

"How you like this job?" Jacob banally continued.

"Love it," the mule driver retorted.

"I would love to try it."

"I would not do anything else in the world," she returned. Murray saw his chance to urbanely interject.

"Love can not be Love which alters when it alteration finds," Murray proudly blurted out one of the very poet's lines that he in fact did not love.

"Whoa!" the mule stopped. "Well done. Sonnet 116." She stared at Murray momentarily, glanced at Jacob, then back at Moore, "English teacher, I presume?"

"Yep," Murray boastfully smiled.

"See you on the bottom, boys. Try not and get yourselves killed." As she turned her body, the mule instinctively moved up followed by the herd. The mule train moved at its steady gait, passed the Three Mile Resthouse, and lumbered on down the trail. Ten mules ambled by the teacher group with a rather tall brunette silently astride the caboose mule tipping her hat as she moved on. Jacob and Murray led their group right on its heels. Though Murray and Jacob struggled to keep pace, the train pulled away. Moments later, Jacob observed that they had pulled decidedly too far away from the pack of teachers and they opted to slow down.

Another hour into the hike, the splintered group marched into Indian Garden, the last refuge of civilization between here and Phantom Ranch. This oasis in a desert canyon ecosystem had been given life due to a creek running off the rim down toward the Colorado River—the same creek that would have quenched the thirst of Native Americans hundreds of years ago. This oasis served as a green patch in a world of browns. Trees grew on an area about the size of a football field. Jacob told the group to refill their water and stop at the restroom, and from behind one of the trees emerged Edward Joseph, dripping with his own swag.

"Well, well, well, Mr. Wilde, I knew it would take you a while to herd this group of teachers down this trail, but I never thought it would take you this long." Jacob, Murray and the rest decided it best to remain silent, for Edward seemed to be sizing them up for a fit of acrimony. "Keep moving down the trail or we will all miss dinner. I will give you girls and ladies a head start down through the 'Staircase' and remember, don't go to Plateau Point. I can read some of my book and take a nap and catch this group."

The slow, but steady plodding methodically continued down the 'Staircase' when the silence became distracted by the sound of a whistle. Jackie Mapes, impressed by the pitch commented, "Nice whistle," when Murray informed her and the rest of the group that the whistle represented a hiking cry of desperation and the needing of help. The teachers moved their heads back and forth unfortunately from one to another, not knowing from where the sound emanated. Finally, Jacob took charge and stated, "Group! We have not passed anyone. So in all likelihood the troubled hiker will not be behind us, and if the distressed hiker should be behind us, Crazy Eddie, or whatever his name happens to be, will find the person. Therefore, we should keep moving forward searching for someone not only on the trail, but more than likely, off the trail. Usually people get overcome by the heat and collapse, sometimes falling off these narrow paths."

All looked around slightly stressed, except Murray; he looked intrigued. Finally his nervous energy effused through, "Hey, I can hike pretty quickly. I will motor ahead and see if I come across anything. If I walk twenty minutes without seeing anything, I will stop and wait."

"Good idea," Jacob approvingly responded.

"I will see you soon," and before anyone could reply, Murray turned and strode away. As he hopped from one cut out landing on the trail to the other dodging the puddles of mule urine— and trying not to smell it—Murray attempted to enjoy the view while gazing all around him for any sign of the distressed hiker. The whistle sounded again. Murray increased his speed down the declivity and made the sharp switchback turn along the canyon wall when he saw the trouble. The Grand Canyon, comprised of two layers, has an initial canyon, where Indian Gardens rests, and an inner canyon carved out by the mighty Colorado. Immediately after Indian Gardens, that inner canyon begins to open up, and precipitously descends in a winding fashion, dropping a good one thousand feet of elevation to the canyon floor near the river. This path, the Bright Angel, hugs this canyon wall wrapping periodically back upon itself in a few nervy switchbacks. Below Murray, down two switchbacks, the couple-hundred-year-old path buckled near a switch and it appeared to Murray at least that a mule or two went over the edge and landed on the path below. He began to jog down the path carefully, desperate to help, but careful not to add himself to the casualty list.

Nimble as a cat, Murray made good time twisting through two switchbacks and moving across the descending path to make it to the back of the mule train where the tall brunette had walked back to meet him. She had a cell phone in her hand as she approached Murray, "Dang thing broke! She had it in her pocket and landed on it when she fell." The Brunette stated pointing toward the mule team leader.

"What happened?" Murray began.

"As we approached the switch, the wall gave way and the path collapsed. Two mules and the guide went down." Now she looked pained. "I think their legs are broken."

"Whose legs?"

"Maybe all of them, definitely the mules' legs. They went down with all of that pack weight on them."

"What about the mule train driver?"

"She keeps going in and out of consciousness. I am not sure of her injuries." Murray tried not to panic. Without a phone, they had to rely on whistles and other hikers to convey a message to someone until that made it to a cell or satellite phone. That could take a while. He didn't know anything about mules, but he felt he should make an attempt to assess the health of the mule train driver at once. "Don't frighten the mules, they might kick you!" Murray moved between the mules and the wall, cautiously placing his hand on their hind quarters and intoning "easy" at them soothingly. As Murray moved up through the mule train and headed toward the switch, he looked up over the animal and down onto the trail below. Murray would not have needed a veterinarian degree to make the determination that the two mules lying on the path had broken limbs—both had lower legs lying nearly perpendicular to their upper legs. Nausea hit him; Murray choked it down. When Murray rounded the switch, he heard another whistle from above. Relief flowed through Murray for he saw Jacob waving an arm in the air. Whatever happened, he knew that the two of them could solve the issue. Murray returned the wave, turned the switch, and then saw the mule train driver. She appeared to have moved herself or had assistance from the tall brunette because Murray could see drag marks in the dirt path.

"Come here! Quick." The mule driver bellowed. "I need your help."

"Are you hurt?" Murray felt confounded, not sure where and how to begin. Murray moved toward her and knelt down beside her.

"You have a name?" she brusquely asked.

"Yeah, Murray Moore. Are you hurt?"

"I am, but I will live. Don't worry about me." She leaned up on an elbow then over up against a rock. "My mules have broken legs. I can't get up." Murray glanced up to see Jacob hustling down the switchbacks with a tenth of a mile or so to go.

"What do you need me to do?"

"You aren't going to like it." She looked away from the mules and up the path. "Are those your comrades?"

"Yes. When my friend gets here, he will be able to help the mule. He used to work a stable with horses."

"Good. It will take a few of you to do it."

"I don't see any wood, but we have hiking poles," Murray felt relieved, but still panicky about working with a wounded animal that outweighed him four or five times over.

"What do you need a hiking pole for?" inquired the mule train driver. By this time the other rider had come back down toward Murray.

"Don't you want me to make a splint for the Mule?"

"You don't know much about the world outside the classroom, eh Teach?" She then looked down, "You can't save them. You can only end their suffering." The full reality of the situation hit Murray. Now, he had never been an animal lover of any sort, but he never obtained much pleasure or satisfaction being around a life about to end—man or beast. Hopefully, he would be able to abstain from any unpleasantries and move out of sight, so out of mind. Now Murray realized that Jacob would be there within minutes to assist him in avoiding the onerous task at hand.

"Hey, I don't know your name."

"Kristin," she paused, "Kristin Fortunski. Now, I will need you to get something out of my saddlebag."

"The other teachers will be here in a minute. They will be able to help," Murray replied as Kristin looked at the other girl.

"Annie," Kristin barked, "you ever put down a horse?"

"No." Annie's horrified face revealed her inexperience. "UK doesn't have its equestrian students partake in that unless they are going to be veterinarians." Murray glanced up, relieved, to see Wilde hurriedly coming to the back of the mule train. He deftly and swiftly moved through the train coming up to the switch and surveying the situation.

"Oh man," served as his summation of the predicament. He looked at Fortunski, "You have a gun?" Murray wanted to denounce the impending doom for the mules, but knew that if a mule train driver and Jacob Wilde with his experience called for the putting down of the animals, he would offer no objection. After all, he possessed no experience in this matter. The Annie girl seemed to oscillate from the reality of the situation to a glazed stare into the canyon; she clearly failed to be a mule boss also—merely a college student engaged in a summer occupation, he conjectured.

"Gruenschlaeger," Fortunski barked again grimacing in pain, "show this guy the pistol." She indicated Wilde. His manifest clarity of the situation clearly exuded itself and Kristin saw it. Murray walked with him and Annie to the saddlebag. Annie opened it; Jacob extracted a Colt 45 pistol and marched to the first mule. By now the entire group of teachers had approached. It didn't take long for the scene to manifest a reality in the eyes of the group. Without a word Aaron Hirst, Nick Kues, and Kyler Humpries approached the front of the mule train to offer assistance. Reluctance grew upon the countenance of Nathan Simon who immediately said, "You will have to excuse me," and he turned to walk up the trail.

"What are they doing?" Jackie Mapes inquired looking aghast. "Surely, you are not going to," her voice trailed off. Both Beth and Francesca approached her for consolation. Jackie did not wait, turned and hurried up the trail after Nathan.

"Hey, man," spoke Aaron, "you need any help?"

"No," Wilde hesitated, "thanks, though." The group had splintered, some obviously disconsolate over the impending doom of the maimed animals. "Guys, could you each grab a reign of the mule and slowly back them up?"

"Gruenschlaeger!" Fortunski bellowed again, "Give them a hand." Kristin's mood had moved from pained by her injury to contentious by their weakness. "You guys that don't have the stomach for the harsh realities of life, best move on up the trail," she finished with a sinister disgust upon her face for Jackie and Nathan up the hill already and a third, Erin Pierce, quickly following. Murray felt the need to defend his professional colleagues, but decided to extend a bit of latitude to the struggling mule leader who painfully lay in the dirt and mule-urine-splashed step of the trail. He only hoped that Fortunski didn't continue haranguing the three leaving. "Soft!" she spit venomously toward the trio. "I can't stand weak-kneed city-raised, egg heads. Completely sheltered and oblivious to the world."

Murray glanced back as the Annie girl softly coached the other teachers how to move the mules back up the trail to lessen their shock to the determined fate of the hapless animals. He then knelt down next to Kristin and said, "Don't be too hard on them. Not everybody can do some of the painful tasks needed in this world."

"Can you?" Fortunski asked him.

"We are going to find out." Murray stood up, "Jacob, what do you need me to do?" Jacob had already walked to the first mule cocking the nearly one hundred year old weapon. "Hold the reign and pat his neck. Bad enough what has to happen, I don't want the animal to be frightened." Moore did as instructed. Looking around, time halted. Murray recognized one of those strange, surreal moments in life when he realized a momentous occasion would occur, and he felt the need to look around to see if anyone else happened to be acknowledging it also. Clearly Wilde recognized it. Fortunski did not take her eyes off either of them. The mules were up and away from the foreboding carnage about to occur. Murray looked into Jacob's eyes, "Have you ever had to do this?"

"No." He approached the mule from behind, extending his arm out and angling it down to fire point blank into the animal's skull. Murray had been patting the mule's neck trying to coax and calm him. Wilde looked at Moore and nodded his head in the direction he wanted him to move. His eyes exuded a painful regret of duty, but resolution prevailed. A raucously, violent concussion rang out. The gun fired; the mule's suffering ended. The second mule audibly cried out in fear, moving its head around. Fortunski still stared at the pair of men. Murray stood up and approached Jacob.

"Here," Murray now upright, advanced upon Jacob, "I will take this one." Jacob displayed a tangible level of regret; he willingly relinquished the pistol. Moore held the hand-howitzer turning from Wilde's pained expression to that of the frantic suffering of the animal. He felt fate had dealt him a servile moment; a steady sobriety lifted that fleeting surreal moment of a few minutes ago. He moved toward the mule, and stroked the animal's mane, and the mule settled down, putting his head in the dirt. Murray steadied his nerve, took a deep breath and extended his arm as he rose to his feet. Without pause, forcing past his apprehension, Murray squeezed the trigger and the Colt exploded with a recoil which forced his arm up and hand around his ear. The two downed mules lay still; the rest of the train brayed loudly. Murray steadied himself, feeling ambiguous about the situation. In his brief moments of preparation, he thought he would feel dastardly about killing a creature, executing it basically. "Putting it down" contained an ameliorated mood, but the reality of this situation warranted reflection and deep down, the veracity of it all made Murray understand, so much so, that a calming relief flowed through his veins. It had had to be done.

"You two did alright," Fortunski spoke attempting to allay their regrets. Murray and Jacob approached her; Murray placing the gun next to Kristin on a rock and Jacob kneeling down next to her.

"What can we do for you?"

"Take your crew down to the River Rest House; it has an emergency phone to the Ranger Station. Call in two mules down and one needing an evacuation. Let them know where we are. If a ranger comes by, I will get the extrication going from here."

"Don't you want us to stay with you?" Murray clearly felt odd walking away from two dead mules, an injured woman, and a college student.

"No, we will be fine. I have Gruenschlaeger. You need to get to the river before the extreme heat of the day. We have plenty of water." As she finished, the audible steps of a rapidly advancing hiker became noticeable. Edward Joseph came like lighting down the trail. Closing the gap rapidly, far faster than any of the younger educators; he quickly surveyed the situation ascertaining all that had taken place and coming to a halt near the three by the felled mules.

"Damn shame to put down perfectly good hard working animals," Edward looked around. "You two, take your group down to the river and head to the ranch, I will take care of this situation."

"Do you want us to call the ranger station?" queried Jacob.

"No, a hiking ranger will be along shortly. I saw her at Indian Gardens. This time of day, she will be heading to the river looking for flatlanders laid out from heat exhaustion. Now, go on and git. I will catch you at Phantom Ranch. Just follow the signs."

By now the rest of the teaching group had meandered down to the top switchback where the mules had fallen, now laying on the trail below. Quiescently, Murray headed down the trail without looking once at the fallen animals. Jacob instructed them to follow, that the situation would rectify itself without their intervention. The group moved with certitude down the hill, all visibly shaken.

CHAPTER FOURTEEN

Befuddled by all that had just transpired, the disheveled pack of teachers marched down the narrow canyon toward the raging Colorado River. The seemingly endless and tortuous twisting of the trail around the canyon wall as it descended down, coupled with the increasing heat, began to plague the hikers. They would have to cover the rest of the three miles to the river alone more than likely, for Edward Joseph would be assisting in the rescue of the Fortunski mule train. Little discussion ensued; most still succumbed to a state of relevant shock. As teachers, they had had little need in their respective lives to put anything out of its misery. As the heat increased, so did the group's perpetual thirst. The awe-inspiring scenery had to be held in juxtaposition with the harsh environment which encapsulated them. Jackie had mentioned a few times from the back what a wretched horror it had been to stand idly by while two mules were shot. Murray and Jacob discounted the complaining because they felt this hike did not serve as the forum for an animal rights debate. As Fortunski stated, this place manifests the harsh realities of life.

As the slot canyon down from Indian Gardens gave way, the inner canyon opened up and the teachers found themselves, all to their amazement, looking upon the majestic and flowing Colorado. A right turn out of the slot canyon, followed by a couple of miles of moderate and undulating hiking along the river, proved placid and serene. Hours had passed since they departed the mule train, and the mule bridge crossing the Colorado and leading into Phantom Ranch could be seen up ahead. Murray and Jacob had been out in front of the pack for a while opining about various theories as to the relativity of this activity with that of managing a school back east, but they always reached the same conclusion—it didn't matter, they were in the Grand Canyon. As the bridge approached, and a wonderful beacon of civilization it seemed, they were overtaken by the indefatigable march of Edward Joseph who seemed more at home in the Grand Canyon than the mules themselves. He passed right through the pack and caught up with Wilde and Moore.

"Howdy, girls!" He bellowed in the most obstreperous manner. Edward's torrid pace allowed him easily to zip past all. "I heard some of the flatlanders you have with you withered in the heat of reality." He kept on walking. "Some have it; some don't," he sent flying back toward them, relegating Wilde and Murray to continue to bring in this particular herd.

"You know," Moore chirped in, "I don't believe that man can pay a compliment."

"Probably right, or that happens to be close." They watched Joseph drive on across the bridge and into the trees of the campground and up towards Phantom Ranch. The teachers eventually arrived—exhausted.

The remainder of their travels to the lodge proved uneventful in nature. But after the mule incident, it would have taken an earthquake to arise their intellect for the group still felt numb. They were met by Edward Joseph, shown their bunkhouses, given beds and told to report to lunch in the chow house/ general store located in the heart of the oasis. The four bunkhouses lined the trail that served as the main thoroughfare of the village. These air-conditioned edifices offered more than rest and comfort; they represented civilization—all found it difficult to leave the crib and head out again into the heat, but lunch called. Each bunkhouse contained five bunk beds, which would mean the four structures could house forty people; the teachers numbered thirty-seven total. Interestingly enough, the entirety of Phantom Ranch for their stay possessed only members of the educator summit.

The group's mood dramatically transformed when they met the avuncular Thomas Charles working the mess hall. Upon entering, Murray's and Wilde's group found that the only other people in the building worked the ranch. The nerves of the group tenuously hung in the balance for all felt weak due to the hike in the heat, along with disheartened after the mule incident. Thomas had sandwiches and cold pitchers of water on the rowed tables, enough for the group.

"Welcome to Phantom Ranch! I heard your hike down became rather eventful. For that I am sorry." He glanced around the room empathetically. "Though I am Thomas Charles, people around here just call me Uncle Tom." His winsome smile and charismatic charm made the entire group comfortable and oblivious to all that had transpired that day. His character seemed the stark opposite of the irascible and vociferous Edward; Uncle Tom served as the quintessence of affability. "Relax. Mellow. Easy big fella," seemed to be soothing phrases he dropped in a long draw to palliate any troubles he overheard from his guests. He seemed an amalgamation of Walt Whitman and Henry David Thoreau, not in look, but in manner. He had them enthralled with his tales of mountain climbing, European touring, biking, and just basically sucking the marrow out of life. He delivered his manner and dialogue without pretense, and within an hour, it became quite clear as to why people called him Uncle Tom.

The blithe mood of the group evaporated when Edward barged into the mess hall blasting out orders for them to grab their gear that the "Box" called their names. The teachers would learn that the "Box" proved to be a viciously hot and tortuous path north through the Grand Canyon. The serendipity of Uncle Tom's company soon faded as Crazy Eddie had them humping up the trail on what he termed a "hardy side hike" up the Clear Creek trail to see the mighty Colorado from a highly interesting position. Most of the group felt knackered and preferred the air conditioning—with the exception of Murray and Wilde who blistered past Edward and out the door. The last thing they heard him say pertained to being back in time for chow.

All throughout their hike up on Clear Creek Trial, Murray and Jacob could not help but speculate as to the rationale for running them out on another hike after they had just slogged 9.8 miles and shot two mules. Jacob quickly ascertained the rationale of it all upon arriving back at Phantom Ranch just in time for dinner. He thought it odd that as they came back into camp from the north, they were told to wait in their bunks until called. Within minutes of getting into the bunkhouse and lying down, Uncle Tom peeked his head in, and told his group of Humphries, Kues, Bockhold, and Klaber that they could go directly to the mess hall. When they arrived, they noticed Beth, Francesca, and Aaron already sitting, along with a slew of other presumable teachers.

"Hey gang, welcome to dinner," Uncle Tom pleasantly smiled, "Tonight we will be having cowboy stew." Charles went on about the serving procedure, ladling your neighbors' bowl and passing it, all the while Murray noticed that Edward Joseph led a group passed the mess hall, down the trail to the mule corral. In his group, which consisted of around twelve, he saw his own group's Jackie, Nathan and Erin.

"Jacob," Murray said in a hushed voice, "Look out the window."

"Where are they going?"

"Hey, remember, the three with us walked away from the mules. You think that could be coincidence? Or are they taking them out?" Murray felt intrigued.

"I have no idea." Both quietly ate, ruminating over the possible ramifications of this group, which by now were not going to attend dinner with them. They counted the room; only twenty-five teachers. The entrance of mule train driver Kristin Fortunski toward the end of dinner walking on her own two feet repulsed any doubt as to what had happened on their hike down. The tests that the Academy of Principals said could perpetually happen had happened.

"Good evening, for you who did not meet me, I am Kristin Fortunski. I am a mule train driver. You guys that happened to be on the trail with me, I wish to applaud you. You took the bull by the horns and did what needed to be done today. In fact, all of you did. Sitting in this room, we have twenty-five of the thirty-seven who started from the top. Each group faced a troubling situation which required the group to take leadership, demonstrate resolve, and make a painful, yet necessary step. My group had to put down two mules with broken legs." No one said a word. All chewing had stopped. If the other groups faced a similar challenge as Murray and Jacob did, then coincidence did not play a factor. All had been staged. Murray remembered how Erin, Jackie and Nathan walked away—couldn't stomach the shooting.

"You had been told everything reflected a test by the Academy of Principals. This group demonstrated a proper skill. Each member remaining here today took responsibility in putting down an animal. Whether you shot the animal or helped with the others in a cooperative manner, this group demonstrated that at times in life, painful choices must be made. Your colleagues who failed are now getting a one-way ride up to the surface of the South Rim. They are effectively out of the Academy of Principals. Though it pains me to set up a situation where animals must be put down, we need to know if the future principals of this country have what it takes to run the schools properly in order to contribute to society most efficaciously."

Murray sat stunned. Jacob seemed livid by the thought of a staged accident where they purposely hobbled two mules with broken legs to see if they would take charge, make tough decisions. Not only did they kill two mules in their group, but apparently the other two groups ran across similar scenarios all having to probably put animals down. It seemed drastic. Then, Colonel Nutt emerged from the back with Alliston and Hauer again. At that moment, Jacob and Murray knew they weren't in Kansas any more.

"Congratulations all, you have passed a key test in moving on toward your principalship," Colonel Nutt perused the room, "I know it seems a bit overwhelming to see us here, along with Fortunski, but I can assure you, your responses today toward adversity have proved excellent."

"Now," interrupted Dr. Hauer, "I would like to clear up some information you have been told. You have been told to always tell the truth and react and act with your gut. You have. This vital information will begin to come to fruition now. You have always known that the principal represents a breed apart from the other educators; that happens to be correct because principals are not educators in the traditional sense any longer." Hauer seemed satisfied with the group of recruits.

"Now," picked up Colonel Nutt, "You will be members of, and participating actors in, the Homeland Security Office. Today should serve as a bit of history for all of you left."

"The principals of public schools," chimed in Jennifer Alliston, "Became part of the Department of Homeland Security following the Great Compromise of 2025." Alliston surveyed the room. "Following the Great Compromise, a system of weeding out undesirable and potentially destructive people from our culture needed to be instituted. The Central Intelligence Agency, along with the National Security Agency and Federal Bureau of Investigation held the perpetrators of evil at the water's edge. However, homegrown terrorism, radicalism, and criminalism also needed to be monitored."

"Furthermore," interjected Dr. Hauer, "Our society radically changed post-G.C. and the public demanded results for their tax dollars. Teachers had to be held accountable for their skills, but new in America, the government decided for the first time to hold students' responsible for their education. The series of examinations set up to determine a student's future saw implementation in the years following the Great Compromise."

"Based upon test scores," continued Jennifer Alliston, "Students received placement in the variety of schools—all publicly funded. Knowing the pertinacious public to ever so shrewdly analyze waste of tax money, coupled with the fact that the Compromise demanded certain rights for the workers, builders, and thinkers of this country—health care for all, education for all, protection for all—teachers found themselves on the front line of the battle for productivity and civility. Mediocrity would no longer be embraced."

"Key to the funding of these programs for the productive," returned Dr. Hauer, "Certain enterprises in the nation found themselves truncated. For instance, welfare, food stamps, government housing and other social programs supporting the sedentary of our society received the budget ax. The unproductive were left to fend for themselves and often turned to crime. The sociologists at the time knew this; however, they also knew that a large percentage of the people, once the proverbial pacifier had been yanked from their dependent mouths, would in fact go to work and be productive."

"That happens to be where the military stepped in," Colonel Nutt re-entered the conversation. "A five year period of social turmoil ensued where the generational welfare recipients revolted, rioted, and attempted to destroy parts of cities all over the country. The public called the military, the buttress of civility, to put down such insurrections. Martial Law had been declared in some major cities, shoot to kill orders on looters and violent protesters instituted. The public applauded, after all, they worked and this lot essentially rioted to not work. After the quelling of Los Angeles, Atlanta, Dallas, Philadelphia and parts of New York City where thousands were killed, the rioting ceased. Criminals rounded up, murderers and insurrectionists shipped to the United States Penal Colony in Guam, and all of the rest of the country settled nicely."

The group of educators sat without much surprise, for all of this knowledge could be learned and had been taught in the electronic textbooks in schools for decades. The only radical information shared, that indeed had been new, centered on the Homeland

Security Association. All teachers knew that something different exuded from the principals, but most felt shocked at this revelation, though it did explain their lifestyle. Now another voice piped in from behind.

"The group of non-hackers are loaded on a mule preparing for departure," added Edward Joseph, "I am here to take anyone else who plans on bailing out." This confused the twenty-five left.

"This folks, I am afraid, requires a decision on your part," Colonel Nutt had stepped forward again. This eclectic mix of educators, military, scientists, and what appeared to be Phantom Ranch employees exhibited a well-choreographed divulgence of information volleying the floor back and forth to one another, keeping the twenty-five teachers' heads moving side to side from one to another. "I must stress that we have reached the fulcrum in the process. If you choose to go forward, the lever, if you can imagine, will tip. The group with the mules failed the test today; they will be returned to the South Rim, enjoy a nice dinner and rim hike, then be returned to their respective schools of origin." Colonel Nutt continued to scan the room; the mood suddenly became tense. "Though you have passed the test, if you have witnessed, participated, heard, seen or learned anything with which you do not agree on a visceral level, you are to exit this hall, follow Fortunski to the mule corral, and proceed back up the Bright Angel and into your classroom. Remember, this represents an all or nothing proposition; if you stay, you are committed," she paused, then emphasized, "For life." Silence. Absolute silence. Eternal minutes passed.

"The mule train for the El Tovar will be leaving in five minutes," chimed in Fortunski. She stood there completely uninjured, an actor in the entire scheme to test the pertinacity and resolve of a group of unsuspecting, city-dwelling educators. Both Murray and Jacob felt the test bizarre; however, since they possessed nothing but the highest respect for principals and so much desired to enter into that world, both, without discussion, consciously made the choice to stay, placing faith in the government which they trusted and the ideals of the country of which they loved. As Fortunski turned to go and headed for the door an ebullient, "Wait!" rang out from the back. Shockingly, Kyler Humphries rose, "I am going." He hung his head and shuffled shamefully out past the stolid figure of the mule train driver. Fortunski scanned the room with an "anyone else" look upon her countenance, and one rose; a woman Murray had not met, and she headed for the door. The resolve of the rest seemed manifestly affirmed. No one else would be taking the mules up today. Twenty-three remained. Fortunski let the door slam and led her two new riders to the mule corral to ascend out of the Grand Canyon and the fraternity of principals.

CHAPTER FIFTEEN

"The woods are lovely, dark and deep.
But I have promises to keep,
And miles to go before I sleep,
And miles to go before I sleep."

ROBERT FROST – 1922
"STOPPING BY WOODS ON A SNOWY EVENING"

Foolish. Absolutely foolish. Murray Mallory Moore stared up at the ceiling tiles feeling like an abject failure, complete and total. No amount of self-abnegation would alleviate his sense of weakness. The medical table of the ranger station upon which he laid proved cold and comfortable especially in relation to the punishing heat outside in the infernal canyon. The day had been glorious; a 5:00 a.m. wake up call followed by a hearty breakfast, then a seven mile hike into the canyon up to Ribbon Falls. He abstained, most of the hike, from frivolous chatter—even with

Jacob Wilde—choosing to take in the tranquility of morning, the seemingly benign trail up the "Box" along the prattling creek as it echoed off the sheer sides of the slot canyon. The solemnity of the hike, the solitude of spacing between himself and the other hikers fostered a proper mood for reflection upon his immediate and far distant future. His intuitive sense that the canyon trip would prove the beginning of the rest of his life began to come to fruition. The consummation of all of his studies throughout his life, impinging here in this glorious setting, laying the ground work for a lifetime appointment as a principal could not be topped by any one single thing Murray could concoct in his mind.

Proof of the genius in the Academy of Principals manifested itself in the very cast of characters placed at all points to measure the fortitude and resolve of the candidates: from the play acting mule driver, to the charismatic Uncle Tom, to the pugnacious Crazy Eddie, to the steady list of professionals and military personnel, all exuded a confidence in Murray of the catholicity of the training. Even the speech of Uncle Tom as they stopped to change their socks and eat a snack upon leaving the confines of the "Box" canyon, where the environs turned into an open desert floor and a widening of the terrain gave the group a sense of relief following two hours of claustrophobic ambling, proved the exactitude with which this enterprise had been orchestrated. He realized that the forum for seminars and lectures were surreptitiously occurring when the candidates least expected it, though he surmised that every word uttered from here to the end of his career would be steeped in symbolism or contain direct rhetoric that would all be applicable to his occupation. While they paused to rest and recover, Thomas Charles took the opportunity to validate the essence of the excursion to Ribbon Falls.

"Please forgive me group, but I have a penchant for symbolism. So do not think it trite when I craft this trail we currently occupy into a metaphor for life. Our goal in the midst of the desert terrain," a pause, "water. Cool clean water, that which will keep us alive." He stood upon a simple, yet utilitarian rock, like a preacher, a philosopher, or a poet. In a laudatory tone he continued pontificating but toward the sky, not the candidates. "A trail, much like a road, delivers man to a destination. Standing here I can hear Whitman undulating the 'Song of the Open Road' or see Jack Kerouac bent over the steering wheel in a jalopy, remembering his characters in *On the Road.* I can envision Thoreau sitting on the stoop of his cabin or feel the presence of Robert Frost standing on the divide of a trail." Until he paused, Murray did not realize—nor anyone perhaps at that moment—that Uncle Tom had raised his arms to the heavens much like a priest asking God for the transubstantiation of the bread on the altar. He stopped, took a breath, lowered his priestly pose to that of a gun fighter standing akimbo, and turned his gaze from heaven toward his flock sitting there, jaws agape, awaiting his next word.

"What a glorious planet we inhabit, my friends, especially when the lost sheep of the world have a shepherd and a trail and a gate-keeper to vigilantly guard us from the villainous vermin and vacuous vagabonds of the planet!" Uncle Tom seemed possessed now, moving from a state of placidity toward a tirade of vehemence. "As principal candidates," he continued gesticulating, "you stand where two roads diverge in a wood! You have chosen the one less traveled. Are you prepared to grapple with the veracity of the order of the world? Can you help maintain the veneer that has been placed in front of the citizens of the United States?" As Uncle Tom wallowed in an alliterative diatribe, Murray strained to focus on the message. What did he mean by the veneer? This, Murray felt sure, consisted of another test, a warning, a lesson like the mules. Uncle Tom stepped off of the rock and took one knee as close to the circle of candidates as he could, imitating a coach and lowering his voice.

"My friends, future principals, your venerated vocation from hence forth will be to maintain society, clandestinely, from the confines of your school. Since the Great Compromise, the destiny of the United States has not been left up to the vicissitudes of the varmints of our verdant world. Your monitoring of your high school—or schools for some—for the remainder of your lives, will be used in conjunction with the Department of Homeland Security to ensure that our society maintains its voluminous opportunities for those who contribute to our society, and not let it shrivel into some viscous muck of waste. You will not vociferously cry out against the degenerates of your world, you will not vindictively point the finger against the miscreants of our society, you will validate your reports to Homeland with data; you will shed a spotlight on those malignant pariahs who, for all intents and purposes, attempt to derail the sheep from the trail, to destroy our society. You will serve as the first line of defense. You will take point. Be the vanguard. You will be the gatekeeper." As Uncle Tom finished his liturgy with the barely audible utterance of the word "gatekeeper," he bowed his head as if in prayer.

Now lying on his back in the ranger station, Murray had ample time to ruminate about the incredible John the Baptistesque rant in the desert. He could only assume that the Academy of Principals entailed more than he had first surmised. That speech, cloaked in metaphors, and bathed in alliteration, served to awake the radical, yet logical, aspects of his mind. Principals served as gatekeepers of society. As he lay there recovering from the heat, an effervescent epiphany developed in his mind; the Academy of Principals had yet to divulge all of its secrets. This thought became exacerbated as he reflected on the later lecture at Ribbon Falls as Crazy Eddie had expounded upon the devils in the desert in the most virulent manner.

Murray's reverie broke as the National Park Ranger—or maybe not—strode back into the clinic area to check on her heat-exhausted patient. Moore truly could no longer tell if people represented their actual title or if, like Fortunski before and Uncle Tom and Crazy Eddie now, indeed worked for the Department of Homeland Security. Either way, Nancy Maushart had been more of a nurse than a Ranger. After making it to Ribbon Falls and listening to Crazy Eddie's rant about the need for civilization to retain only the contributing masses and expunge the excrescence, he found himself getting thirstier and thirstier until his second trip through the narrow part of the canyon called the "Box" found him dizzy and experiencing cold chills in 110 degree heat. He skipped the bunk-house and found himself force-marched to the Ranger station to make sure he avoided collapse, or worse, heat stroke. He recalled the humiliation of it all, for he had needed to put his hand on Jacob

Wilde's shoulder for support. His shame only became exacerbated when he had been relieved of his pack by Beth or Francesca, for everything became blurry when he arrived at the Ranger station.

"How are you feeling now?" Nancy inquired. "I hope the air conditioning, the electrolytes, and salty snacks have you feeling a bit better." Truth of the matter, not yet, Murray thought; however, he kept that to himself for he feared that his physical weakness may exclude him from the academy. Though Wilde and Moore quietly and secretly competed against one another, Jacob would be traumatized if Murray proved weaker than him. To be sent home as Wilde advanced in the program would have devastated Moore.

"I feel a little better, but to be honest, I am so comfortable at this moment, I would like to continue to rest here. That okay?" Murray subjugated himself.

"Stay as long as you need," Nancy checked his pulse, temperature, and the level of his glass, which needed refilling. "I am going to top off your drink. You eat the pretzels and peanuts." She quickly administered to her patient, handed him the snacks, then continued, "I need to make my rounds. I shall return in fifteen to twenty minutes. You should be ready to go by then." Murray smiled; Nancy left. The ceiling tiles became the focus of his attention again as he shuffled himself on the table and settled back to close his eyes.

He thought of Crazy Eddie standing in Ribbon Falls, letting the water cascade down on him, pummeling his head, neck and shoulders. Throughout, most avoided close proximity with the irascible Edward for fear of a verbal evisceration; he hiked at a torrid pace so avoidance proved easy. Now, the crew all sat on the bank—if you would call it that, more of a rock—of the small pond which grew from the twenty to thirty foot waterfall that seemed to explode out of the earth. Moses Falls seemed more apropos. Amazingly, the rock that Ribbon Falls hit possessed a green mossy blanket soft to the touch and slick to the death. The falls then cascaded off the rock into a pool, and in that pool most of the candidates soaked. That of course offered Crazy Eddie the opportune time to climb off the rock and stand on the bank preaching to his flock—the scene felt Biblical.

"Look around," he raised his arms in much the same fashion as Uncle Tom. "Here we sit in absolute desert and desolation. Remove the water and we die quickly. On that path we hiked here and will soon use to go back to Phantom Ranch; you are bearing witness to a plan, a destination, an engineering project. That path will lead you back to Phantom Ranch. Think of it folks, in the middle of a desert, at the bottom of a hole 5,000 feet deep, man has eked out an oasis with water, air conditioning, food, showers, luxuries, beds, clean sheets, and hell, we even have steak. Everything at Phantom Ranch reflects logistics in moving materials and supplies, hard dedicated work in building and maintaining trails, engineering and science to harness the energy, provide clean water, and recycle sanitation. Nothing located at Phantom Ranch made it there through laziness, incompetence, criminality or any other characteristic you find in the worst forms of life in our society." The group sat enthralled, focused upon every word. Crazy Eddie had become Logos Eddie all of the sudden.

"Life in Phantom Ranch bears a stark verisimilitude to life on this planet and in this country. Think of the planet as the desert, the United States as Phantom Ranch, and you will quickly realize that the country, like the ranch, cannot be maintained by non-hackers, folks filled with lassitude and welfare types with their hands held out. We can't have the mules bringing food down to people who are not performing a task. This philosophy explains why your training had to be held here in Phantom Ranch. Take this back to your schools. If you won't work, you starve! If you won't find water, you die of thirst! If you won't contribute to society, you get the boot! Be part of the team, or get off the trail. You guys and gals have proven yourselves. The metaphorical hike tested your will and nerve to make decisions, to toughen up against nature, and to search your souls." Crazy Eddie scanned the crowd receiving the visual approbation he sought. He finished with, "The nature you will be combating back in your schools will be human nature. Find and burnish the leaders, serve as a buttress for the ideals of this great nation, and sort the wheat from the chaff, or work the system to go against the slackers. Remember, from here on out, you will be the gatekeepers of society."

All in all, Murray reflected; the day had been enthralling. He thought of all of the points in society which seemed to operate smoothly, from the criminal justice system to the public educational system; and to think that he would have a firm grasp upon the steering wheel, controlling the direction of the country, seemed intoxicating to him. Unfortunately, the intoxication of power which seemed to be eddying about him caused him to lose focus on staying hydrated, for as he mulled over his powerful position in the future, he became lax on the hydration. While he should have been drinking, he had been ruminating. Fortunately, the team stuck together and recognized his symptoms and quickly ushered him to the ranger's station where he sat awaiting his verdict. Would he be shipped out like the other weak candidates? He prayed not. America had always been the land of equal opportunity, but for too long, those who did not want to take an opportunity got easily by on the backs of the worker. Atlas truly did shrug post-Great Compromise. The country evolved into a pseudo professional sports team, if a player devolved into a rapscallion who could ruin the fabric of the team, that player would be cut; if a player decided not to participate, practice or play, then that player would be sent packing. Who would fill the void? Call up from the minors? Steal a solid player from another team. Therein lay the immigration policy. Come what may regarding the Academy of Principals, Murray Mallory Moore felt adequately prepared to take on the position and fulfill his duty. Though unsure about the career when first approached by Principal Feinauer, Murray felt he had proven himself, even taking into consideration the setback of being overcome with the heat. Moore had performed his duty on the trail concerning the mules and then accepted the challenge as an appropriate test for the academy. He felt a level of certitude regarding the academy; he would rise to the challenge.

CHAPTER SIXTEEN

"I am not interested in preserving the status quo; I want to overthrow it."

NICCOLO MACHIAVELLI **(1469-1527)** – *THE PRINCE*

Murray Moore reported to his rendezvous spot in the small Northern Kentucky town of Clayton. He had recovered from the Grand Canyon excursion; Ranger Maushart proved more than up to the task of nursing him through his dehydration. The hike out with the other candidates proved uneventfully blissful. They flew back to the Cincinnati area, and as far as Murray knew, all of the candidates were given furlough until the big trip to Lord of the Flies Island—so he always thought of it. He loved that sobriquet. More commonly referred to simply as Guam by officials not wanting to drag out the phrase "United States Penal Colony System," in casual conversation, most used L.O.F.I. During their week off, they were sent home to prepare for their final leg, prepare to move, and meet with a Homeland Security Officer in a local part of town. Murray didn't feel that Northern Kentucky exactly constituted local, but the drive proved less than forty-five minutes. Not ever having much need to go into Kentucky, he found himself quite pleased with the area. After taking the interstate to Grandview, he drove down Route 8 into the quaint nook of Clayton, a rather posh and eclectic neighborhood. Murray's instructions consisted of a relatively terse statement, "Meet agent at Buona Vita, Sixth and McKinney, noon, Thursday."

Having never been to the area, Murray arrived early and decided to take a walk around the neighborhood—absolutely gorgeous in every way. Most of the houses were a hundred and fifty to two hundred years old and highly maintained. The styles apparently had been saved from being razed, for these types oftentimes were bulldozed and newly built structures replaced them. He knew nothing of the area, but thoroughly enjoyed walking down the obvious main avenue of the town and seeing the vibrant, small businesses. The town bustled with activity. From the coffee shop, bookstore, and art gallery, to every form of service such as: hair care, pet care, lawn care, etc., this town with its homely restaurants seemed a wonderfully eclectic village. The nearly one hundred-year-old restaurant in which he now sat appeared to be a refurbished bank from a bygone era. When he provided the maitre d' with his last name, he found himself relegated to the most apropos setting in which to eat, a table in an old bank vault.

About ten minutes prior to noon, in walked Nick Kues, a Kentucky candidate from Louisville whom Murray had met in the Grand Canyon, and finally, Jacob Wilde. Upon their arrival, the server immediately advanced toward their table. Murray felt surprised; for he got the impression that this meeting would be more of a tête-à-tête and not a group discussion.

"Good afternoon gentleman, I am Carling and I will be taking care of you this afternoon." She pulled her tablet up to type in the order.

"Carling," Nick circumspectly repeated, "Odd name. How about the last?"

"Just Daniels. Nothing fancy."

"Well Carling, what sort of wine list do you have?" Nick continued as he received a suspicious look from the server who seemed in Murray's eyes to carry herself with a demeanor of an expelled Catholic schoolgirl who would live in denial of all of her faults for the rest of her life. There seemed something eccentric about her mannerisms.

"You are not to be served alcohol," Carling returned, stupefying her clientele.

"Says who?" Nick Kues invectively retorted.

"Says him," Carling chucked her head to the side and a wizened, aged man stood up from a table which had nothing on it but a glass of what appeared to be water. Heading toward the table, a man sporting a goatee, pastel shirt with coordinating tie, and wearing sunglasses, seemed to drift across the dining area. He stepped to the edge of the table, spoke, then sat with the three men.

"The name, Louis Cottonwood," He glowered at Kues, "No alcohol! This ain't no casual date my friend. All business." Nick appeared nettled, Jacob satisfied, and Murray, as usual, intrigued. "Boys we are going for a walk. When you get to me, you are in the fold, the fraternity, the society. I hope to satiate your inquisitiveness."

"No offense Pops," Kues wantonly spoke, "but what are you going to teach us?"

"Son, I am fifty years older than you, had my back broke once, spent time as a prisoner of war, and sometimes use a cane, and on my worst day, I could teach you something, you snot-nosed punk," Cottonwood rose as if to prepare for a pugilistic resolution.

Kues, in a recalcitrant response uttered, "Please."

"I will say this, son, you sure are sassy; I would show some respect to a man with five confirmed kills! Mind your mouth son, or I will have your liver on a stick eating it as you bleed out. Capiche?" Kues sat silently.

"Five confirmed kills?" inquired Jacob.

"You will learn boy. You will learn. Now, if you will follow me. You have quite a bit to take in and understand about life, the universe, and everything." Cottonwood gazed around sizing up his two, quiet charges, then turning back to Kues, "You are an arrogant upstart boy filled to the brim with chutzpah. Remind me of myself a bit. That spunk got you this far in the process. I advise you to keep your mouth shut, do what you are told, when you are told, and every time you are told and you just may come through this process alive." Kues, taciturn, chose to bite his lip. "You two wall flowers, taking it all in I see, offering nothing, quizzical looks plastered on your melons, well, I trust the system knows what it wants in candidates. Get your gear boys, we are going walking. Carling will save the table. We eat later." Cottonwood climbed up out of his seat and moved toward the door with all the swagger he could muster. Kues, Moore, and Wilde followed, glanced at Carling, received a disgusted grimace for their trouble, then the coterie moved toward the door, following on the heels of their enigmatic host.

The group of men meandered down the main boulevard glancing at the quaint yet opulent looking antique houses along with the multifarious businesses conducting their daily work. One unique manifestation in Clayton which struck the men with a sense of glee took its form in the electronic bookstore, library, coffee shop and massage pallor called Erudite-e. This type of entertainment chain had been in existence for decades and though Murray frequented the Mayfield establishment, Jacob had never done so, and apparently Kues had only gone infrequently. This massive edifice's only rival in girth happened to be the local gymnasium and Y.M.C.A. Intellectuals frequented the establishment, downloading books or music onto their tablets, tuning out the world via headphones, and then relaxing with any manner of fifteen to sixty minute massages, depending upon a given patron's funds. Oftentimes, this process preceded a coffee, cappuccino or tea along with the perusal of a healthy in-house library of classical "coffee-table" books perfectly made from a bygone "paper" era to engage the patrons in casual conversation about their content. This intellectual hotbed rivaled the local health nuts that descended upon the health spas nightly to exercise and maintain their physicality. No one spoke, only observed.

The men window shopped up the avenue, turned down Irvin Terrace and rambled across Fifth Street, then down into the lower numbered byways, all gazing at the lush gardens, immaculate houses, and distinct air of snobbish-ness that accompanies a neighborhood where a community purposely maintains two hundred year old houses all to foster a tranquil ambiance of a foregone era. Cottonwood led them into a corner park where assumingly a house once stood, for it clearly manifested itself to the group that this town boomed as a working class neighborhood around the turn of the 20th century in an era where houses were literally built in endless rows on blocks with only a walkway wide enough for a person to amble to serve as a buffer. Fences and walls were common in that era along with the feeling of living in a pen like animals. Now though, the blocks contained probably one half to a third of the normal houses allowing spacious yards between and in this particular "block" layout, a public park on the corner. Cottonwood took rest upon a park bench; the three silent followers imitated their leader.

"Well, what do you see?" Cottonwood, though seemingly healthy, rasped out this question, his energy a bit drained following the brisk pace he had set.

"A pretty nice neighborhood. I like it," Murray replied.

"And you, Wilde? Kues?" Nick, still taciturn, however, chose not to answer.

"I see economic success, a highly desired community in which to live," Jacob now responded.

"You are sitting in the neighborhood that Louis Cottonwood molded, my boys." The gaffer looked around with a hint of nostalgia in his eyes. "After my military service, boys, I joined Homeland Security in 2027. At thirty-five years old, I had seen some brief military action, killed a few well-deserved enemies of America, found myself a prisoner of war for a brief time period, and ultimately made it home, finished my tour, then came back to my home town Clayton." Louis stared at them. "This town represented the type of cesspool America had become, with huge swaths of the population lying around on their duffs, collecting a government check. Scum! Vermin!" Cottonwood now looked over their shoulders with what could only be described as the "fifty yard stare."

"I grew up in this pit of slothful humanity; but of course, I did not realize how reprehensible these people were until I came back after serving this country. I suffered, I agonized, I killed to preserve this country, a country where nearly half didn't pay income taxes and quite close to the same amount became accustomed to food stamps, government assistance, and/or free rent. I tried to get back into the Army—told them my level of disgust. They sent me to the Department of Homeland Security." He leaned back upon the park bench drawing his face into a smile. "Boys, after I passed a series of idiosyncratic tests, I came back home to Clayton; I made this town. I affected change. The type of change you men will help to foster in your role of principal. You will be working with men like myself—indirectly of course."

Kues and Moore sat intrigued, Wilde a bit more befuddled. Murray could hold back no more, eager to know all, "How and what did you do?"

"After the Great Compromise, the politicians decided that welfare would go extinct. Food Stamps the way of the dodo bird! Criminals would be punished. No longer would the worker have to sit as Atlas holding the Earth trying not to shrug. I had studied a bit of sociology in my military years, so I had been chosen to live in Clayton and report firsthand on the changes wrought by the Great Compromise. After a year into the program, the politicians had made us to understand that the period of transition would be painful, but necessary."

"I sat here as the new 'anti-working' government policies kicked in; those filled with lassitude became motivated, those perpetually incorrigible shipped to L.O.F.I., and the willfully useless either starved, or became depraved, and ultimately faced neutralization. I watched as the unemployment benefits began to dry up, shriveled 10% each month until gone. The effect manifested itself immediately. Family units pulled together and took those jobs 'beneath' them. The gas station attendant job certainly would be beneath anyone when he or she could sit at home on food stamps, a government check, and dine on a steady diet of cigarettes and Budweiser watching nothing but satellite television. When the nipple had been plucked, those who had adopted 'learned helplessness' suddenly had their reality shaken, thus stirred, they took on occupations. With health care provided for all working Americans, much of the job issues resolved themselves."

"When the food stamps were cut 20% a month until gone, a massive scrambling of the obese masses began to move. The educated workers of the world used the poverty of third world countries to demonstrate true penury. Only in America could someone on welfare not only be corpulent, but they coddled obese pets as well. Free food gone, government checks gone, people went to work. They took any and every job. Family units solidified, teams if you will, formed. The first part of the congressional plan worked to perfection."

"Louis," interrupted Murray, "What does that have to do with this neighborhood?"

"Clayton, the people, the town, exuded all of the qualities of a cesspool. This town exemplified all that happened to be wrong in America at the time. Most of the people were renters using government housing vouchers. The amount of food stamps, single parent households, and non-working staggered the imagination. Towns like Clayton existed ubiquitously across this nation—disgusting. However, when the programs were cut, the herd had been prodded and began to move. Some refused. As their food stamps dropped and government money dried up, they turned to crime. The government, in all of its newfound wisdom, took the money saved from wasting it upon the human offal of this town and every town like it and hired police, detectives, and myself—money well spent. As the human excrement began to sell drugs for money, rob their fellow neighbors, steal from local establishments, they were met by unsympathetic mobs of vigilantes and others in cahoots with the law—a esprit de corps formed between the law enforcement and the citizen worker. With war declared upon the useless, and times desperate for the criminality, oftentimes these miscreants hit multiple felonies per arrest. The plan proved perfect."

The age upon Louis Cottonwood's face seemed to ebb away. This trip down memory lane served as the proverbial fountain of youth for him. "Yes, boys, the population of this neighborhood dropped by a third within two years. Between the murders, the suicides, the arrests and convictions, this simple application of logic and demand of personal responsibility had led the rest of the animals down here to toe the line. This neighborhood proved the norm, not the exception. Targeted application of law enforcement helped reduce the population in the lazy areas of major cities by a third. Needless to say, the unemployment level plummeted, government expenditures flattened or decreased, tax revenues skyrocketed, health care became funded, and the malaise inflicted upon this country by the leaches it allowed to attach itself lifted. America headed in the right direction."

"We know all of this," interjected Jacob Wilde looking at both of his teacher colleagues. Louis Cottonwood's rancorous vitriol slung at the Claytonians of the past had made approaching him in any conversation seem risky. The teachers did know all of this history, though all three would admit this had been the first time someone historically present had explained it to them. All of their knowledge had been obtained in school, or books, or historical documentaries. Louis Cottonwood served as the incarnation of this historical transformation. It had been a tumultuous time in America. Food riots occurred by the "poor." The workers, along with law enforcement backed by the military, countered the implacable vagrants with a force of their own. The civil unrest proved brief, for the sheer antipathy for willfully unemployed ebulliently erupted around the country. With Europe's economic collapse a decade before due to its attempted financing of the nanny state, Americans had a prelude of the turmoil to come. The ranks of the non-workers began to shrink as many took jobs, realizing the fate of their movement. All of this had been taught.

"Yep, then the immigrants came," Cottonwood offered up. "Many thought it crazy to open the doors to the world, but once the country settled down, L.O.F.I. became one of the most densely populated parts of the country. There truly did exist a shortage of workers for the unemployment rate collapsed. The crazy plan for paths to citizenship for those here and a one-way ticket to GITMO for anyone who invaded, later ended all of that controversy. Sure, some guys bellyached in Congress. The Moderates shouted 'em down. People were tired of the partisanship. Common sense dictated a plan needed to be formulated. That Senator Schmitt proved a shrewd businessman; turns out, he served as an educator as a previous occupation."

"Look, I gotta be square with ya boys," Cottonwood paused, "I didn't think that immigrant policy would work. But, by God, every job had to be registered in a national database; the government always knew what America needed and the world eagerly supplied the talent to fill it. Back then, the term 'big government' had been anathema to many, a pejorative, but I gotta tell ya' boys, a proper application of big government will get the job done. They carefully planned to immigrate a diversified populace—a steady mix from the planet to truly make this country a balanced sociological enterprise. With the propaganda from television and movies that inter-racial marriage would be copasetic, along with the institutionalization of gay marriage, along with the old generation of the 20th century dying off, well, this country changed, and for the better. Hell, I remember a debate at a town hall meeting when some fogy challenged Senator Schmitt on his advocacy of same-sex marriage. That senator looked this geezer in the eye and said, 'Boy! You ever seen a gay couple on welfare? I don't give a hoot in hell what people do as long as they don't think they are going to suck off the government teat; furthermore, if you think God will banish them to Hell, let God do his own dang work. We have a country to run down here.' By God, that ended the debate there and continued to quell the conundrum nationwide. Live and let live boys."

"Again, Mr. Cottonwood," Wilde continued a tad frustrated, "We know this; we teach it. Why did the Academy of Principals want us to drive down here, meet you and walk around this neighborhood?"

"Simple. You don't know everything yet boys. Your final step into this secret society if you will, this fraternity, will occur on the way to Guam. The powers that be wanted you to meet me; as a principal, you guys will be working with us—the boots on the ground if you will. I represent the rubber that meets the road. I cannot elucidate any further. I can only say, trust the system. Trust the government for its infallibility exists all around you." He spread his arms around indicating their need to view the village. "Ready you are. The next time we meet, you will fully understand that which you shall undertake for the rest of your lives. Happy travels to L.O.F.I. boys."

CHAPTER SEVENTEEN

Murray awoke suddenly and violently, troubled by a dream. As an intellectual, the dream horrified him, for in it he taught, but in a world where pathetic literature had become endemic in the schools. He often had this recurring nightmare where he forcibly had to teach a book on vampires or zombies or worse, love. He shook his head of the cobwebs as he tried to ascertain his location and his thoughts. Other than abhorring the books of infinitesimal importance in theme, development, and pragmatism in the world, he struggled to figure out his last thoughts prior to falling asleep. Murray glanced around the room realizing that he had fallen asleep in "Little Britain." He began to have pellucid thoughts concerning his rationale for hiding in his hermitage the night prior to the trip to Washington D.C. to prepare to fly to The United States Federal Penal Colony on Guam. He felt cramped and sure he slept quite a while. Murray pushed down his recliner and moved out of "Little Britain," putting the Conrad book back upon the shelf.

Murray moved out into his empty classroom. Being July, not only were the kids gone, but the school felt like a recently abandoned civilization that comprehended man would never return. Eerily he moved into the room stretching, looking upon his wall, catching the mural of Jonathan Swift running, knife and fork in hand, with a dialogue cloud above his head, "Cook me the babies!" Murray laughed for Swift and his adherence to logos often gave him cause to smile; his own infectious, irreverent humor encouraged mural paintings such as this, for the students remembered the material better if he provided a good "one-liner," or in this case, a good "one-image." The painting often whetted the appetite of his students who excelled in the area of ethos and/or pathos, but who generally discounted the realm of logos. Reflecting back, Murray remembered the last time in class he discussed "A Modest Proposal" and the intellectual conflagration that followed.

"Mr. Murray, I have a question."

"Yes, Toren."

"I have a question about a modern application of Swift's idea," again, Toren represented the rare minority left in America; his completely black family tree put him in the same unique category as himself, for Murray's genetics offered nothing but white ancestry. With the huge influx of immigrants from all around the globe, the abandonment of inter-racial taboos and the dream of Dr. King nearly coming to full fruition, Toren and Murray represented a unique mono-colored demographic, although society viewed it not as racial superiority nor inferiority, but just a quirkiness—like a guy six foot ten inches tall.

"Toren, ask away!"

"In modern America, why such a harsh treatment of bad parents? It seems as radical to ship bad parents to L.O.F.I. as it did in Swift's time to eat unwanted children. Why not punish them and leave them in society?" Toren's question proved provocative, for in any given room, a teacher would almost certainly have one, if not more, fostered and/or adopted child. Though he felt a tad apprehensive about starting the conversation, Moore knew that this proved to be his function in American culture. Here quantified the teacher's value to society, answering the difficult questions without a series of platitudes, augmenting the next generation's intellect and extolling upon the virtues of the late 21st century dynamism that exuded from the United States at that moment.

"Can anyone answer Toren's question?" Moore figured he would toss the hot potato out to the class. Several hands extended. "Ellen Davis, by all means, divulge."

"One of the most important aspects of society today would be the raising and rearing of children. Improper parenting leads oftentimes to poor citizens," Ellen glanced around the classroom, "Besides, if you don't want to have children, our health care system provides adequate prevention methods."

"Excellent, Ellen. Now, why not just take the children away. Why punish the parents? Wouldn't the removal of their children be enough?" Moore felt the need to press on, for this social restructuring evolved directly from the Great Compromise. "Whitney Jo, please expound."

"The removal of a child and into foster care for adoption costs the state an inordinate amount of money from childcare services to monthly stipends for the adoptive parents through the first eighteen years of life. Though the child bears no culpability in the situation, the parent, fully aware of the responsibilities of being a parent, bears full responsibility for the child. Their burden thrust upon society should be viewed no less than any other crime which costs the citizens of this nation years of annual salaries."

"Whitney Jo, Ellen, Toren, anyone, what do you think of the policy?" Moore pushed to see if they could quantify an opinion on the matter.

"I think it draconian to convict them of a felony per each child permanently removed," inserted, until then, a quiet student.

"Miss Singleton, why?"

"Well," Amanda continued, "the parents only committed one crime, neglecting their children. It should only be one penalty."

"Absolutely not," Toren chimed in, "Each child has had a crime committed against them. Society will have to pay and care for each child. If the mother killed them, she would receive three convictions for murder, not one."

"Excellent Toren. Excellent. Our society has decided to hold its citizens personally responsible for bringing children into the world. If the child became a burden to society by no fault of their own, their parents will be held responsible." Murray loved the law, mainly because he felt it closely adhered to the practices laid out by Swift hundreds of years ago. "If the child, in being neglected, malnourished, abused must be removed, then the parents must pay the penalty. Now, provided that the parents performed his and her duty and the child chooses to buck the societal norm, well, now you know why we have expulsions."

"What about fathers who run out on their families?" inquired a normally quiet Justine.

"Can anyone answer Ms. Kaminsky?" Moore did not have to wait long, "Ah, thank you again, Ellen."

"Absent fathers hunted down by the law can be convicted of a felony for each child abandoned. A father who deserts three or more children will receive a one-way ticket to Guam," Davis's eyes panned the room, "And it serves him right!"

"All of that correctly stated," Moore continued, "Remember this kids, you bring it into the world, you keep it, you clean it, and you feed it. No more, no less. Not one American wants to work harder because you can't manipulate contraception. Be a responsible citizen and contribute positively to society! And with that, class dismissed."

His reverie broken, Murray surveyed the room. This could be his last time to meditate reflectively in his oasis from the world. In heading to D.C. in order to catch a flight to the Island of Guam, he would miss the next couple of weeks. Upon his return, he would be placed in a new school. All of this would be gone. Bobby Feinauer had told both he and Jacob that the existing principal's duty, when one of his/her teachers flew to L.O.F.I. for final phase of the indoctrination to the order, had to be the hiring of a crew to organize and pack up the teacher's material to be shipped to that teacher's new placement. Lugubriousness began to set upon Murray like a pall. Though he didn't mind the moving of his flags and other relics of the world, the most disturbing thought lay in the fact that his new school would be without the art he helped to have painted in the hall, the offices, and the classrooms. From the jocularity of a Swiftian figure shouting, "Cook me the babies!" to the solemnity of Lennie, with back turned toward the class, walking toward a bunny as George followed with left hand on his shoulder and right concealing a gun bent up behind his back, to the painted ajar door frame with 101 blazoned upon it and "Abandon all hope, ye who enter here" above it, each just made his soul soar. The blending of such aforementioned literary scenes, from the irreverent humor of infanticide coupled with cannibalism, to the grim realities of *Of Mice and Men,* all provided him with the motivation to teach, to instruct and most importantly, to lead. He strode to the back windows looking out over the empty teacher parking lot, the lake and State Route 4 busily hurling cars north and south.

Just a few days prior to the end of the school year, and possibly his teaching career, a poignant moment occurred when once again he had to admonish the two stooges—so he called them—Jordan Chappell and Christopher Schlegel. Though not quite recalcitrant problems, they were related more closely to wandering sheep. Their classroom transgressions tended to be more of the venial and not mortal kind.

"Boys! You are out of your seats and at the window again."

"Yeah," blurted out Jake Tunnell, as the fourth of the group, the stately Mr. Scheer, chose his normal course of silence. "Get 'em Mr. Moore!"

149

"Thanks Jake," Murray attempted to regain class. "What now boys?"

"Oh yeah, Mr. Moore," Chappell could barely control himself, "I am trying to think of the feeding word."

"What?" Murray became perplexed.

"Feed to animals word," Chappell literally appeared to be ready to run in circles.

"Fodder, you dolt!" Schlegel rapped him upside the head gently knocking his glasses askew. Tunnell began to guffaw while Scheer shook his head in a despondent Yoda-esque manner.

"Jordan," Murray began to move toward the window, "Explain please."

"Fodder for class. You have fodder for class in the parking lot," Chappell puffed out his chest and scanned the room looking for signs of approbation for the proper application of elevated diction.

When Murray reached the window, Jordan's observation proved accurate. A chain gang walked the parking lot—thirty to forty of them, arms length apart scouring the pavement looking for any trash. Frequently the general public would witness a sea of misdemeanor offenders fulfilling their community service, all wearing bright yellow shirts with black lettering reading, "Bound for L.O.F.I.?" This crew, free to roam, followed by two police officers had free reign to offer the community service they would like to perform. For instance, in the winter you might find them descending upon a neighborhood like a benevolent pack of locusts, shoveling walks, assisting motorists, checking on invalids and the elderly or any other manner of winter work. In the spring time, they might arrive in a neighborhood, take the lawnmowers from the citizens and help them conduct their work. Once they fulfilled their hours of community service, the officer would acknowledge them in the middle of their endeavors, and the highly visible shirt would come off and be handed to the officer. The custom of the day proved to generally be a round of applause from the others on the chain gang, along with the residents. All respected the men and women who completed their service, for they sinned against society and their transgression had been repaid in the form of service, and since the common man could find himself in an equally displeasing state for violations such as: too many traffic tickets, drunk driving, public intoxication, disorderly conduct, drug possession, etc., the common man usually did not castigate the man repaying his debt to society—plus the community viewed such behavior distastefully.

"Mr. Moore," Schlegel interrupted Murray's thoughts, "Why do they call it a chain gang? They do not have chains!"

"Well class, did all hear the question?" Here, Chappell's teaching fodder manifested itself. "Come on over and have a look. Anyone know the answer?"

"The original prison details from the 19th and 20th centuries chained the convicts together and forced them to work," Sean Scheer shared without enthusiasm as if all in the room knew the answer.

"Brilliant once again, brave Sean."

"I would be gone!" Jordan impetuously blurted out.

"No you would not meathead," Tunnell stood up from his desk. "Anybody arrested and put on the chain gang has a data chip implanted with a list of their offenses."

"Yeah," Schlegel responded smacking Jordan again, "When you run, you go straight to L.O.F.I."

"Very good!" Murray glowed. "Anyone else? Why?" He paused then called on a student, "Mr. Kuertz."

"Because Mr. Moore, you get slapped with three felonies," Ray unctuously poured out his answer in a accent that seemed to move from Brooklyn to Jersey, "One for felonious fleeing, one for felonious public endangerment and one for your original misdemeanor being automatically changed to a felony. You'd have to be stupid to run."

"Yes. Yes. Yes. Excellent boys. Back in our seats class," Murray moved toward the front of the room. "Now, this type of punitive atonement can only exist in what type of government class?" A hand went up. "Justin Smith."

"A meritocracy," Justin offered.

"Like which novel?"

"*Starship Troopers.*"

"Good Justin, you read it." Murray beamed.

"My brother didn't read it," Justin pressed a sly grin upon his face.

"Kevin Smith, why didn't you finish the book? You had plenty of time!"

"I don't know," Justin shook his head; his twin brother, Kevin, looked away, Murray became a tad crestfallen, but only momentarily. He coveted these times. And yes, not all of these guys would go on to a full university; some would opt for a two year college and the rest would go into a customer service and business trade school, but the system, though not perfect, approached infallibility. Murray's muse moved from his blithe memory to the reality of his current quandary—he must give up the classroom to run a school. He found solace in the decision knowing that Jacob would accompany him. Not only on the final leg in Guam, and the trip to Washington D.C. to catch the plane to L.O.F.I., but apparently in the present for his audible, quick shuffle of feet always proved a foreshadowing visit and in the deserted building, a thunderous omen.

"I knew I would find you here," Jacob waltzed in.

"Ruminating. Reminiscing. Feeling a bit melancholy," Murray examined Jacob; he felt the pang of leaving. "I will miss them." Jacob knew no platitude would suffice to ease their anguish. He would not give one, nor would Murray wish to hear one.

"What do you say we walk out to the faculty court yard, have a stiff drink and commiserate upon our occupational loss and celebrate upon our career gain?"

"Not a bad idea." For years, each knew how to pick the other up. If Murray knew Jacob completely, he could guess what would follow. "Any beverage?"

"Please," Wilde's disappointed countenance revealed a disbelief in asking the obvious. "Tsingtao for me and Coors for you. Iced and next to the door waiting to head to the courtyard." He smiled, "You game?"

"Yes, sir." A thought exploded in Murray's mind. "Feeling a bit nostalgic, the evening seems cool, how about a small fire in the pit?" Moore's mind raced gleefully, he knew what would cheer him immensely and would brighten up this little sojourn in the cloistered courtyard under the few stars visible due to the light pollution.

"We will need some paper to get it going. Some wood still there."

"Don't worry; I have the paper. Plenty!"

"Wait!" Jacob knew that look on Murray's face—the look of some sophomoric act about to be committed. The very enthusiastic glow that would cause Murray to quote Shackleton, Mallory, and Scott and would cause himself to sycophantically follow Moore up a mountain in the rain, running across sand dunes away from thunderstorms and up a canyon to a waterfall in the snow. "What are you going to burn?"

Murray scurried into "Little Britain" laughing the hideous mad scientist laugh. He shoved passed his Union Jack chair and pulled on his bookshelf moving it at a forty-five degree angle allowing him to get to the back door of his neighboring classroom. Wilde recognized that indomitable spirit of Murray he admired, for when he had one of his visions and set a goal in front of him, nothing would stop the tsunami coming.

"Murray, why are you sneaking into Sammy Reed's room?"

"I am going to give this jackanapes a souvenir and provide him with an intellectual service." He cracked the unlockable door, slid in and bolted, for some unknown reason, to his bookshelf. "I am going to save you, Sammy Reed, from your own ignorance." Murray pilfered Reed's bookshelf.

"What are you planning to torch?" Wilde called from "Little Britain." Murray slid back into his hovel, closed the door, pushed back the shelf and turned holding some books Wilde quite frankly had not read: *Hunger Games, Twilight,* and *Fifty Shades of Grey.*

"It will be a pleasure to burn!"

CHAPTER EIGHTEEN

> *"Government's view of the economy could be summed up in a few short phrases: If it moves, tax it. If it keeps moving, regulate it. And if it stops moving, subsidize it."*

RONALD REAGAN SPEECH **1986**

The final phase of admittance to the Academy of Principals had begun. From all of the correspondence and discussion, Jacob Wilde and Murray Mallory Moore had come as far as one could go without total commitment. Late one Friday night, the two future principals finished their beers, burned pathetic literature, slept a final night and left Mayfield High School without fanfare to catch the train to Washington D.C. Since they had to fly from D.C. to Guam with all of the other national candidates, Murray pushed for a nostalgic train ride. Jacob agreed to take the long journey in hopes of getting to pick at Murray's brain about their future. The night of beers and Murray playing Montag offered no real opportunity, for the evening turned into a rant about poor story development, pathetic diction, and dystopias without reason as Murray maniacally shredded his colleague's books and offered the pages up to their controlled conflagration. The train ride offered no more chance at discussion, for Amtrak felt the need to show back-to-back-to-back the *Albus Severus Potter* trilogy. Murray, a rabid Potter fan, disappeared as soon as he saw the line up. He vanished into the film car and immediately joined the round table dinner and discussion which followed. The ten hour train ride allowed Murray and Jacob only twice to come into contact with one another. Wilde felt sure that Moore had known of the films, and could not for the life of him fathom why Murray would invite him on this mode of transportation and turn this into the Hogwarts Express knowing full well that Jacob possessed a disdain for literature, and furthermore loathed this pandemic fantasy which seemed to keep breaking out across society. Not until they had checked into their hotel, visited the National Holocaust Museum, and exited out onto the National Mall did Jacob feel he had the opportunity to bring up a discussion with his closest friend.

"Well, what did you think of the museum?"

"Disgusting! Nauseatingly revolting," Moore emphatically exploded.

"I agree; the slaughtering of six to eight million people horrifies me."

"Please," Murray rudely spouted. "The population of the planet now rests at 9.5 billion. If you think all of that life happens to be precious you have lost your marbles." Murray Moore prided himself on never equivocating and in this sense he chose not to again, plus he enjoyed getting Jacob riled up so that he would perch himself upon his constitutional soapbox and preach. "I am sure 6 to 60 million could easily be disposed of. The proverbial herd of humanity needs to be culled. My disgust arises from the fact that Germans—chock full of intellectuals—found themselves so bent upon a warped sense of perception and social Darwinism that they chose to exterminate the brightest, most talented, intellectual and amazingly productive people on the planet. That would equate to hating bad baseball players then going on a shooting spree at the All-Star game. Really?"

Jacob Wilde felt an existential crisis landing on him, and he inadvertently provoked the Semitophile, who now went off the deep end with a supercilious rant about non-productive, able-bodied people over-populating the planet and nearly destroying America a couple of generations ago. This historical, spiritual and philosophical sojourn on the Capital Mall had not started as Jacob had wished. He decided to endure the rant as they walked past the Washington Monument, skirting around the World War II monument and its crowds on Independence Avenue, and headed in the direction of the Lincoln Memorial via the Martin Luther King statue. They walked silently taking in all the pomp, marble, bustle and history that encapsulated Washington D.C.

"Murray, I hope you don't mean that?"

"Mean what?"

"The wholesale slaughter of millions just because they don't fit your notion of what humanity should embody," Jacob moralized. Murray strode on impervious to this sudden rash of ethos.

"Are you kidding me? You wouldn't take all the drug cartels, murderers, rapists, terrorists, anarchists, and unproductive societal leeches and place them on a raft out to sea? I am not advocating the elimination of a race, or political group, or religion or ethnic group." Murray stopped, looked incredulously at his friend, then continued, "What has gotten into you today?"

"Look, if you advocate the killing of millions just because you don't agree with them, that makes you equal to Hitler, Stalin, Mao or any other mass murderer."

"Hey, if you want rapists and murderers and drug dealers in your neighborhood fine. I don't. I bet most of the Americans around you would agree," Murray continued on, stepping onto the Reusch Bridge crossing the Tidal Basin, flipping his head from left to right taking in the Jefferson and World War II memorials at a nauseating rate. Moore tried to decide if Wilde's mood here reflected sincerity or not. Generally, when he would rant and rave, Jacob would nod his head, smile, roll his eyes, and then attempt to placate his mood afterwards with some words of Gandhian wisdom. Blocking his view of the Martin Luther King, Jr. Memorial stood the statue of a man standing next to what appeared to be a grizzly bear, standing and looking up at the man who had his arms extended out much like a preacher. Murray thought he would change the subject, "Check out that statue."

"Senator Colin Reusch from the state of California."

"I recognize that name."

"You should; he fell off the top of Mount LeConte in Tennessee just prior to the Great Compromise." Wilde often discussed the Senator in class when teaching the Great Compromise, for Reusch made a name for himself as Senate Minority Leader, great advocate of Egalitarianism, crusader for Gay Rights and enemy of the rich. Wilde often wondered if the Great Compromise would have occurred had Reusch not fallen to his death. He surely would have filibustered ironically to his own death, any notion of the United States Penal Colony System, though he would have lauded the new marriage act, immigration act and health care act born out of the compromise. He often wondered how an idealist such as Reusch would have faired in that legislative revolution. Some would have called him a partisan, a liberal, a socialist; however, Jacob, who had read his autobiography, viewed him just as a compassionate human, a pacifist, and an idealist.

"Hey Jacob, shouldn't that grizzly be walking?"

"I thought you were the master of symbolism Mr. English teacher?"

"Huh?" Murray stood befuddled.

"It symbolizes how California stood still at the passing of their great Senator," Wilde spoke reverently.

"Hah, falling off the mountain would be more like it," Moore responded irreverently.

"You are a brute; the arms are extended for his advocacy for all people." Murray knew with this last comment that Jacob had settled into a peculiar mood. He emanated an aura of moral gravitas all of a sudden. Murray had not noticed this on the train, but of course he had found himself consumed by the *Albus Severus Potter* series and could not be bothered. Come to think of it, maybe Jacob had felt like this on the train; it would explain why he had agreed to take Amtrak—to talk. They had had little to no time with one another since the quaffing of the last beer back at Mayfield. Why didn't Jacob talk about his angst then? Did he not have it then? Or had he selflessly put his qualm aside to help Murray over his melancholic hump of leaving the classroom? Murray knew the answer. Jacob always sensed when Murray struggled with any emotional trauma. Murray, who spent his life myopically focused upon his personal goals, often neglected those close to him. Moore knew he lived for his students and his classroom; therefore, he rarely concerned himself with anything outside of that sphere, unless it could efficaciously be applied to school.

Suddenly, Murray felt the sting of separation from his students again. The last week of school contained one of his favorite customs held in the American schools—Demographics Day. Some would call it Multi-Cultural Day, others Melting Pot Day, but the day served as a reminder of America's amazingly successful cultural diversity. Students across the nation, during their senior year, would research their family history. If they belonged to the minority of whites, they would try and figure out from which country their ancestors derived—which proved difficult after generations and generations of American family ancestry. If they could not, their job would then be to hook up with another group and teach the other students about the cultural diversity of Europe.

The true fun came in the mixed or bi-racial or bi-ethnic groups. The student then would take his or her non-white heritage and follow that back to its place of origin. In cases where the students proved a mix of multiple non-white ethnic or racial groups, they found themselves free to choose their "favorite" of the bunch, much like the all white students could study their given German heritage over their Irish. The goal of simply drawing student's attention to the hodge-podge of genetic, cultural, ethnic, religious, and racial variety worked with amazing efficacy. Any given year, in every mega high school, when Demographics Day would occur, the news media outlets would arrive, interview students, take pictures, and post them on the web. Students would share information about their home country, even if they were removed from that country a hundred plus years ago.

Not only did Murray love Demographics Day, but so did the parents, especially the first generation immigrants. Still tied to their homeland, often by language, if not accent, it did them a spiritual good to see their children carry on the home traditions, if only for the fleeting moment of a generation. Truth be told, the second generation often held onto the culture minimally through life, oftentimes marrying into the American "Melting Pot," diluting their own culture. Though assimilation did not happen to be the law of Congress, it effectively manifested itself into the law of the land. The administration would close off the main and auxiliary gymnasiums, along with the cafeteria, and the underclassmen from every variety of life, every nook of the globe, every expression of faith would be peppered with a cornucopia of cultures, religions, ethnicities, customs, clothing, and most importantly, food. The American custom had turned Demographics Day into an unofficial national holiday, though there had been talk in congress of replacing a current holiday. The day had all the air of opening day for baseball. Because Demographics Day occurred in the spring, many, major, county-wide high schools would put the show out on the fields—football, baseball, or soccer—then at times have parades involving faculty, staff, parents, and students. The idiosyncrasies fluctuated from place to place, and with the country's targeted immigration policy—highly selective and demographically conscious—the government purposely spread a healthy influx of multiple cultures, races, ethnicities, and religions around the country. This kept any one group from occupying certain sections of the country or a city. Since potential immigrants applied for green cards around the globe at Statue of Liberty Stations, potential candidates were interviewed and vetted on their given home soil at the time. Immigration and Naturalization Service utilized its nationwide database, listing all of the currently unfilled occupations. Since every United States Embassy around the globe possessed a Liberty Station, the government could calculate, maintain and balance the variety to ensure not only diversity, but could snuff out any radicalism from the highly selective process. If immigrants passed muster, they would be granted a temporary visa contingent upon their children living up to the graduation requirement. It worked. Pockets of left over radicalized liberals and religious zealots would still clamor about allowing masses of poor and downtrodden into the country, but the majority of the nation just furrowed their brow at them and moved on with their daily lives.

This particular Demographics Day found Murray Moore making a beeline for a booth which bore all of the traits from one of his students. A placard above a booth read "Goodbye, Britain!" with a Pakistani flag draped on the left side of the placard and an Indian flag draped on the right side. He zigzagged through the crowd to view a group of students he held in high esteem. He approached the booth to investigate this collection of culture he felt sure would be from British India.

"Mr. Murray," waved Saadiq Sayani, "Check out this." Saadiq pulled out a remote control and pointed it at the projection screen, and it went into motion displaying all the marvels of Pakistan. Images of a mosque, major cities, industry, professionals, workers, and landmarks fluttered across the screen. "What do you think?"

"What mosque did you flash up there?"

"The Faisal Mosque in Islamabad, Pakistan."

"Well done," replied Murray as another student, Parth Patel, snatched the remote control from Saadiq's hands who magnanimously relinquished it.

"Oh no, Mr. Moore," Parth politely interjected, oblivious that he had mildly affronted his partner in the project. "I would be very pleased for you to see the wonders of India, sir." Parth fumbled with the remote frantically pushing buttons, "I have located photos of elements of the British Raj; I feel that you would be most interested in these edifices of the empire, sir." The projector began popping Indian images up for all to see. "If you just look here sir, the Akashardham Hindu Temple represents a wonderful imitation of the Khajuraho and Vijayanagar kingdom architecture. Furthermore, Mr. Moore, please view this stunning pictures of the Himalaya Mountains." Parth loquaciously continued flashing pictures and celebrating all of the achievements of India over the past 100 years. Having studied

Forster's *A Passage to India* with these two students, along with his other Indian and Pakistani students, a bond formed between the groups. Murray loved to read about British India, and they thoroughly enjoyed the literary and historical perspective he could teach them through the eyes of an outsider—a fresh view to contrast with the history learned through the direction of their immigrant parents.

"Mr. Moore! Mr. Moore! Look what I have created!" He turned to see the owner of the new voice, Shireen Desai, waving in front of him a paper-mache elephant. "Look Mr. Moore, I have expanded my cross-cultural enlightenment—an Indian piñata!"

"What do you have inside?"

"Well, I am making ten total and each will be filled with a different type of dyed powder except for one; that one will be filled with candies."

"Zoroastrians," Parth shook his head.

"Blah, blah, Parth. Have some fun," Shireen embraced the word assimilation, refusing to wear traditional Indian attire, forgetting most of her culture and embracing everything that America put in front of her—an amazing feat for someone raised by two immigrant parents. The last of his Indians, young Shahnawaz, arrived bearing his perpetual smile.

"Hey, Ehsaan," chimed in Saadiq, "help a fellow Muslim out and get the remote back for me that Parth stole."

"Keep it up gang!" Murray belted out as he waved and moved on to head toward what could only be "Little Salt Lake." He meandered, ducked and contorted his way through the throng of Mexico, Italy, Cuba, and Russia, heading for the promised land of Salt Lake, for the Mormons seemed to—rather comically—draw all of their people to their religious center. So the LDS booth would have not only the American Mormons there, but also those Mormons who emigrated from other countries, usually from the continent of Africa. School didn't mind, nor the country, groups could form up by religion or ethnicity, but most chose country. For instance, the Catholics never formed up from Latin and South America, but occasionally the Catholics of Eastern Europe may combine to talk about that oft forgotten part of the world, no greater example than the Buddhists Booth of the Orient. He approached a coterie of seniors ranging from Taiwan, China and Vietnam.

"Nice looking booth, Johnny Lin!"

"I had plenty of help," responded Johnny. He observed the screen with the Far East map as each of the respective countries lit up, expanded in view, and offered up statistics about the country fluttering up the side of the image.

"I heard you guys were called by some special universities. Ms. Shao, where are you headed?"

"I have been accepted by Boston College," Diane responded.

"Beware of the Catholics," Murray smiled. "Vu, where are you headed?"

"I am going to Purdue for Industrial Manufacturing so that I can come back home and buy the company my father has worked with for the last eighteen years in order to come to America."

"Noble Mr. Nguyen, I knew you would do Vietnam proud." By the time Murray worked his way through the cultures from Latin and South America heading toward the Mormon booth, the time had expired for release back to class. He smiled internally and apparently externally.

"Why are you smiling?" His daydream had been broken by Jacob, bringing him back to reality and the bustling streets of Washington D.C. with the stony face of Senator Colin Reusch and his pausing Grizzly. "Can you not focus on anything?"

"Well, I can concentrate on burning trashy novels," Murray offered a smile; Jacob continued to walk on passed the small monument on toward the glorious image of Martin Luther King, Jr.

"Have you thought about the fact that after Guam, we will be separated? Sent to different schools." Jacob exuded a palpable pang in his voice.

"Not really," Murray embarrassingly replied. "I guess my excitement about the process cluttered my mind." In his typical myopic fashion, Murray had been so focused upon the conquest that he had forgotten his friend's concerns. He had always pushed forward too far in life, and Murray had done this on climbing trips with Jacob in the past. On more than one occasion, Moore had put the two of them in precarious situations. "Don't worry man. We will have hiking trips in the summer time and social media during the school year." Murray felt that their friendship would remain intact; however, he would miss Demographics Day.

CHAPTER NINETEEN

Murray and Jacob, though nearly shoulder-to-shoulder while walking, felt as if a crevasse had opened up to separate them. Jacob felt furious for Murray's lack of attention; while Murray experienced a sense of bafflement as to why Jacob could be so upset, sitting upon the verge of a career advancement, a paid working island vacation, and a trip on the greatest aircraft in the world. Moore could not understand Wilde's sudden scrupulousness concerning the idea of social Darwinism to eradicate non-participating slugs of society concerning their civic duty in the process. As for his mind drifting, why wouldn't it? The pell-mell cognition going on inside the head of the restless Murray Moore could not be controlled.

"Not sure why you happened to be so bent out of shape, I am only flippantly speaking," Murray attempted to mend the bridge he had apparently rammed, but not quite burned with Jacob. "Look, we are about to embark upon the greatest journey in America. Tonight you and I will board Air Force One with the other national candidates and fly to the Island of Guam, and we, unlike others, shall return."

"Look," Jacob finally spoke, "Therein lies the issue. I have an uneasy feeling about all this."

"About what?"

"The principal position."

"Are you nuts?" Murray barked. "We leave tonight! Tell me the issue."

"I am baffled. I can't name it. This whole process has begun to take on a certain je ne sais quoi."

"Jacob, firstly," Moore attempted to assuage, "Don't use French in our nation's capital. Show some respect." He smiled; Jacob did not. "Secondly, what could possibly be the problem? You will be running schools; we were born to do this." The two made it to the Martin Luther King, Jr. Memorial.

"I can't put my finger on it." They stopped and gazed at the white marble jutting out of the mountain. "The oaths, the canyon, shooting mules and that crazy interview with that Louis Cottonwood guy. Something seemed amiss there—like he didn't reveal it all."

"Man relax and check out Dr. King. Awesome!"

"Yeah," Wilde ignored the monument another moment, "I don't get this Homeland Security business. Why would the position of teacher fall under the umbrella of education, but a principal all of a sudden works for Homeland Security? That doesn't bother you?"

"Have you chosen this moment to go temporarily insane? You live in the greatest country in the world. We have the greatest economy of the world! We have been the lone superpower for nearly one hundred years. Low unemployment! Good schools! Health care for all! Retirement for all! Low crime rate for all! Equality of race, religion, creed, gender and sexual orientation for all! And look," Moore pointed to Martin Luther King, Jr. looming over them, "How do you think this guy would feel?"

"I don't know," Wilde being perplexed internally had baffled Murray. Moore could not fathom Jacob's brewing struggle; he had no words to express it.

"Look," Murray threw his hand in the air, "I have a dream that one day," he raised his voice to the heavens and poorly attempted to imitate the voice of the civil rights leader, "Little black boys and little black girls will be able to join hands with little white boys and little white girls as sisters and brothers." He paused, waiting for Jacob to respond; he didn't. "Damn man, how can you be so sullen? MLK hoped they would play together; they have been having kids together for half a century without any social stigma, along with every other group of people on Earth. How can you have any misgivings about this move to a position that will help ensure this country continues as it has?"

"I know," Jacob conceded reluctantly.

"Plus," Murray now found himself on a roll, "Think of the end of that speech—black men and white men, Jews and Gentiles, Protestants and Catholics, will be able to join hands and sing 'free at last, free at last, thank God Almighty, we are free at last.' Hell, King didn't even have Muslims, Buddhists, Orientals, Indians, etc. etc. Come on, man! This country serves as a beacon of light for all of the cesspools of the world, and here we are, man, Washington D.C., heading to Guam, joining the Academy of Principals, and we will be defending, controlling, and ensuring these principles! Embrace it, Jacob!"

"You're right," reluctantly Jacob admitted. "Let's go see Abe, before we have to head back to the hotel." Murray bolted forward knowing that Jacob withheld more of his feelings; however, overcome with intrigue, Moore needed to press on.

The walk through Ash Woods across to the National Mall proved to be a meditative and silent trek as both men contemplated the conundrum of Jacob Wilde. Moore accepted the post, along with its oaths and odd initiations, in a state of mind that lay somewhere between patriotism and sycophantism—Wilde's skepticism, on the other hand, confused him. After all, Jacob Wilde exuded nationalism incarnate. Besides the myriad Presidents hung on his wall, the miniature model of the Presidential limousine, and an Air Force One model hanging from his ceiling, he had pictures of every form of Americana that should evoke the need to belt out, "My country tis of thee, sweet land of liberty." As they strolled down the mall, Reflecting Pool on the right, Lincoln Memorial dead ahead, with the surreptitiously placed Korean War Memorial on the left, Murray's contemplation turned to elated enthusiasm. Though he feared flying, no amount of fear could mitigate his enthusiasm for boarding Air Force One. That the plane happened to be a retired Boeing 747 hardly mattered to Murray or Wilde—the Man flew in that jet; the Boss, the President. Night could not come soon enough.

After a brief waltzing reflection through the Korean Memorial, the two men turned their ears, eyes and attention to the strumming of at least one guitar and a singer. As they came through the trees, they could see two young men playing acoustic guitars, singing folksy songs. As they approached, Murray tuned into the lyrics and could just catch the end of the tune, "Oh Lord, I'm stuck in L.O.F.I. till the end."

"What on Earth?" Murray inquired.

"Anti-L.O.F.I. protesters," answered Wilde.

"You are kidding me right?"

"No. Free country you know. Not everyone thinks the United States Penal Colony System represents the fundamental values of our nation." Moore became myopically focused upon the signs the two young men had placed behind them. "Stop the Injustice!" behind the one on the right and "Shutter LOFI" and "End Cruel and Unusual Punishment" scrawled on the left board. Murray became intrigued, and he knew the scene would warrant a conversation between them and Jacob. Wilde loved protesters—said they manifested the principles of the Bill of Rights and all that tommyrot. Moore generally found protester ideals a load of radical hogwash that could not work in American society. Before, Jacob could reach the two lads, the music and lyrics began with a twang.

"I hear the plane a comin'
It will be landin at land's end
And I've been seeing sunshine
Since, I don't know when…
I'm stuck in LOFI prison,
And time keeps, draggin' on,
And I hear that engine hummin'
All the way from San Antone.

Way, way back in high school,
Our teachers told us, 'Son,
Always stay a cit-a-zen
And never shoot a gun'
But I shot a man in a casino
Just to watch him die
And as I hear that airplane idle
I turn my head and cry."

Jacob patiently awaited the boys to finish their passionate song; Murray tapped the side of his leg thinking it a catchy tune. The Lincoln Memorial manifested its usual bustle as tourists from every corner of the world came to pay homage to the man and the edifice. Everyone moving hither and thither in the frenetic pace that represents D.C. seemed far too engaged to pay these two any mind. As soon as they finished, Wilde descended upon them.

"Excellent tune, lads," he affably approached. Murray continued his visual perusal of the crowd. "Where are you two guys from?"

"I am from Colorado, and my buddy, he hails from Virginia."

"Wow, how did you two fall in with one another to harmonize?" Wilde with his amiable tone and non-imposing mannerism waltzed right up to the two men and began shaking their hands.

"We both attended Harvard Law School."

"Why aren't you two making some prolific money?" Murray could no longer sit still. "Two future attorneys with those kinds of educational credentials should be in a courtroom shipping degen-erates to L.O.F.I. not singing against it."

"Ignore my lame friend," Jacob replied as Murray snorted in disgust.

"Some things are more important than money, man." The kid drug the word 'man' out in a manner that intimated that he prob-ably singed a copious amount of his medicinal marijuana recently. Murray surmised that the THC fumes cleared just enough so he could stand up and shake Jacob's hand. "I'm Chris Shafer, man." *God, he drug out 'man' again* thought Moore.

"Good morning, sir, I am Jake Daniels," The Jake kid extended his arm to shake Wilde's hand; neither even glanced Murray's way which suited him just fine. At least the second kid, in Moore's opin-ion, retained the bulk of his brain cells. "We feel the injustice done to the convicted of our country warrants, at the very least, a moder-ate protest."

"What brings you guys out today? Or are you here all of the time?" Wilde inquired politely.

"The Academy of Principals leaves from D.C. tonight. We are hoping to catch the attention of some. They leave at night so the teachers can tour during the day. Are you guys teachers?" inquired the Daniels kid.

"No," lied Jacob; Murray couldn't figure out why.

"Yeah maaan," he drug it out again, "Those guys, man, are get-ting a raw deal. What ever happened to the Bill of Rights, man? Number VIII says no cruel and unusual punishment." He paused, or passed out, Murray could not ascertain; then his eyes flickered a bit and his moaning continued, "You, me, we need to liberate those people, man." His voice inflected the word "liberate" and "man," which continued its perpetual audible slog. Murray assured himself that if he had the tool, he would club this whining whelp to death like a baby seal then spit on his corpse. He hated protesters.

"You guys are to be honored. Americans died to establish the right to freedom of speech. Keep up the good work, Jake."

"We gotta stop the violence on that island, man!" The Shafer kid, much to Murray's chagrin, continued to vomit his opinion from the bowels of his romanticized idealism. "People are dying, man! Women are put in there, man. People killing one another and the government lets it happen." Murray had heard enough of this diatribe of a bygone era and decided to move in and verbally blast this kid into submission. However, before he could formulate a statement to engage an attack upon the Shafer kid, he heard a profound voice scream behind him.

"Hey! Hey, you scum sucking bag of vermin! I told you to go back to Cali or wherever the hell you came from!" Murray and Jacob turned, stunned to hear such vitriol on the steps of Lincoln's Memorial, and they saw a beast of a man rampaging up the stairs wearing a Chicago Blackhawk's jersey of all things, carrying a Bible in one hand and what appeared to be a tomahawk in the other. Jacob did not move; the boys fumbled, stood up, and walked in front of their guitars, and Murray thought that the morning would be getting entertaining now.

"Sir," continued Jake Daniels holding up his hand in a pleading fashion, "We have a right to protest the cruel imprisonment of our fellow Americans."

"Be ye afraid of the sword," he held up the tomahawk-looking weapon, "For wrath bringeth the punishments of the sword, that ye may know there will be judgment!" By now the bizarre interloper reached the two young guys and loomed over them in the most intimidating manner. "What are you two pukes crying about now?"

"Just because they are criminals, man, America can't treat them cruelly."

"And these shall go away into everlasting punishment: but the righteous into life eternal. Get a job you pot smoking hippie."

"Sir, please do not cause a scene," interjected Daniels as civilly as possible, "You are free to express your opinion…" The big guy cut him off.

"Listen here scumbag, if you want to protest, fine. Protest something that matters. How about singing a song about the tens of millions of native tribes raped, murdered, and expelled from their lands to make way for the Europeans? Protest that!"

"You are correct, sir. A terrible injustice occurred when the…" He could not finish for this evangelical prophet came at him with such ferocity the Shafer kid cowered behind the Daniels boy.

"You think it a terrible injustice, muttonhead? Marching men, women and children native to the Eastern Woodlands of America across the damn country at gunpoint out into the plains of Kansas and Oklahoma, you think that a terrible injustice? Women, kids, elderly—dying as they walked! Then shut your mouth. Sitting here in the Capital, spewing your bile about murderers and rapists sent to a tropical island. You make me sick!"

"Sir, I respect your Native cause, believe me. However, that happened in the past; L.O.F.I. currently houses anywhere from 35,000-100,000 inmates. We have no idea because the government keeps the numbers secret. We need to stand up for them."

"Behold, thou hast driven me out this day from the face of the earth; and from thy face shall I be hid; and I shall be a fugitive and a vagabond in the earth; and it shall come to pass, that every one that findeth me shall slay me." The man's Blackhawk emblem heaved as he breathed fire and brimstone from the Bible. "So God gave Cain, we gave it to them all!"

"Dude," from behind his partner in protest, Shafer reared his blood shot eyes, "Two wrongs don't make a right, man. America can't send them to L.O.F.I., man!"

"Let death seize upon them, and let them go down quick into Hell: for wickedness will be in their dwellings, and among them. You two pukes best give up this cause, for as the Lord said, 'It shall be more tolerable for the land of Sodom in the day of judgment, than for thee.' Get a life!" The two young guys grabbed their guitars and looked as if they would attempt one more statement to defend their cause, but the big guy slammed the Bible shut and landed his gnarled piece of wood the size of an Irish shillelagh that Murray originally thought a tomahawk at a distance down upon the Bible with a thud. The boys moved on. Jacob walked on with them; Murray found someone to talk to.

"Well done my friend. You brought the fires of Hell down upon those useless sacks of flesh. I am impressed."

"Nothing sickens me more than someone protesting that damn earthly island of perdition man made to hold the scoundrels of this country until their final judgment. Only a jackass would bellyache over the fate of murderers, rapists, gangsters, and every other form of felonious scum that crawled across this earth."

"You, uh," Murray hesitated due to the rage of the man, "Have quite a fervor for the Native Americans."

"You are damn straight I do."

"Are you tribal?"

"No, I know that a tremendous injustice has been done to those people—people who exhibited nothing but peacefulness in the beginning. Then those murderous Spaniards, cloaked in Christianity, but bearing the gun of conquest and gluttony started a veritable tsunami of European immigration and the destruction of a noble race of people." The big man had visibly calmed down, slowed his breathing and relaxed. "We owe those people and their ancestors."

"Well, either way my friend, I am glad to have met you," Murray extended his arm, "I am Murray Moore."

"Phillip Money. Likewise."

"Keep up the good fight, Mr. Money!"

"But with righteousness shall He judge the poor, and reprove with equity for the meek of the earth; and He shall smite the earth with the rod of His mouth, and with the breath of His lips shall He slay the wicked." Phillip Money read from his opened Bible and upon conclusion snapped it shut. "Good luck in your endeavors, Mr. Moore. I suspect that you are indeed a teacher bound for L.O.F.I., am I correct?"

"Very perceptive."

"Two guys, middle aged, intellectual looking, walking the historical monuments of the this nation on the night of the Academy of Principals' nationally reported flight to the United States Penal Colony on the Island of Guam; it seemed obvious."

Murray smiled. "I need to be heading back to the hotel. Air Force One will be calling."

Phil Money shook his hand and patted him on the back. Moore continued, "Plus, I have to catch my colleague."

"You better watch that one. He has a liberal streak in him."

Murray smiled and waved, turned, saw Jacob Wilde standing alone now by the Reflecting Pool, and trotted off towards him, remembering the words of the hockey-jersey-wearing evangelical preacher.

CHAPTER TWENTY

"Nothing in the world can take the place of persistence... Persistence and determination are omnipotent. The slogan 'press on' has solved and always will solve more problems of the human race."

CALVIN COOLIDGE – (1872-1933)
30TH PRESIDENT OF THE UNITED STATES

Murray Moore had sat down in his seat of the presidentially retired Air Force One. Every minute more involved in the Academy of Principals, Moore found substantially more invigorating than the last. After the interesting incident on the National Mall with the protesters, Jacob and Murray enjoyed a relatively peaceful stroll back to the subway station and rode to Crystal City Metro in order to walk to the local Marriott. After the fracas upon Lincoln's doorstep, Murray bore a mood of jocularity, while Wilde appeared more subdued. Moore perceived a palpable drop in the amount of verve Jacob possessed in recent days and weeks, especially in their generally congenial political bantering. He decided that Jacob would have to work through his own demons; for once he, himself, felt an enormous sense of conviction for going forward.

With the plane due to depart at 9:00 p.m. from Ronald Reagan Airport, the nearly twenty-four hour trip seemed to Murray a death sentence of sorts; however, knowing the spaciousness of the plane, along with their scheduled meetings, he had at least been hopeful concerning the idea of the trip not being mundane. After the shuttle from the hotel to the airport, Murray and Jacob, along with other candidates, were escorted into an airport conference room for an itinerary briefing—along with various restrictions—prior to the flight. Inside the room, a gathering of what could only be presumed teachers received their instructions and were told to wait until being called before they proceeded through the door in the front of the room and out to the awaiting jet. Once airborne and after release from the captain, all of the candidates were to convene in the meeting room aboard Air Force One.

Only moments later, the report of a candidate's name growled through the door. A middle-aged woman rose and grabbed her bag and departed. Murray's level of acumen had been honed over the recent weeks; he figured he knew what procedure would be conducted behind the door. He leaned over to Wilde who sat next to him, and since the woman's last name began at the top of the alphabet; consequently, he could only assume they would be close to last.

"Your final escape clause my friend."

"You think?" Wilde inquired.

"Absolutely. Man, once you get on the jet you are all in. Think about it—all the warnings about bailing out, all the caveats about secret society, and all the tests that at the time we didn't know were tests. It all makes sense. This will be it."

"Getting rather astute in your old age," Murray scanned Jacob's face for any sign of resignation. He intuitively felt that Jacob could still be a tad apprehensive, but for the life of him, could not figure out why. All that Murray felt to be right with America seemed to be directed by the Congress and defended by Homeland Security along with the other agencies. To think that principals, besides living a life much like clergy, would be working in the vanguard of this endeavor of preserving the apogee of America's economic and global dominance made Moore's sense of pride, self-worth and patriotism soar. He could not wait to be a full member of the Academy of Principals. Numerous candidates were called; they all filed back with none returning. Murray notice that the same twenty-three that survived the canyon were all assembled here tonight for the trans-Pacific flight.

"We shall see if you are correct," forewarned Jacob.

"Murray Mallory Moore!" a voice called from the front.

"See you on the other side friend," spoke Murray as he rose and moved. He quickly passed through the doors, down a hallway to the end, which held a door ajar. At the end of the hall towered a young lady he recognized but not entirely at once. He stewed on the face momentarily as he slowed his walk to a plod. The face seemed familiar; however, the expression seemed disconnected with his memory. The girl, he presumed an agent or guard, stood motionless, eying him up. He gazed around the hall, attempting to find anything in his surroundings to forestall his passing the girl in hopes of a visual clue to reacquaint him to his context of knowing her. Then she gave a furtive look through the door, turned back and presented him with a wry smile prior to speaking softly.

"Glad to see you survived the Grand Canyon." Exactly, Murray recalled.

"You were on the mule train! Let me guess, you do not attend the University of Kentucky for equestrian studies."

"Hardly, I studied medicine and chemistry at Morehead State University."

"I suppose you work for Homeland Security."

"Yes. Agent Gruenschlaeger. My assignment to your mule train served two priorities for your canyon test."

"Agent and doctor," surmised Murray.

"Welcome to the Academy of Principals," she smiled opening the door and directing him into a small room. Murray returned the smile and passed the agent, arriving in front of a table with a familiar cast of characters. Before him sat the immutable trio of Hauer, Alliston, and Nutt. Despite the grave ambience, Moore experienced an inner tranquility; he fully comprehended the elephantine nature of his decision. Yet, he concluded before asked, he would proceed onto Air Force One—conviction resolute.

"Mr. Murray Moore," spoke Colonel Nutt. "I am sure you understand why you are here."

"Yes, ma'am."

"Through your years of teaching you have been nominated for vetting for the Academy of Principals. You sufficiently possess the educational credentials; you have proven yourself for years in the eyes of another member of our society, Principal Feinauer; you have easily passed the mental questions, the physical examination, and the field trials and tribulations. Now you stand on the threshold of an 'all in' decision. Once you take the door on the right, you will board Air Force One bound for Guam. You will be educated on the flight to the penal colony along with receiving information of a classified nature. Finally, you will complete your initiation on the island; then finish training. Upon your return to the mainland, you will be bound as Principal for the duration of a term of service of twenty-five years and a vow of secrecy for the remainder of your days. Do you accept these terms?"

"I do." No hesitation, absolutely zero debate. Murray felt intrigued; he could not wait to see what his future held. Whatever the Academy of Principals had in store for him, he felt assured of its beneficent nature.

"You may proceed sir to the plane. Good luck." The three stood shaking his hand as he bottled up his excitement and skittered toward the door and the awaiting Air Force One. Murray couldn't help but wonder; would Jacob hesitate?

Air Force One presented and fulfilled every notion that had saturated Murray's mind. The amenities were without privation; from its opulent décor to lavish dishes displayed. Presumptuously, Murray partook in various foods and a beverage while waiting to be told to take his seat. As he stood and mingled with other principal candidates, he found himself shocked to see his tour guide of Clayton, Kentucky, Mr. Louis Cottonwood standing in front of two much younger men that he could only presume to be Homeland Security Agents. Cottonwood caught his attention and struggled over to him, for the years clearly left its mark upon this man who seemed more antediluvian than just aged.

"Well done my boy. You made it," Cottonwood croaked.

"Yes. I am just waiting for my buddy Jacob to get through."

"Good. Good. I would like you to meet a couple of men you will be working rather closely with." Cottonwood, redoubtable as ever, scanned the room receiving salutes from obvious agents. "Here comes our man. Wilde!" Louis bellowed in his raspy bellicose voice. Jacob immediately spotted the group and headed for them through the now twenty-three candidates.

"Louis Cottonwood, good to see you again."

"Right. Now that I have you both, I want to introduce you to the other agent of the Cincinnati area along with the new inductee. This young whippersnapper will be taking my place upon my retirement. Long overdue, I might add." He nodded at the young man indicating his need for self-introduction.

"Zachary Hatfield." The young redhead extended his hand to both Moore and Wilde in a rather enthusiastic manner.

"Young Zack here will be working closely with you two. Major cities have a pair of agents who cover the metropolitan area. So Northern Kentucky, Southwest Ohio, and Eastern Indiana will be handled by Mr. Kues right here and this young pup straight out of the Navy Seals and Homeland Security." Louis Cottonwood extended his arm and put it around the middle-aged agent. "This here young man, Luke Kues, will be a valuable asset to you in completing your job and helping you to clean up your numbers."

Murray and Jacob had no idea what "clean up your numbers meant" but both figured the top-secret briefings would clear that up. Jacob spoke first.

"Kues, didn't I hear that name elsewhere?"

"Yes sir," Cottonwood hissed, "His younger brother boarded this plane with you—Nick, the principal candidate from Louisville."

"Right," Jacob expressed hinting at his realization. The older agent stepped forward.

"I am Luke 'Top-Gun' Kues. My friends call me 'Top-Gun.' You aren't friends."

"Where did you get a name like that?" inquired Murray.

"I earned it, I can most assuredly tell you," Luke stated with a bit of self-aggrandizement. "Now, if you will excuse me, I must find my kid brother." Luke Kues strode away without further look.

"Don't mind him boys," Cottonwood aridly stated. "He has the brazen chutzpah of his brother. Let me offer this caveat; call him Agent Kues until he tells you to call him 'Top-Gun,' things will be smoother."

"Does he have a problem?"

"No sir, Mr. Moore, he likes to bust the chops of the new principals. He earned that title 'Top-Gun'; he has quite a number of confirmed kills." An intercom interrupted the conversation warning them of take-off. Hatfield and Cottonwood found their seats. Moore and Wilde found theirs.

After the flight had been in the air for a couple of hours and dinner had been served, the candidates were all sitting in the main passenger seating area of the 747 when a distinguished looking Chinese-America man walked up from the back and turned to address the group as a whole. Murray judged the man to be his own age and found himself impressed extremely quickly by the distinguished man's speech as he took command of the soon-to-be principals.

"Greetings," spoke the man with a palpable level of aplomb, "I am Dr. Benjamin Ko. I am one of the two doctors in charge of running, monitoring, and reporting on the condition of the United States Penal Colony on the island of Guam. I have been assisting in the maintenance and experimentation upon the island for five years now. I possess a general medical degree along with a doctoral degree in socio-psychology." Scanning the room, Dr. Ko found nothing but attentiveness. "I monitor and study the mental, physical, and sociological health of the island. To state my occupation as stimulating would be an enormous understatement. You will meet the other doctor of the island, Dr. Carran, upon our arrival. His degrees specialize in areas different than my own; I will allow him to divulge."

"Not only do I monitor the inmates living upon the island of Guam, or as you the general public refer to it as L.O.F.I., I welcome the new batch of candidates, and I chair the board of doctors and military personal who monitor the general health and well-being of our extremely important personal—the proverbial boots on the ground if you will—the principals of America." Dr. Ko, still scanning the room for questions, found his audience all encompassed about the information forthcoming.

"Our immediate itinerary will be simple. In a moment, I will have all of you move into the meeting room in order to show you a video. I cannot stress the significance of this video for it will serve as not only the first bit of clandestine information to remain top secret, but also the most important. For this class of candidates has proven itself worthy to become the next generation of principals, you will be welcomed formally into the fraternity in a moment." After perusing the room and seeing no befuddled looks, Dr. Ko continued.

"After your inculcation into the inner circle of information, thus providing you clearance status, there will be a series of discussions, information sessions, historical documentaries and time to sleep. Tomorrow when we arrive at Guam, Air Force One will circle the island for your omniscient view, and then we shall land. Finally, I want to ask you to hold questions until after the impending video and ask you to head up to the main meeting room. Oh, and welcome to the fraternity." Dr. Ko dismissed the group who energetically moved toward the next stop in their indoctrination.

On the way up to the meeting room, as Murray and Wilde moved with the herd, Jacob seemed to come out of his funk, even if momentarily, and began a conversation asking, "Can you name the worst student you ever had?" Moore, perplexed by the suddenness of the question, hesitated and did not respond. When he surreptitiously glanced at Wilde seeing his inquisitive look, he felt he should respond.

"Why do you ask?"

"Well, thinking about L.O.F.I.," Jacob opened up, "I remembered Sam Wolfe. Do you remember him?"

"Yeah, intelligent, border-line genius, with a certain disregard for the rules. I believe circumvention and circumlocution manifested his two best attributes," summarized Moore adjusting his half-mooned spectacles.

"You are correct," Wilde picked up, "He would move right around any obstacle in his way due to school rules. And he certainly could wiggle and wheedle his way out of trouble and into any forbidden realm."

"I thought I told you that I saw him cuffed and arrested in the teacher parking lot earlier this year. Why do you ask?"

"Well, Sam Wolfe crossed my mind as we headed toward Guam. What if the rules set up by society caused him to rebel? What if, let us say, in a European setting where their typical laissez faire attitude, Sam happened to be raised. Don't you think that Wolfe's creative mind may have flourished? Blossomed? Did you ever think that we push these kids over the edge? Maybe we are the problem?" Here again returned the now recurring theme of doubt in Jacob Wilde's mind and not good timing either; they were in!

"No man, you are looking at this all wrong. This happens to be the greatest country in the world; we help educate it. All students are provided with every opportunity for success, and most of all, the price of no success hangs in their faces daily. Poor scores offer little chance in college; no college offers lower wages. Failure to work means starvation," Murray felt he must pour it on in order to assuage Jacob's trepidations. "Look, I think the worst kid I ever taught would be Jake Neyer—a real piece of human offal. He had great potential, but too much free will. His well-read nature caused him to incessantly question the meaning of everything and trust in nothing. He began skipping classes, engaging in recreational drug usage and then petty thievery. His rebellion consisted of rude and disrespectful behavior leading to his poor grades and subsequent expulsion."

"Look," continued Murray, "that boy had free will, and he chose malevolence. Would God be mad at Himself for creating creatures that inhabit the world and destroy its beauty and fellow humans?" Wilde offered nothing. "That answer, no. Therefore, we should not mourn them; they opted for a life of crime."

"I know I should feel that way, but sometimes I have such reservations!"

"Don't! I dare them to break rules! I don't care if Jake Neyer and Sam Wolfe currently can be found in a ditch dead, in drug rehab, on a chain gang or in L.O.F.I.; they deserve what they get. Anyone brought up in America with free education, funded social programs, a robust economy, universal health care and the world's envy of personal freedoms and then decides to take that liberty and destroy some small part of the whole of society, well then they need to go."

Murray took a seat in the meeting room; the conversation seemed finished. Murray looked up at the tele-screen. Only moments passed prior to the lights dimming, for the two educators represented the last group to arrive. As they nestled in, the screen lit up and a man reclining in a chair sat there looking into the screen. Jacob recognized him immediately, Murray had that terrorized haze of knowing the man, but not being able to place him, let alone name him, but then he spoke in a deliberate and authoritative manner.

"I am Johannes Schmitt, and I have come to speak to you from the grave."

CHAPTER TWENTY ONE

Jacob Wilde sat upright in his seat, mouth agape and eyes bulging in a most apoplectic manner; Murray Moore thought *I have heard of that guy.* An indescribable emotion hung upon Wilde's visage from shock to trepidation; for since this icon upon the screen had taken it upon himself to record a message prior to his demise, Wilde realized immediately the full implications of the message to come. Wilde quickly looked at Murray with a grotesque expression of lament upon his face, "Here comes dangerous dogma," he whispered. Moore felt a somberness overcome him, not for what would come from Schmitt, but for not having any inclination as to the ramifications of a dead senator speaking from the grave. The screen continued to talk.

"As I said, I am Senator Johannes Schmitt from the great state of Tennessee, and I felt it necessary to greet all of the new principals, even after my unfortunate death. If things are still perpetuating as I set in motion prior to my demise, then I should be looking out upon a meeting room of candidates for the Academy of Principals—an institution that I helped to found. By now, you have all passed several tests, interviews, trials and tribulations. Now, you have but some secrets to learn on this trip and one last initiation on Guam to fortify your readiness for your lifetime appointment. Since I have no idea how long the Academy will show this video, I have no possible method of addressing any isolated issues of that time period." Schmitt paused.

"Now, due to the circumstance, I will be doing all of the talking; you will have to trust the staff there to fill in and rectify any issues. The reason for my video will prove quite simple. I want to explain the Great Compromise; I don't want you learning it from some fancy textbook written by some recent college graduate born after the fact. You will hear the truth, the whole truth, and nothing but the truth. I won't blaspheme with a 'so help me God,' for I may be beyond redemption, for what I am about to divulge must be held in the strictest of confidence for it represents privileged, and thus top secret, information. Prior to judging me for my past and present, please keep this in the front of your lobe, I did everything for America first, America second, and America third. God had to wait." Murray Moore once again had his imagination piqued by intrigue and his mind whetted by these controversial ideals he had been learning: the fraternity exhibited by the guild of principals, and the Academy developing the next generation. Schmitt continued.

"Now, you must understand the background and circumstances of the world in 2025 that made that era the most opportune to accomplish the Great Compromise. You must understand that America had developed into a myopically focused culture where everyone became centered on just one thing, me! Not me Senator

Schmitt, but 'me' the individual. No one believes in the principles of fraternity and egalitarianism any longer. Bumper stickers on cars, along with tee-shirts, social media updates, etc., all advocated the phrase, 'As long as I get mine'; this self-centric mentality allowed the filthy rich to cry foul when asked to pay more taxes, and the over-weight welfare recipient to demand more alms because they kept propagating the species without any manner or care as to how to provide for and raise their heathen offspring. Criminality ran the streets because of the overly worked police and judicial system; this country needed a wake up call."

"Furthermore, the lack of civic mindedness by that social-media obsessed culture gave them satisfaction in playing video games, watching football and all other manner of sports, posting pictures on the web, and watching reality television, all of which led to an apathetic and ignorant populace. Worse yet, the only people politically active were the damn radicals. Every election, those mud-slinging 'fringers' would inundate the internet, radio, and television with voluminous amounts of vitriol and animus. Hell, the jug heads at home, minds filled with barley or bong resin, did not have a clue as to whom to vote for because all they saw in politics amounted to ad hominem attacks ubiquitously sprayed on the television like bullets in some third world, hell-hole, country."

"And though I love our Founding Fathers, not all of their great ideas were coming to fruition. God knows the country tried to educate those ignoramuses, but when your options are work hard and pay taxes or don't work and receive welfare, well the damn Japs made a hell of a lot of money on video games for those deadbeats to play all day. Scum sucking pigs laying at home smoking, drinking, fornicating with generations of worthless children because they had been raised by worthless parents. Teachers got the blame for trying to teach the uneducated masses of lazy, good for nothing, non-motivated children. Hell's bells, I left the classroom because of that rhetoric and got into politics. Well, without enough major wars to cull the herd if you will, it only took a couple of generations to send Europe into the trash heap of civilization and put America on the rampart overlooking oblivion ready to leap in head first." The only thing audible on Air Force One beside the outside whining engines would have been the breathing of this audience waiting for the punch line, the coup de grace of the speech.

"Well, when you take the mindless rabble of proletariat and couple that with the radical jackasses who were involved with the political process, you got yourself one dysfunctional sclerotic quagmire in Washington D.C. Every year, primaries filled with radicals, the moderates pushed out because of the 'base' needing to be appealed to because they slung the money into every form of political action group and campaign coffers they could find. Radicals versus radicals in every damn election in the nation, with each political group, Republicans and Democrats, using their herds of unthinking automatons as their voter, with ideals implanted into their heads by sound bites and headlines, using specious and spurious arguments. Disaster! Well, ladies and gentleman, you know that the good moderates in this country, the middle, the independent, found themselves caught in the morass with no possible way to break the stalemate. The ideologues proved too cunning in controlling the dullards on both sides of the aisle. What America needed, besides a good kick in the rump, would have to come from within. That 'within' would be me, boys and girls. As Senate Majority Leader, I gathered me a group of moderates, equally, from both sides of the political aisle, and formed me the Inklings, and we plotted and performed a coup d' etat which the populace still heralds as the finest political wrangling and successful string of legislative laws ever enacted upon this great country. And to think it all started when I threw that leftist bastard Senator Colin Reusch off the front of Mount LeConte." Silence. Schmitt leaned back in his seat to allow all in the audience to listen. His speech, well planned, had calculated the pause to allow the revelation to resonate. He lit up a cigar and began to puff upon it. None spoke, Jacob looked horrified, and Murray smiled with a look of intrigue. As the planned paused served its purpose, all had time for Schmitt's admission to sink in; he leaned back up into his chair to continue.

"Now understand, I liked Senator Reusch; hell, I loved the guy. Great politician. But, by God, America found itself stuck partly due to his leftist, idealistic policies, and he packed a following. Young senators feared him; they called him the 'hammer.'

After his tragic death, I helped engineer the advancement of another closet moderate into the minority leader role. With my buddy Congressman Lopina, along with the other Inklings from the mountain—Belarski, Young, Reed, and Emma Bower—and those who joined later, we infected Congress with bi-partisan moderatism unparalleled in history. Within months, I had mobilized with Lopina in the House. Utilizing the knowledge that I had about the innumerable closet moderates who would defect, I knew I could pull the numbers together to ostensibly control the House and Senate, along with ensuring their own re-election for the radicals would be stamped out, we would revolutionize the country. Then, damn it, those two throwbacks, Congressman Jon Stupak of Massachusetts and Senator Cate Adams of Maine, decided to get in my way, the way of the movement, and the advancement of this American legislative revolution. They came after me and my cohorts with smear tactics and partisan balderdash. I told Lopina that we are just going to have to kill those two sons of bitches."

The aforementioned hush turned into a rapid staccato firing of hissed whispers around the cabin of the meeting room. Murray sat trying to grasp why Schmitt would admit to killing two politicians that Murray knew were killed by terrorists in the Congressional Massacre of 2025. Jacob, sitting next to Murray, sat incredulous at the idea that the Great Compromise, even though it caused the United States to turn a crucial corner in its history, came about because of murder and mayhem set up by a senator from the South. Murray ruminated upon all of the trials they had faced, the questions they had been asked, and the speeches they had heard. An epiphany blossomed in Moore's mind; he turned to whisper to Jacob, since on the screen Schmitt leaned back in his chair puffing away upon his cigar.

"Jacob, it all makes sense. The shooting of the mules, the questions they asked me about literature—the shooting of Lennie and the sacrifice of Mr. Spock—it all prepared us for this moment."

"Wow. My historical questions revolved around painful sacrifice and controlled ruthlessness." Both men noticed that Senator

Schmitt leaned up in his chair and prepared himself to speak. Those tests and those inquisitions served to measure each candidate's visceral response to their own perceived immutable ideology.

"Alright, alright. I can only imagine the fervor in the room. Settle down." He looked from left to right and right to left, giving all present to watch, the impression that he indeed sat alive upon the screen. "Folks, you have to realize that the august nature of America sat in the balance. The nanny state had become endemic. I had the Senate and House in my hip pocket preparing to turn the ship a full one hundred and eighty degrees in the right direction, and these two unscrupulous demagogues figured they would assassinate my character through defamation. Much to my chagrin, right there on the House and Senate floors, they commenced to cause such fracases with their rabble-rousin' speeches, I thought the two firebrands would destroy all that I had set in motion. We nearly had a full-blown donnybrook on the House floor between the remaining few radical liberals and my fighting moderates—bloody pandemonium. Something had to be done or all would be lost." Schmitt edged up in his chair looking abrasive and belligerent. The audience attempted to acclimate to the stunning revelations coming their way. All tried to remember that they had taken oaths, knew clandestine information would be coming to them, understood that they now worked for the government, and would participate in Homeland Security's vanguard ensuring the peace and tranquility of America, but not sure how that would happen in the public school.

"Where I come from in Tennessee, if you want to get rid of the pig in the house, you first see if you have a wolf at the door. So I contacted the head of the Central Intelligence Agency," Schmitt said leaning back complacently, "A fine lady that I helped appoint to that post. I gave C.I.A. Director, Elizabeth Gruenschlaeger, a call and asked about any credible terrorist threats. We had been watching a few in the various House and Senate committees. Turns out we had an agent undercover working with some animals from Yemen wanting to hit the Capital, taking out some politicians. Well," Schmitt leaned back puffing upon his savory cigar attempting to repress a smile, "We opened the door and let in the wolf.

Now before you self-righteously disparage my plan, understand America stood on the doorstep of ruin due to partisan gridlock. Senator Reusch had already paid the ultimate sacrifice, God rest his soul. I would not let him die in vain! Knowing the last days of the House and Senate were convened, I made my fighting moderates, the Inklings, over one hundred strong, meet in a joint House and Senate session far away from the impending melee. Our inside guy let these Yemeni animals in with some real explosives from a couple of 'home grown' terrorists."

"The plan proved flawless, even if a bit truculent. I knew with the moderates meeting for one more day, it would cause the radical left and also the radical right to gather in order to try and cling to and defend their outdated dogma and selfish ideology. To maintain our deniable plausibility, I had our operative lead them right to my meeting in the Hart Building. In collusion with Gruenschlaeger, I made sure she would be at some contrived C.I.A. and Homeland Security meeting nearby. All went as planned. Sure, over one hundred people died with nearly half being Senators and Congressman, most of them tied to the political ideologues. All of the terrorists were killed, America galvanized behind the President and the Senate Majority leader. With a bit of artifice and political prestidigitation, I worked on the remaining Senators and Congressmen not on board and got them to agree to vote on the changes in the Great Compromise and just to wait until November to replace those lost. Amazing what kind of accomplishments happen when you are consecrating ground for falling Senators and proposing statues being built and bridges renamed for dead Californian liberals." Schmitt once again paused, puffed away vaingloriously upon his stogie. He sat inviolable, safely in his grave, unable to pay for his Machiavellian patriotism.

"Look, before I end this political opus, don't think I won't go to my grave without compunction for my actions. I have blood on my hands that won't wash away. I have spoiled the seas incarnadine! But judge not lest ye be judged, my fellow educators. Presidents have ordered men to war sacrificing hundreds, thousands, hundreds of thousands and even millions. Unlike Abraham, I spilled some sacrificial blood; I broke the Washington gridlock, killed partisanship, solidified the country in the middle, and helped foster a fifty year apogee of economic, social, and global progress unparalleled in the planet's history. Not bad for a Southern boy! Don't let July 18th of that aforementioned year stand as a day of infamy, but effable sacrifice worthy of this nation's gratitude." He paused, crushed the cigar and looked visibly pained. "Go forth, my principals; you will be pointing out the wolves at the door! You will be in the vanguard, leading this country from the inside, while Homeland Security and the C.I.A. protect it from the outside. Do not let the sacrifices of those before you—some with their lives and some with their consciences—go wasted. Defend America; keep her the envy of the world." Senator Schmitt sat back and the screen went black.

CHAPTER TWENTY TWO

"And as he journeyed, he came near Damascus: and suddenly there shined round about him a light from heaven: And he fell to the earth, and heard a voice saying unto him, Saul, Saul, why persecutest thou me?"

ACTS OF THE APOSTLES **9: 3-4**
THE HOLY BIBLE

As the lights brightened and the screen went dark, Murray noticed a familiar face striding toward the front of the meeting room. He recognized her easily; she had been at the door at Ronald Reagan National Airport as well as on the trail ride down to the Grand Canyon. It had become abundantly clear to Moore, and Wilde for that matter, that every person who had crossed their paths in the last few months had been members of Homeland Security or some other form of covert government agency. As this augmented the resolve of Moore, it served to unnerve that of Wilde.

"Hello again," she stood tall in front of the room, "If you remember, I am special agent Annie Gruenschlaeger, and I have been asked to speak first following Senator Schmitt's posthumous speech. As you may have heard, C.I.A. director Elizabeth Gruenschlaeger worked in close proximity with Senator Schmitt and helped orchestrate the unfortunate events of July 18, 2025, the Congressional Massacre. As you may have concluded, the C.I.A. director happens to be my mother. She brought me into the agency after my graduation from college with a medical degree to serve as an agent with a specialty in my field. I want all in this room to understand, the secrets revealed today were learned by all present here and in other classes of the Academy of Principals, along with Homeland Security agents, at this juncture of their individual training. All of us experienced the similar sense of shock, and maybe even horror, upon the discovery of these brutal facts. My mother lamented her decision for the rest of her days; however, upon her death bed twenty four years later, she informed me that though numerous fundamental ideals had been violated in those early days, it proved worth it, for America had not only rebounded, it turned into the moderate, centrist, meritocratic state in which we live. As she told me once, I had to be cruel to be kind. I challenge you to think about your own careers and reflect upon times when you were working in conjunction with your principals where you would have displayed ideas or thoughts consistent with what you have learned today and experienced in the last few months. Though I wish our modern American prosperity and stability had developed from a more peaceful and ideal set of circumstances, that does not happen to be reality. Put that past aside and remember that our job now revolves around the preserving of this nation with its global, economic and military dominance that it has enjoyed for the last one hundred and fifty years. Very little occurs economically, politically, and militarily without the intervention of the United States of America, and due to that, we have the highest standard of living, lowest amount of poverty and greatest education, not to mention a lifestyle that can only be called the envy of the world." Agent Gruenschlaeger looked around for a sense of approbation. Murray Moore began to clap and soon had a sporadic, and then a full-fledged ovation as the whole room gave her applause. As soon as Murray stood, the room conformed, and though Wilde stood and clapped, it lacked enthusiasm, as if peer pressure forced his inclination.

After a few more speeches by other members of the Academy, the candidates were sent back to their areas where bunks had been installed to accommodate them for the near twenty-four hour flight on the antique Air Force One. Murray found himself comfortably on the top bunk; Wilde restlessly on the bottom. Murray had known Jacob long enough to know when he needed to talk, for Jacob fidgeted endlessly until Murray addressed the issue. It did not take extraordinary vision for Moore to know what ate at Wilde's soul.

"Out with it Jacob!"

"What?"

"I know when you are bothered, especially ethically bothered. We have had enough political discussions over the past ten years."

"How do you feel about what has been revealed today?"

"Like you, stunned. Hard to believe our own government worked with our own defensive agency to take out politicians and conduct a terrorist attack on its own people, but it happened."

"Are you comfortable with all of this?"

"I am comfortable with America's state," Murray replied.

"But man, this sullies all in which I believe."

"Why? You believe in it, even if you don't think so at the moment."

"Why do you think I believe in it?"

"You have stated so in front of Principal Bobby Feinauer more than once."

"When?" incredulously asked Jacob.

"Oh, come on!" Murray related the story of one of their "Wall of Shame" students, Iain Warrell-King, an affably obnoxious young man who unequivocally turned for the worst. Though he started out benignly enough, he began to renounce all of the ideals of the United States ironically upon a trip to the capital, Washington D.C. He went "AWOL" during the trip, got caught kissing a girl in the back of a Senate chamber tour and so thoroughly shamed

Wilde, Jacob sent the student on an early flight home. After that fiasco, Warrell-King began to find himself in hot water over disrespectful comments to the staff and actually verbally attacked the Mormon students while they studied with their religious teacher before school one morning. His anti-religious rants in the hallway, on social media and in class against every denomination on Earth landed him in counseling and in the main office for discipline. His sophomoric behavior stood in stark contrast with the country's ideals and therefore the ideals the nation's principals instilled in America's schools. Soon, his behaviors smacked of drug involvement, his grades plummeted and his discipline referrals increased until the point of expulsion. Jacob Wilde had been the main educator in forcing Iain out of the building. Murray knew, as he recounted the history of Iain Warrell-King, that Jacob Wilde had chosen to selectively forget this type of historical past when confronted with the history learned from Senator Schmitt. "Do you remember what you said to Bobby Feinauer when you went to see him that last time?"

"Yes."

"Well?"

"I said he should be put upon a raft with only a gun and a bullet and shoved out to sea," Wilde hung his head in shame.

"Make sense why we are here? That does not represent the only time that you or I have talked in that manner about a student to the principal. Have you not figured it out yet? We have been observed and vetted for years. In your years as a teacher, you have perpetually talked the talk; do not be afraid to walk the walk. Wilde sat reticent in his bunk while Murray moved his feet and legs over the bedrail when they heard an audible, "Knock, knock," from outside their drawn curtain which offered a slight amount of privacy, if privacy could be had on this air chariot of the Department of Homeland Security.

"Howdy, boys! Mind if I pop in?" Thomas Charles, a.k.a. Uncle Tom, from the Grand Canyon peered around the curtain. This solidified all that Murray had just divulged to Jacob about the perpetual observation. "I heard you boys chatting." Murray thought momentarily that the possibility that their area may be being monitored seemed likely—only minutes into this touchy conversation, the always affable Uncle Tom coincidentally arrived.

"Come on in!" Murray sounded out.

"Just cruising by, looking for grandma, and thought I overheard a bit of despondency."

"We were just discussing the past and present," answered Jacob attempting to repel Uncle Tom.

"Did you say grandma?"

"Yes sir, grandma always has the answers," Uncle Tom looked up, then down, and then around all the while he patted his pockets front and back, then he produced what seemed to be a flask. "Ahhh, grandma. Have some." He offered Jacob and Murray a drink from the silver container. Murray reached out and took a pull of the recently produce flask. The sweet burn from palate to stomach left him feeling invigorated.

"Oh my, Grand Marnier!"

"Boys, sometimes the meaning of life and the purpose of hiking coincide, when you hit a rough patch, take a breath, have some 'grandma' and mellow." Uncle Tom continued to musingly look off into some imaginable horizon. Jacob took a pull off the flask and handed it back to their philosopher who immediately took a robust swig. "My sister, Mary, always told me, 'Thomas, sometimes you just have to face the facts of life, bite your tongue, accept your duty, and move on.' I love my sister Mary, but the one thing I add to her advice, Grand Marnier." A hardy quaff again. "You boys need to vent on Uncle Tom?"

"Jacob, relax! Think about it," Murray glanced at Jacob ascertaining his level of discomfort talking in front of Uncle Tom. "Look, accept the fact that the Academy knows more about us than we do."

"That bothers me. I forgot about the trouble with Iain."

"Yeah, you also forgot your level of infuriation with Warrell-King when he crashed the Mormon religion class and offended our favorite Mormons, remember?" Murray goaded Jacob on to acquiesce to this new reality that the two of them must embrace. "The Degraw triplets, Sarah, Jeffrey and Curtis? Remember? You were ready to rip his throat out."

"I know," Jacob relented.

"And Brittany Simpson, in tears due to Iain's irreverent rant? And here you sit, worried about other pieces of trash like Warrell-King getting removed from the equation all for the betterment of the world."

"Well, that makes an enormous difference. Expelling Iain juxtaposed with murdering Senators and Congressman can hardly be equated."

"I beg to differ there pilgrim!" The sound of a raspy voice hissed from behind the curtain, which then found itself rent backwards and flung wide open. "That, my friend, justifies my career and existence. You see, your compadre there hit the nail on the head. In fact, the differences in this case could only be stated as minute." Louis Cottonwood entered the personal space of the two men attempting to bed down for the evening. Jacob felt multiple worlds and philosophies beginning to impinge in front of him. "I distinctly remember receiving an electronic dossier on a young man to be marked and neutralized when an opportune time manifested itself." Cottonwood grinned for he saw Uncle Tom nip at his flask; he extended his hand, which immediately had been filled by the alcoholic container.

"What are you talking about?" Jacob inquired as Cottonwood swilled the Grand Marnier.

"Boy, when you sat down with Principal Feinauer, what exactly did you report to Bobby concerning all of the data you and the other teachers gathered on Warrell-King?" Wilde sat perplexed, not understanding the relationship between a dead, former student, his expulsion report, and murdered politicians nearly fifty years ago.

"Relevance, Louis?"

"I shall provide you with relevance, boy and pay attention," Cottonwood stood up taller than his agedness generally permitted. "His expulsion resulted ultimately from his religious intimidation, a societal taboo along with racial, ethnic and cultural intolerance. We got no room for it. However, that does not serve as the summation of Mr. Iain Warrell-King's list of school transgressions and possible civic crimes. Mr. King allegedly partook in, and sold drugs to go along with his blatant disrespect for the staff. His pathetic grades in his nationally funded education, not to mention his documented felony charge of religious harassment, all added up." Cottonwood took another hit of 'grandma.' "Tagged as a pariah of society from your principal by you, my teacher friend."

"How do you know all of that?"

"It happens to be my occupation. My profession, sir. What did that fiend's death certificate say, hmm, let me see? Oh, I have it. Dead on Arrival in Churchill Woods from two gunshots. Death consistent with homicide; one gunshot to the chest and another gunshot to the back of the head." Cottonwood's stony glare frowned down on Jacob Wilde. "In the business, we call it execution style."

"How do you know all of that?" The flummoxed Jacob looked around the area for some semblance of clarification.

"Remember when I told the Kues boy to show respect to a man with five confirmed kills?" Louis Cottonwood wheezed.

"Yeah. How does that relate to Warrell-King's murder."

"Son, for a teacher you ain't that bright." Evidence of an epiphany enlightened Murray Moore's countenance; Jacob Wilde sat incredulous. "You helped expel that boy and mark him as a pariah to society for his anti-religious rhetoric and potential drug usage. I followed Mr. King for two weeks and, during surveillance, proved not only his drug usage, but also his narcotic distribution. He met the criteria."

"What criteria?" This time it happened to be Moore asking.

"Full expulsion, son."

"What does that mean?" now inquired Wilde.

"Do you need me to paint you a picture? Spell it out for you? I shot that miscreant in the park. I followed him to the park, waited for him to get out of his car, approached him, inquired for drugs, and before he knew what hit him, I shot him in the chest. Didn't kill him though. Tough son of a gun. Even though I put him down, he tried to get up and run, but fell. I tapped him with one in the back of the skull. Full expulsion, son. The world ain't got the patience to convict them all three times."

"Sweet Mother of God!" exclaimed Murray, "You are an assassin?"

"Son, I have been called many things; I just think of it as taking out the trash."

"You murdered Iain Warrell-King?"

"Damn, you are dense boy; you expelled him from school, his anti-religious rhetoric, along with his drug distribution, expelled him from society, and I expelled him from this world. His own mamma doesn't even miss him. Good riddance to bad rubbish!" Cottonwood looked at Uncle Tom, "Grandma?" Thomas Charles tipped his flask over displaying that indeed its contents had been drained. "Damn, I need a drink! Edward!"

"Yo!" bellowed a booming voice from down the cabin.

"I need a drink!"

"Hell son!" Storming up the aisle of drawn curtains into the wide-open area with Wilde and Murray, along with their inter-lopers, Louis Cottonwood and Uncle Tom, came Crazy Edward Joseph, bearing a bottle of something resembling wine or whiskey. He held out the bottle and Cottonwood guzzled a quantity provoking Edward Joseph to snatch it back. "Easy son, you aren't drinking hillbilly moonshine!"

"Damn good," confirmed Cottonwood.

"It should be big fella, Taylor Fladgate Tawny Port, aged ten years. Sip it, son." Crazy Eddie looked around, "I know this party. Which pup happens to be struggling with reality and the world? Moore?" Murray Moore and Jacob Wilde pondered just how many of the people they had encountered in the last few months would be on this plane bound for L.O.F.I.; Murray wondered why he had been suspected as the weak one.

"No, Wilde's compunction crashed into the proverbial wall of ethos," added Uncle Tom. Jacob tried to assess it all, but felt beset by this coterie of what he could only now assume were agents.

"Hell son, the way you put down that mule, I figured Moore hit the wall." Wilde let all of this settle in his mind.

"Let me ask you Cottonwood, you stated you had five confirmed kills in our first meeting and just now; those weren't in combat were they."

"Nope. Not in the traditional sense—call it urban combat."

"You have killed five former students?" Jacob inquired tentatively.

"Hell, no. I have killed far more than that. I have killed five of *your* recommended students," Cottonwood's truculent answer nearly knocked Wilde out of his bunk.

"What do you mean he recommended?" interjected Murray Moore with a defensive temerity hoping to assist his evidently flabbergasted friend.

"Son, you two boys need to realize that every student you have expelled poses a risk to the fabric of our society, whether they turn to crime or vagrancy." This time Crazy Eddie interceded. "America's 'work or starve' policy pushes some to a life of crime. For the last fifty years, we, as a country, have been shipping the worst off to the Penal Colony. If the teachers and agents could perfect their craft, L.O.F.I. could cease to exist; unfortunately, even with crime down, the penal colony still serves a purpose to absorb the excess criminality."

"Moreover," interjected Uncle Tom, "The slow hand of the law doesn't always keep pace with the criminal world. This, my young bucks, reflects the veneer, the proverbial façade which you have been entrusted to keep. As teachers you had your finger on the pulse of the school; you knew the students; you knew who would turn out productive and who would not."

"Wow!" Murray exploded. "All of those data meetings, mining through tests scores, behavior reports and discussions on the students; all were used to determine who would be killed."

"Hell's bells, son! We ain't killers!" Cottonwood shouted in an apoplectic rage. "We follow strict guidelines. We monitor certain expelled students or potentially expelled students and verify that they will be, and are, a detriment to society. With that confirmed, we get the green light from Homeland and take them out," he looked disgusted. "It represents a science steeped in logos. Why waste time on the scum sucking pig? Slaughter him first."

"So let me get this straight," Jacob cut in, "The United States of America has a policy of murdering people it does not approve of?"

"Boy you are dumb!" Again Cottonwood retorted as ferociously as ever.

"No," Uncle Tom tranquilly responded. "Homeland Security takes interest in any and all people who may disrupt society. The judicial system removes the hardened criminals to Guam. But the philosophy of Homeland, for the past fifty years or so, has been to eliminate threats with a proverbial pre-emptive strike. Teachers know the next generation, you provide the data; the principal makes the call. Agents such as Cottonwood and my friend Edward here cull the herd if the pernicious and potentially seditious students proved positive to exhibit what the principals charge based upon such data. Really, a simple formula that has worked for a couple of generations."

This concatenation of memories, ideals, dogmas and flashbacks hammered at Jacob Wilde's moral compass; Murray Moore's level of intrigue evolved more and more. Jacob glanced around the less than commodious space and reached out for the bottle of tawny port that Crazy Eddie had raised. Wilde's country that he loved, cherished and taught revealed its dark underbelly; consequently, it failed to sit well at that moment for him.

"Let me ask a question," Wilde inquired hoping to exhort some sense of grip upon this new reality he had just had thrust upon him. "You said five kills Cottonwood. You know anything about Kyle Medley? I taught him a few years ago, committed suicide not long after dropping out of school."

"I love that story," piped up Cottonwood. "It took me a full half hour to drown that scoundrel. I have never had someone drunk struggle so much."

"Jesus! You murdered him, too."

"First son, Jesus ain't got nothing to do with it," scolded Cottonwood. "Second, your exit report on his dropping out of school read something about being a potential reprobate for society to deal with in the future, but more than likely, a leach on society for his total disinterest in the advancement of his own personal self. Hell boy, that served as a red flag. Sociological studies reveal that social deviants like that never commit three felonies. Sure, the murderers and violent criminals go straight to L.O.F.I., but the Kyle Medley's, with their periodic felonies and decadent behaviors, serve only to slowly degrade society. God knows how much trouble you saved the community writing that data analysis."

"Have another drink son," Crazy Eddie added holding up the bottle of Taylor Fladgate tawny port.

CHAPTER TWENTY THREE

"The mind 'manifests' its own place, and it itself
Can make a heav'n of hell, a hell of heav'n."

JOHN MILTON *PARADISE LOST* **1:254-255**
[WITH AN IMPROVEMENT THAT SHOULD MANIFEST ITSELF]

Murray Moore awoke to the steady hum of forced circulated air and the distant whine of a multi-engine aircraft slightly bumping through the atmosphere at a steady six hundred miles per hour. The fumes of the night before had worn off as he shook the cobwebs from his mind. Not long after the finishing of the tawny port, the captain sounded over the intercom that lights were being dimmed and all should consider resting, for a momentous day lay ahead. As he lay languorously in the cot, he heard Jacob Wilde stirring below him in the bunk. Murray had camped often enough with Wilde to recognize the cacophony of noises he made—clearing his nose and throat—prior to rising and stretching. He felt the evening prior lamentable, for Murray became painfully cognizant of heterodoxy arising in Jacob Wilde, which could not and would not be acceptable. He needed to convince Wilde to come to grips with this new occupational reality but Jacob must do it under his own volition. It would not do to force ideology down his throat; Wilde must transcend his reservations and face the consequences of being a gatekeeper of society. The conversation must address the ethos of the matter, for Wilde would not be won on logos alone. Murray thought that if he could convince Jacob to set his compunction in a momentary state of abeyance, Murray could foster in him a logical moral settlement of Wilde's qualms.

"You awake, buddy?"

"Yeah," Jacob listlessly responded. Moore remembered the last thing that Crazy Eddie instructed him to do prior to breaking up the party the night before. He said, "Get your boy in line." Coupling that incarnation of a threat with Uncle Tom's piteously empathetic, "He'll come around," Murray Moore felt the clock ticking for Jacob Wilde to make a verbal commitment.

"How about some breakfast? They are serving in the main meeting area."

"Yeah, okay," ambivalently replied Jacob as he swung his feet upon the floor. As the two men headed for the breakfast area—one waltzing, the other trudging—Murray racked his brain trying to remember an instance that could help his friend come to terms with his inner conflict. Jacob's chief moral dilemma seemed to stem in the backroom ruthlessness of the maintenance of society. However, he needed examples from class and their career that would help him navigate this tortuous road he would have to travel. "Hey, Jacob."

"Yeah?"

"You remember that young girl we had in class a number of years ago from Japan?"

"Yeah, what about her?" Jacob paused, "Ayumi. Yes, Ayumi Ogawa. What about her?"

"Well, she just popped into my head. What a great kid! Well, probably a woman by now," Murray felt the palpable tension built up around Jacob begin to evaporate.

"The girl you terrorized while she studied here," Wilde furtively gave him a look of condemnation.

"What are you talking about?" Murray pretended to be surprised; however, the idea he engendered to bring Jacob out of his funk began to move toward positivity.

"Oh please, you would try and humiliate her on a daily basis as she entered your classroom."

"What?" Murray elongated the enunciation of the word to imply complete befuddlement.

"You would not let her into your room unless she would pronounce 'hamburger' with the enunciated 'h' on the beginning and 'r' on the end, knowing full well that her linguistic background made this all but impossible."

"Oh relax," Murray felt he had his friend back, at least momentarily. "She came to America to learn the culture and language, I assisted with that; furthermore, I had to teach the kids about linguistic differences, and have a bit of fun, of course." Murray could ascertain by Jacob's mien that a casual conversation could now take place and lead him back into the fold. "Do you know what she does now?"

"Who, Ayumi?" Jacob paused, "No, I do not."

"Veterinarian in Tokyo, Japan."

"Nice, a fine occupation. Tis a shame she went home to Japan," remarked Jacob dispassionately. "America could use someone of her intelligence."

"Yep. Tough job being a vet sometimes." Murray added as Jacob nodded in agreement while they moved into the meeting area for breakfast. "Sometimes as a veterinarian you have to make tough decisions on animals."

"Wait a minute," interjected Wilde. Murray feared he incautiously advanced the subject, for Jacob retorted, "Are you comparing the putting down of an animal with the willful murder of a human being. Sick man!"

"What?" Murray observed Jacob's now querulous mood blossom.

"You are talking about two different creatures: man and beast."

"I see no difference. We put animals down when they are of no use to man or themselves, not to mention when their very existence threatens the herd."

"Don't even start this comparison, Murray," Jacob now growing cantankerous, "The mule and man are vastly different."

"How so? Are we not animals ourselves?"

"We, sir, are sentient beings! We have dominion over the animals."

"Firstly, I refuse to believe that all humans possess sentience. Secondly, if you would like to quote the Bible, we have dominion of man. See some of the laws in the Old Testament."

"I will not have a Biblical debate on this. You will lose. Jesus never advocated any of this activity in which we will now be engaged." The two sat down at serving tables in the meeting room of Air Force One and were immediately given menus.

"Look Jacob, what must man do with a rabid dog?"

"Spare me your rhetorical questions."

"We put it down. We put it down for it can harm the animals around it. You do it for the good of the herd."

"Then, why not kill the crippled? People with Down Syndrome? Huh, why not put them down?"

"They don't try to destroy the society. Also, they did not chose to be crippled or a burden upon society. The malcontent had every opportunity and chose to buck the system, to throw a wrench into the works; they don't deserve anything else."

"Then let the crime be committed, the person charged, tried and convicted. Let the courts work the way they were intended!" Jacob's vehemence exploded.

"So, if I monitor a student through school, evaluate all intellectual and personal data on him for a few years, find evidence that he may become a social deviant, a murderer, or rapist, tip off our agents, catch him in the act, you are saying that you want him to be able to commit the crime, get punished, and then have a chance at two more felonies? He can commit three rapes, and then have to be caught three times to be convicted three times by his unreliable peers before we ship them to L.O.F.I."

"It would be better that one hundred guilty persons should escape than that one innocent person should be condemned."

"Look, that Piggy attitude may have worked in Ben Franklin's day, but that type of liberal idealistic philosophy landed this country in financial trouble all through the previous two centuries—not to mention terrorized America with crime and frustration. Now crime has bottomed out, and the budget has money to fund beneficial programs for the industrious of the country such as health care and retirement." Moore thought of William Golding, "You now have the conch, my friend."

"I would prefer to drop the subject. Let us agree to disagree."

"That roguish behavior won't suffice in our new job. You can't play the maverick."

"I will work through it," Jacob's level of perturbation continued to increase, "Now, I want to eat breakfast."

Murray decided throughout breakfast to let Jacob stew in his own moral dilemma, for the captain had announced that Guam would be reached within a few hours, and he felt a sense of ebullient excitement at the prospect of seeing the island which had fascinated his mind for years. While the candidates ate a steady meal, out marched the omnipresent Colonel Elizabeth Nutt, who seemed to be a ubiquitous figure in their lives; along with Nutt came a familiar looking, swarthy hued gentleman sporting a Fu Manchu and wearing it well, for his Oriental roots stood in stark contrast to the Occidental heritage of the military woman standing shoulder to shoulder with him.

"Good morning candidates," Colonel Nutt began, "As you have heard, we are only a couple of hours from the United States Federal Penal Colony located on Guam." She gazed about the room sternly. "Apparently, we had a mild breach of etiquette last night involving a couple of agents and candidates. I assure you disciplinary action will be taken. Since the itinerary has been haphazardly circumvented by a couple of tipsy agents, important revelations concerning the workings of Homeland Security were divulged prior to my schedule. I have Doctor Ko here to elucidate upon the matter."

"Greetings again," the Orientally mixed doctor spoke, "I am Doctor Ko, and my function with the Department of Homeland Security revolves around the logistics of clandestine affairs. I won't bore you too much with my aforementioned credentials; suffice to say that I have attended medical school at Harvard and finished a doctoral degree at the Sorbonne in Paris. Besides socio-psychology, I have varying degrees in natural sciences focused upon evolution, basic medicine dabbling in neuroscience, with minors in sociology and anthropology—though I possess a penchant for classical literature. I am a humanitarian of the first order, a pacifist at heart, and a professional intellectual who also struggled with some of the more unpleasant activities of the agency." He scanned the crowd and then continued.

"I learned very early on in the agency that I would prefer to rule in Hell than serve in Heaven. After my graduation from the universities, I reconnoitered the world searching for a country that could satiate my romantic notions of man and his existence on this God forsaken mud ball, and sadly, a utopian society of man where the citizen educates himself, takes ownership of his fate and civic responsibility to ensure a safe, orderly and egalitarian existence did not exist as I had desired. The closest in practice and intent I found existed in the United States of America; however, despite all of her problems, I found myself called, or recruited, to serve in the Department of Homeland Security. Though my scruples and compunction struggled with the 'dirty work' of the bureau, I experienced an epiphany. The vapid, vacuous miscreants, along with the pernicious malcontents born into any land would only serve one purpose; destruction of the society."

"Thus, being a Darwinist, if you will, and pragmatist—not to mention a man desiring to live in a free, peaceful, and opportunity filled land—I accepted that a small amount of disagreeable work now would result in a better society tomorrow. So much like the childcare provider does not enjoy changing the diaper, the dog owner does not relish following his canine picking up his warm excrement on the side of the road, nor the custodian long for a clogged toilet, they clean up the fecal matter of their world, for if left undone, ruin and disease shall befall their charges and themselves.

Candidates, you are the gatekeepers of society. You don't have to change the proverbial diaper, or follow behind the symbolic dog or free up the hypothetical toilet; your requirement shall be this simple: call the person assigned to such tasks. Your agent will confirm the problem—diaper, dog or toilet—then your agent will save the community from the human waste." Again, Doctor Ko silently scoured the crowd.

"I completely understand some of you may find this morally offensive. When we land on Guam, take the opportunity of the tour to find some modicum of solace in your soul to rectify this to yourself, as gatekeepers you will ensure the pedigree of this great country of America. You are not judging people upon their race, color, creed or ethnicity; you are not judging at all. A simple application of logos shall suffice; analyze data and predict. Let the agents know your concerns; the field agents will confirm your prognostications. If they prove accurate, the agent and the agency will deal with the aforementioned person. Understand, no matter a citizen's fate, the process reflects a sedulous and rigorous checklist that the agent and agency work through. No blood will be on your hands. We are here when L.O.F.I. just does not provide the protection America, the greatest country on Earth, needs. With that folks, I shall leave you to your breakfast."

Not long after breakfast, the candidates were instructed to return to their seats, for the approach to the island of Guam had started, and Air Force One would be landing at Andersen Air Force base on the north shore of the island within the hour. Murray had benefited from a bit of luck; his window seat would allow a terrific view of the upcoming island; a bird's eye view of the penal colony that had him intrigued. Anxiously awaiting his view of L.O.F.I., he sat silently next to the still reticent Jacob Wilde. He could feel the plane begin to descend and hear the myriad mechanical noises of the aircraft preparing for landing with a series of banking maneuvers. It had long been a desire and dream to see the island even though it strictly banned tourism for obvious reasons. Up until recently, Murray thought the only way to see the island existed through joining the Air Force, Navy or Marines, which ensured that the inmates remained on the island.

In class, because of the island's literary sobriquet, the Language Arts department taught William Golding's *Lord of the Flies.* Though it had never been the intention of the government to refer to the United States Federal Penal Colony as L.O.F.I., as Moore taught in his linguistics class, you cannot stop the English language from bubbling up. If the masses called it L.O.F.I., then beware Oxford English Dictionary, a new word would have been born. Murray remembered a class that he had asked Jacob to attend, for the discussion of the day stemmed upon the subject of the novel and the actual island. One of Murray's favorite mural paintings in the hall of the Languages Arts department had centered around a pig's head on a stick bearing an open mouth with a conch shell in it. A bit more irreverently in his own room, Murray had had painted the bloated Piggy, blindly reaching for his glasses with the corrupted quote, "Some one show me a rock upon which to sit please." In class, earlier in the year, Murray had encouraged the students to break up in their web-based group research inquiry projects and build either computer or real models of both versions of the island—America's and Britain's. As they met for class in the conference room, to allow better ambiance for presentations, Moore had called the attention of the class after a group's presentation.

"Guys and gals, come forward and check out these scale models." The group had moved forward gawking at the model of Golding's island and America's version. "Who crafted these?" Two hands had risen in front. "Well, done Katie Toensmeyer and Anna Braam. Like two Alphas plusses, always over achieving!"

"Mr. Moore," a hand from Arlie Turner went up, "Didn't the British and French empires utilize penal colonies? They didn't work did they?"

"Good question, Arlie," Murray drew the class in for discussion. "There were differences." He paused, "Good, Ms. Fowee!"

"The British colony at Botany Bay and Van Diemen's Land, along with Georgia in our country, were not permanent settlements necessarily. Many could work as indentured servants to pay their debt to society. The prisoners could be released."

"Very good Allie." Murray saw another hand, "Becky Taylor, you wish to add?"

"Didn't they have colonists living near the penal colonies?"

"Excellent, they did. Convicts could gain their freedom and then actually move in around the very people who may have sentenced them there—a poor policy. Can anyone name the difference between ours and theirs?"

"Oh, I know!" shouted Katie Reece. "When you go to L.O.F.I. you can't come back."

"I think it wrong to banish them forever," interjected Kristen Bevins.

"We've got to have rules and obey them. After all, we're not savages. We're Americans, and the Americans are best at everything!"

"Ray, relax," interceded Moore for Master Kuertz had a way of stoking the proverbial fire if a political debate could be seen on the horizon.

"Sorry, Mr. Moore," Ray dejectedly glanced down, "I'm just sayin.'"

"Remember class, all people on the island of L.O.F.I. have been tried and convicted of first degree murder and received life imprisonment, or they have been tried and convicted in a court of their peers for three felonies. Superfluous pity for those who categorically reject society shouldn't enter your mind."

"I know Mr. Moore," cried out Bevins, "But that island has to be dangerous."

"I am sure that day-to-day life mimics a perilous verisimilitude to life on the Serengeti. Survival of the fittest."

"Mr. Moore?" inquired Ben Forsyth from the back. "How did that not violate the eighth amendment of cruel and unusual punishment?" Moore witnessed Wilde's spasmodic shudder in the back corner of the room. Murray knew he would be apoplectic if not able to respond.

"I believe Mr. Wilde wishes to address that issue!"

"Stupid, Ben," muttered Matt Van Houten.

"Yes, thank you Matt, stupid!" Jacob blasted, "Forsyth, just what part of the stratosphere did your mind occupy last week when we discussed the Belarski Amendment?"

"Uhh," Ben glanced around receiving copious glares of disapprobation from the class.

"Mr. Wilde! Mr. Wilde," called out Murray, "I believe young Sam Chang would like to respond." Jacob's fury relented and he subsequently relinquished the floor. "Samantha, please."

"Senator Mahatma Belarski proposed an Amendment to the United States Constitution which ostensibly stated that any citizen who commits three or more felonies by their own actions shall serve as a renunciation of his or her citizenship."

"God and the fourteenth giveth, and Belarski taketh away!"

"Very frolicsome Eric Lee!" Moore shouted above the raucous laughter of the class. As they simmered down, "Correct Sam."

"Why did he push the amendment?" Wilde spoke up from the back of the class.

"Someone had to do it!"

"Okay," Moore attempted to reign in the class, for it teetered on a brink of dysfunctional excitement—which he enjoyed, for it provided the best discussions. "Whitney Jo, explain."

"It had something to do with the immigrant and naturalization policy enacted after the Great Compromise."

"Good," Moore paused, glanced around the room, spotting Jordan's hand, "Mr. Cavalaris, explain."

"It had to go before the Supreme Court. Since immigrants were going to have to prove their worth to stay in the country by filling a needed position and raising children who graduated from America's schools, it seemed only fair that America citizen's were held to some standard."

"Our standard seems easier," commented Anna Braam.

"True, but Senator Mahatma Belarski had Indian relatives immigrating to the country, and it clearly represented an injustice for productive immigrants wanting nothing more in life than to move to America, assimilate to the culture, produce robustly for our economy and live a life of freedom raising a family," Murray summed up.

"Besides," Jacob Wilde broke in, gathering every student's attention, "We all know that a system of government granting citizenship to people just because their parents in an act of lustful, animalistic pleasure brought into the world an unwanted or unexpected child truly represented a folly of the 19th century Congress."

"Amen, Mr. Wilde! Amen."

"May I ask a question prior to dismissal, Mr. Moore?" Jacob perked up in the back. "Extra Credit of course."

"By all means."

"What court decision had to be overturned in order to push through the Belarski amendment?" A hand immediately sprung to life, "Anna Braam!" Eric Lee sat disgusted as usual with her.

"Afroyim vs. Rusk, a decision of the 1960s," Braam glowingly respond. Wilde nodded much heartened by his prized student's response.

"Ten points for Gryffindor!" blurted out Elizabeth Sarvak and the class exploded into laughter. Murray knew a modicum of decorum could not be restored to finish his thoughts on the social benefits of the revocation of the 14th amendment, nor the successfulness of the immigration policy enacted during the Great Compromise, and the economic juggernaut which followed the shipping out of the criminality, importing the world's talent and cutting out the handouts for the generational welfare recipients. *Oh well, another lesson for another day* Moore contemplated. He had reluctantly finished, "Class dismissed."

CHAPTER TWENTY FOUR

"I cannot but conclude the bulk of your natives to be the most pernicious race of little odious vermin that nature ever suffered to crawl upon the surface of the earth."

JONATHAN SWIFT
GULLIVER'S TRAVELS

On the approach to the island of Guam, the pilot of Air Force One circumnavigated the oasis from 10,000 feet. Murray's window seat allowed him to enjoy a bird's eye view of the island; furthermore, in preparation for the visit, he had read a brief history of Guam multiple times and already knew that the island consisted of 209 square miles of land with nearly every inch of it occupied by the convicts. Two areas of non-inmate occupied civilization existed on the island. On the western shore, a small naval base wrapped itself in the Apra Harbor and consisted of possibly 5% of the island's land mass. On the northeastern portion of the island, Andersen Air Force Base took up about another 5% of the island. Both sections of civility appeared from the air—and Murray knew from the history—to be protected by a double wall system. The landing proved banal, for the fly-over failed to display much of the island except its minuteness lost in the vastness of the surrounding sea.

After touching down, the candidates grabbed their miscellaneous carry-on bags, and as they headed into the Air Force Base, the plane taxied to a stopping point where they were greeted by a band of all things playing "Stars and Stripes Forever." The candidates were then loaded onto two small shuttle buses and taken directly to the Commissary. Though hot, the breeze off the sea exemplified that of a tropical resort. Murray, intrigued as usual, followed the group into the main dining area of the Commissary adjacent to the base's store of sundry goods. Wilde, looking dejected as ever, stood in stark contrast to the other twenty-two candidates who seemed to swallow, with no moral qualms at all, the realities of the world, along with their new positions and duties in life. As they emptied out onto the tarmac and approached the buildings, the candidates were awestruck by a thirty foot tall statue that had neither been mentioned to observe from the air, nor highlighted by anyone when planning the trip to Guam. The statue, to any literary scholar, would be immediately recognized as a corruption of the Jonathan Swifts' *Gulliver's Travels'* statue of judicature. The statue appeared to be stepping forward as if being chased. The distance between the stride proved large enough for a man to walk through unscathed. Near the statue's feet lay a discarded bag lying open, spilling coins onto the ground displaying that Justice had preferred to reward as opposed to punish; however, dropping from the left hand of the statue turned out to be the scales of justice and the blindfold, and the right hand had a drawn sword raised in anger and/or retaliation. Murray felt intrigued.

The cast of characters in its entirety emptied the airliner and filled the banquet hall from the officers down to the agents. Murray observed Louis Cottonwood and his two young protégés, Zack Hatfield and Luke Kues, along with Colonel Nutt and Hauer with

Alliston. Murray recognized Dr. Ko as he approached a podium with a microphone in the foreground and a projection screen in the background. Just as Murray thought Dr. Ko would speak to the group, out walked a sveltely dressed uniformed woman, clearly highly ranked in the United States Air Force. Though small in stature, she strode lankily into the room standing before the fresh batch of candidates.

"I am Lieutenant Colonel Hannah Weeger! Graduate of the United States Air Force Academy in Colorado Springs, Colorado class of 2057. I am the supreme commander of this facility here on this island. This facility should be viewed as a war zone. On the other side of the Great Wall of Guam, you have nearly 250,000 examples of the worst forms of human life. While on this island, you will be subjected to a regimented schedule; this will not be a pleasure holiday." Weeger glanced around the room receiving complete attention by all. She continued, "While here, you will be flown on a tour of the island in a vintage Marine One helicopter; you will be briefed in several seminars on the history here at the United States Federal Penal Colony of Guam. You shall be privy to information that ranks as top secret. You belong to the fold now, the fraternity; honor it; stick to the code. We here have a greater responsibility than most Americans can possibly fathom. We literally stand on the wall between anarchy and civility. You will be inducted into that responsibility with your final test. A test which shall be observed by all that you have met in the past couple of months." Lieutenant Colonel Weeger glanced around the room. "Tech Sergeant Keith Turner will lead the two groups out onto the tarmac. There will be two former Marine One helicopters there ready and waiting to provide you with a more personal view of the island. Afterwards, we shall reconvene and continue on with the agenda. Please follow Tech Sergeant Keith."

"Alright! You heard Lieutenant Colonel Weeger, move out!" The candidates followed the Sergeant towards the doors of the Commissary. Keith embodied the quintessential differences between the Air Force and the Marines, being a bit under the average height, his wearing of glasses demonstrated to the world the intellectual threat that he posed instead of the physical one. As they

headed through the doors and the sounds of the outside perme-
ated the hall, the thwacking thump of propeller blades could be
heard pulsating—a magnificent adrenaline fueling sound. Murray
experienced a visceral flooding of jingoistic patriotism breaking
out into the sunshine to see the incarnation of metallic grasshop-
pers slowly and methodically hissing, thumping and thwacking endlessly. He felt he would explode from excitement. As he glanced
around at the other candidates, this tangible exultation manifested
itself upon all of their countenances. Sergeant Keith counted the
first twelve up to him and pointed to the Marine One chopper preparing to touch down on the left landing pad, and then he counted
the last thirteen and pointed them towards the beast descending
in its landing routine on the right. As the two Lockheed Martins
touched down, they seemed to freeze in time—all except the fan
blades still thumping and thwacking as the creature hissed incessantly—as they seemed to wait for the most opportune time to
open up and swallow their elated and eager passengers. And then,
with excellent military uniformity, both helicopters dislodged their
respective stairway platforms, flipping down, allowing two smartly
dressed Marines to descend the steps and take up a post on either
side.

Both stood in a ramrod straight posture, effusing magnificence.
Moore hung back, hoping for some unknown reason to be the last
onboard the aircraft. The group hurriedly marched aboard both
helicopters, intimidated by the voluminous sound they exhorted.
Murray took up the rear slowly walking up to the stair platform first
looking into the face of the Marine on the left, then right and then
at their nametags—Davis and Sanders. Moore committed Sanders
and Davis to memory, wondering if he would then see them some
other place on this epic odyssey. He trotted up the steps, ducked
his head, stepped in and pushed back his half-mooned spectacles.
Most of the candidates had sat or were preparing to sit; both sides
of Marine One provided small yet comfortable swivel chairs, allowing the passengers to look out a window or spin around to see the
passenger in front, behind or on the side. Moore plopped down
in front of Wilde, who for the first time in a while, had disposed of
his sullenness and exuded an air of childish excitement. Above the

cockpit door, a telescreen came to life as Sanders came in followed by Davis, who then commenced to close the door to the aircraft. Upon the screen flashed a full-faced pilot donning the headgear anyone would expect of a pilot.

"Good day candidates, I am Captain Chris Meyer. I will be conducting you around the island today on an aerial tour. Enjoy yourselves." Murray peered inquisitively at the name labeled above the forehead on the pilot's helmet; it read "Jumbo." A noticed increase in the vibration of the craft and thwacking of the blades made it clear to all that lift off would be immediate. "Just sit back folks, seat belts on. Here we go!" Jumbo's screen remained on as the craft slowly rose from the deck. As the chopper lifted and gained altitude, it moved out toward the sea, due north then banked at a forty-five degree angle to turn east looking out over the endless expanse of the sea. The aircraft seemed to hover over the ocean for an unnerving amount of time, then moved again at a forty-five degree angle and turned south. Murray, by noticing the second helicopter turning to follow, conjectured that the pause allowed the machines to stay together.

"Candidates," Captain Meyer addressed the cabin, "As you look out the right side, you will see the island of Guam in all of its murdering mayhem. If you glance back you will see the area we just left, Andersen Air Force Base. Below you," and he tipped the chopper so slightly, "You can see the double wall which separates the base from the inmates." Murray observed two walls, height indeterminable from this elevation, running in an east-west fashion then taking a forty-five degree angle in a north-south direction. From the air, it appeared as a double arrow point and it separated the base from the rest of the island. Much to Murray's intrigue, the wall extended into the sea a good one hundred yards on both ends, as if to ensure that inmates could not circumvent the obstruction.

"We will be flying over beaches and circumnavigating the island. Due to safety concerns, we will not fly directly over the inmate population. Since the best viewing will be through the starboard side windows, please be courteous and move to allow those sitting on the port side to gain a view." Jumbo Meyer's revelation of flight pattern disheartened Moore, and probably the rest of the candidates, he even heard Nick Kues, who sat near him, spit out some form of disgusted disappointment. However, upon reflection, it would seem foolishly idiotic to fly the numerous dignitaries who visit the island for various inspections over top of a zone that, if an accident occurred, the greeting the survivors would meet on the ground would be unconscionable.

As Marine One skirted the island, the candidates could visibly see people; they appeared to be lounging upon some of the beaches. Moore found himself surprised to see the appearance of civilization in the inmate area. Clearly houses stood, streets existed and farming evidenced. The chopper moved at a steady clip down the coast; Jumbo continued, "If you look out over the island you can see abandoned AB Won Pat International Airport. We call it 'execution alley' because the prisoners who have formed their own tribal laws will execute inmates in full view of all cameras placed at various points around the island. If you look toward the right of the abandoned runway," and Jumbo forced the aircraft to rise so that a better angle could be had, "You will see what the military has deemed 'question eight.'" Moore noticed a Roman numeral eight made from what appeared to be multiple felled trees stretched in a pattern of a least thirty feet in length laying boldly in the open. Behind it, equally as large a collection of rocks, stones and boulders had been gathered together forming a question mark. "Apparently, the last thing the animals remembered prior to their citizenship revocation and deportation would be Amendment Eight of the Bill of Rights. I guess they can remember some of their schooling." Jumbo cut the microphone but could be seen visibly chuckling in the cockpit.

Murray peered through the starboard window wondering if the debris on the abandoned runway did in fact represent executed bodies. The aircraft bounced and banked providing more views of what appeared to be three distinct settlements upon the island. North of the AB Won Pat International Airport seemed to have a collection of cleared trees and vegetation with visible smoke from possibly cooking fires. To the south of the abandoned airport on the eastern shore a relatively settled area with similar activity seemed apparent. As the chopper rounded the southern extremity of the island revealing rather large but uninhabited beaches, Marine One headed north revealing a third settlement immediately south of the Guam Naval Base, the candidates' apparent destination.

"As you can tell," Jumbo Meyer broke in, "There exists on the island three definitive camps occupying the former towns of Dededo in the North, Yona in the East, and Agat in the West. The former capital of Hagatna has mostly been destroyed and looted over the last fifty years—much of it burned in the Guam War that raged from 2026 to 2032. Brutal! You will learn about it on the base. The center of the island ostensibly could be called 'No Man's Land.' The three villages live in a perpetual state of war with one official truce; no one group will interfere with another group if they slaughter someone on 'execution alley.' A bit of civility among the barbarians." Chris Meyer paused, "Make sure you are buckled up, we will be landing in a couple of minutes."

The landing near an abandoned airstrip inside the confines of the Guam Naval Base proved uneventful. The two Lockheeds touched down on two different well kempt helicopter pads which were marked brightly on a much larger concrete pad. The anti-quated strip proved a relic of World War II so many years ago. Immediately off the heli-pad, the candidates were taken into a modern building standing between the landing area and the road. Passed the road, a lush, green, slight declivity rolled down to a cliff which promptly dropped into the sea. Murray and Jacob marveled at the double-walled system via which the Naval Base had secluded itself from the rest of the island. Inside, they were greeted by an entrance hall of dignitaries and ushered into a large classroom four times larger than it needed to be on this occasion. Many of the faces inside were now becoming familiar—all but one.

"Welcome, to Guam Naval Base. I am Vice-Admiral Timmy Truong. I run this facility in conjunction with Lieutenant Colonel Weeger of the U.S. Air Force." Truong represented another exam-ple of the majority bi-racial mixture which had come to define America so much of the past half century. Murray thought the name Truong denoted a Vietnamese origin, but it had become so difficult to tell these days, plus its significance only mattered in the realm of cultural assimilation and victory for racial integration. Truong continued, "Lieutenant Colonel Weeger and I manage the military strike team of the island and ensure the safety of the island, the protection of the citizens, and the integrity of the facility." Murray noticed Truong did not say people, but citizens.

"Outside of the military theater of the island, two doctors are in charge of monitoring the inmates and studying their progress. The first doctor you met on Air Force One, Dr. Ben Ko. The head scientist will join us in a moment, Dr. Spencer Carran. I am here to provide you with some basic data about the island which may not be common knowledge back in civilization." Murray felt intrigued. The plethora of new information he had come to grips with recently could only become more wondrous the further from Mayfield he went and the closer to the L.O.F.I. walls he crept. "Ah, here he comes. Dr. Spencer Carran everyone."

Murray stood flabbergasted for the visage in front of him bore all the truth to the stereotypes of the world. Here before him stood a man who rendered doctoral introductions superfluous. This man had an aura of knowledge about him; it hung like a pulsating fume of function. His age could not be determined—somewhere between 35 and 65—Murray had no clue. Peeking through his disheveled mop of a head of hair hung a Henry David Thoreauian beard that would have shamed the hermit himself. As he came to the podium to address the crowd, he looked out at the audience but never really looked at them—maybe did not even see them. His countenance screamed that his whole being, his existence upon this planet could amount to one thing and one thing only: thinking. He wore a demeanor as he stepped to the microphone that he had been huddled behind a desk, or hunkered down in some back room library with anywhere from two to four lap tops or tablet computers working simultaneously as he formulated this, calculated that, all to predict something. It served to humble Murray Moore, for he knew that on his own greatest intellectual day, he could provide no nugget of knowledge to so much as move this man's intellect one iota in either direction. Moore sat in awe of greatness, for in front of him stood scientific investigation incarnate.

"Hello," the scientist glared into the abyss, "I am Dr. Carran; my field of study includes ecology, biology and evolution. My charge here consists of monitoring, supervising and advising all anthropological, psychological, sociological and evolutional experimentations upon the inmate populous of the island." He went on to explain that he had been in charge of the island for the last twenty years, so that assisted Murray in narrowing down his age, as if that mattered.

"Folks," interrupted Dr. Ko, "On your short visit here, we hope that you will learn or gain a better understanding of what we learned about man's primeval self as exemplified by the hordes of civilization-rejecting subjects. The abject evil, racism, barbarism, and non-humanism that conduct itself on this island should solidify your duties as principal and allow you to sleep at night conducting your work. Being the 'boot on the ground' your job as gatekeeper will be to snuff out potential candidates for this ninth level of hell here on earth. We want you to label and target these potential animals for verification; that will be the extent of your work. Homeland Security agents will take your sociological and psychological data on the former students and monitor them. If the data does indeed prove the school's prognostication, then that aforementioned pariah can be, and will be, dealt with in an orderly fashion. Now, rest assured, no blood indeed shall be on your hands. Your special agent will verify your data, receive verification from higher authorities, and nothing that you submit will automatically insinuate a death sentence. We learned from the past that the teacher possesses a pretty good sense of who will turn out right and who will turn out wrong. Now, we quantify those assertions with data and carry out the exercise with the promptness and expediency of a plumber fixing a pipe or a garbage man taking out the trash. I know Dr. Carran would like to speak briefly on the multifarious predictions social scientists supplied fifty years ago about what they believed would transpire when prisoners with death sentences and life sentences were placed without restrictions on this island to govern themselves." Dr. Ko smiled, "Dr. Carran, I yield the floor."

"Yes," again not paying attention to the crowd, it seemed Dr. Carran's mind indeed happened to be elsewhere—like a room full of sitting chess players, and he moved from table to table attacking them all. "Although many theories had been postulated by the leading minds of their times, this would represent my favorite farce of some dimwitted, pie in the sky pacifistic numbskull: that the men would unite in a common cause to revolt against their harsh treatment and unjustly cruel and unusual punishment. The pragmatists and pessimists of the day coagulated together if you will to surmise that man, being evil in nature, would divide up and engage in a violent struggle, eradicating all other groups with only the strongest surviving." Dr. Carran's up-until-then expressionless face, displayed a glimmer of humor. "Very unprofessionally, the leading minds of a half century ago sunk so low as to wager upon the situation. Some believed that the men would unite, strong versus weak, some old versus young, some prison versus prison, but most believed they would descend quickly into an animalistic and violent racial war. The results of the confluence of prisoners deposited upon the island of Guam did indeed erupt into a racial holocaust."

"Yes, thanks Dr. Carran," joined Dr. Ko. "As you flew about the island, you would have seen the city area in the center destroyed from perpetual and incessant warfare. The battle lines stabilized after the race war of 2026-2032; the black population occupied the western edge of the island, the whites the northern range and the Hispanics the eastern edge. However, as the 'pure' races began to kill one another over the years and the island began to see the motley mixes of today's America over the last thirty years, the groups' original lines of hatred have became a muddle. It has been a sociologist's dream controlled environment—not to mention Darwinist."

"One of the most illuminating aspects of the carnage," Dr. Carran added, "involves the fact that no group will accept the East Asian population that periodically will be dropped on the island. Every attempt the Oriental people have made to set up a village has been destroyed; likewise, when Orientals attempted to establish unity with another racial group for protection, it has been slaughtered. Their population fails to make any progress, for they just don't have the numbers."

"Are there any questions at the moment?" Dr. Ko inquired. He looked around, "Oh, yes, you sir."

"What stopped the carnage and bloodbath causing them to divide?" Murray felt stunned for Jacob Wilde had become inquisitive again.

"Well, the Mormon Mission of 2035," answered Dr. Ko.

"Uh," interrupted Dr. Carran pulling on his beard as if plotting three chess moves in his head for victory, "I do believe you mean the Mormon Massacre."

CHAPTER TWENTY FIVE

---

*"Proclaim ye this among the Gentiles; Prepare war, wake up the mighty men,
let all the men of war draw near; let them come up: Beat your plowshares
into swords."*

JOEL 3: 9 - 10
THE HOLY BIBLE

The ensuing history divulged via Dr. Ben Ko and Dr. Spencer
Carran reflected some information not known initially to the
general public on the mainland. Feared that Americans and
lawmakers would cringe at the barbarism of the United States
Penal Colony System, the circle of radical moderates, the Inklings,
squelched all of the news for a while coming out of L.O.F.I.—
which truly earned its name in horrific accounts. The students
back home at Mayfield unfortunately, if they knew the truth, would
take a far greater interest in the subject of the Correctional Facility

Transition, as referred to in the electronic schoolbooks, but called the L.O.F.I. Death March in military circles.

Murray remembered an encounter earlier in the year when two students had debated in class, the morality of the Correctional Facility Transition. The nationalized common core curriculum required the students to research, read, and dissect the Federalist Papers, the Bill of Rights, and the Constitution among other Founding Father documents. A particularly heated exchange had occurred when a student, Lori Ann, revealed her liberal tendencies arguing the injustice of shipping the hardened criminals of America—first federal prisoners and then state prisoners—from the prisons in waves across the seas to this remote island where social scientists had predicted over-population and starvation.

During their time studying *Starship Troopers* by Robert A. Heinlein, the discussion of crime and punishment, meritocracy and civic duty afforded many conversations not only in his own classroom, but in Jacob Wilde's also. The revocation of a person's citizenship had proved a sticky wicket in American politics for the last fifty years equivalent to the *Roe v. Wade* abortion law set a little over a century before and the Civil Rights Act a century and a half prior. The debate had proved an excellent way for budding intellectuals to cut their proverbial political teeth on the discussion which still had an annual march in Washington D.C.

"Look, the debate on the legality of citizenship revocation has been law for fifty years," Gregg Jordan went after Lori Ann. "Just read Chief Justice Taricia Lightfoot's majority opinion."

"I don't care what the Chief Justice of the Supreme Court wrote fifty years ago," Lori cut right back at him.

"Don't forget," chimed in Toren Chenault, "The Supreme Court at one time advocated and defended 'Separate but Equal' then changed its mind a couple of decades later."

"Yes, but Toren," carefully responded Gregg, "The Supreme Court in that racial issue decided it had erred and rectified their decision. I contend the same thing has happened here."

"Your meaning?" another student, Jordan Cavalaris, inquired.

"Meaning, the court recognized the idiocy of allowing someone to remain a citizen when it had to be painfully obvious to all of the tax paying citizens around them that his or her life of crime against society advocated for his or her removal from said society." Gregg Jordan, when on his educational game, had always handled himself quite well in class debates, which would have had a different feel altogether had the class known all the information disseminated to the candidates. The public schools had taught how the government systematically emptied out the male prisons of each state, first sending to L.O.F.I. the death row inmates, and then the lifers. Murray had recalled a time during the class debate when he had had to explain the transition.

"A specially fitted squadron of C-130s would take around ninety shackled passengers to the island at a time. In 2025, when the program commenced, the United States had a little over 4,000 inmates on death row. With ten C-130 prison ships in the fleet, each plane in flying four to five sorties from the mainland to Guam, cleaned out the death row inmates of America." Moore had known his students always loved the logistics of the Correctional Facility Transition. "Now interestingly enough, with nearly 2.5 million inmates nationwide, 160,000 or so had life sentences to serve. This would take the ten C-130s 16,000 sorties to transport them all. At first, the Government wanted the program to slowly transition the prisoners out, so as not to overload the island, the staff, the military or the unemployment market (as prisons began to consolidate)." Murray and Wilde had loved to hear them debate. The callow, irrational student would say it would be cheaper to shoot them; the humanist or liberal would cry 'cruel and unusual punishment'; all the while the government just kept on shipping them.

"Why did they move them so slowly?" Murray remembered the inquisitive Katie Toensmeyer asking.

"Class?"

"I know," Murray had acknowledged the speaker, Ben Forsyth, "They wanted to give the inmates time to construct housing, start growing food and begin clearing the land."

"Well done, Ben"

"Mr. Moore, what did they do with the people who lived there?" This time Kristen Bevins had asked.

"Who knows?" Erik Hoffman had come to life.

"I think I read that residents received ten years' wages to relocate to the states, or they could take a lifetime guard position on the base if they joined the Marines."

"Very nice, Erik."

"Mr. Moore," called out Gregg, "How about the positive effects?"

"Okay, fair enough, what positive effects?"

"Why don't you ask Lori?" Gregg goaded.

"Who cares that the crime rate plummeted and the rate of convictions declined precipitously. That does not excuse the wanton cruelty inflicted upon those American citizens," Lori Ann fumed.

"Listen to what you just said." Erik jumped in, "The crime rate plummeted because the citizens feared the punishment. Also, you are forgetting the money saved the taxpayer as these facilities closed."

"Besides," added Gregg, "They are not citizens! Sure cultures of the past did diabolical things to their citizenry. However, unlike the Romans, America did not toss into the gladiatorial arena sprouting religious groups or political prisoners; unlike the Nazis they did not round up the best and brightest of their civilization and exterminate them; America, like Christ discussing the rapture, gathered its refuse after it had gleaned the wheat from the field and tossed it into the proverbial fire. Jesus adamantly stressed not to judge; therefore, America did not judge their fellow man; they simply removed them."

In the present, Murray sat with the candidates learning the true horror of releasing convicted murderers into a 209 square mile "prison yard." Apparently the government landed the first ninety prisoners at Andersen Air Force Base and released them into the "wild." Once out past the old chained barrier fence of the base, groups of men began attacking one another. The men immediately formed into gangs based upon color, and the carnage that ensued reflected bloody hand-to-hand combat. The permanent crew of Air Force guards fired tear gas into the fighting, but little else. As the first ten sorties landed, discharging a total of 900 plus inmates into the island, still functioning traffic cameras, satellites and Predator drones recorded the carnage. After twenty sorties had been flown and nearly 2000 inmates released, the Department of Homeland Security called for a three day moratorium in order to assess the progress. Since the inmates all had microchips tracking them, it became easy to ascertain the extent of the carnage or as the government spun, proof of Darwinism at its finest. Of the 2000 inmates released in the first weeks, less than 400 were alive during the hiatus. Not surprisingly, on the twentieth release of prisoners, a group of whites charged from the woods and immediately hunted down the blacks with spears and other hand made weapons. As the Hispanics ran and the newly released black prisoners were being mutilated, the other tribe of blacks counter attacked—apparently late for the C-130 landing—and caught the assaulting white tribe unaware. Horrifically, the full battle could be watched because the melee took place in front of the base fence cameras and continued for so long, Predator Drones were flown in to fire upon the combatants in hopes of ending the slaughter.

"This represents a crucial Great Compromise turning point in American history," Dr. Ben Ko interjected. "During the hiatus, Homeland Security met with the Inklings—especially Senator Schmitt—to discuss the ethics of the matter." Ko looked around the group of candidates.

"Predicted slaughter by some social scientists, but ignored by the then people in charge, prompted a new approach," added Dr. Carran. "We would like you to view the following video recorded by Senator Schmitt less than five years after the opening of Guam." The lights began to dim and the screen lit up. Senator Schmitt of Tennessee sat in his office, leaning up on his elbows, puffing and chomping on a cigar.

"Senator Johannes Schmitt here! I am speaking today upon the decision to not only maintain the current policy of inmate release into the Penal Colony on Guam, but to no longer maintain this as a clandestine enterprise." Chomping away at the cigar, Schmitt's gravelly voice, with a touch of southern twang, contained an ominous tone. "Ethos loving morality types, extremists in other words, need to get the full-fledged horror of these animals we have removed from our midst. If God can banish Cain from civilization and I quote, 'a fugitive and a vagabond shalt thou be in the earth' then America can expunge its legions of Cains to exile. And you whining religious whelps that wish to cry out God's words of warning, 'whosever slayeth Cain, vengeance shall be taken on him sevenfold,' I say, 'thy will, be done.' We ain't slaying the bastards; inmates, like animals, are free. If our Cains choose to kill our other Cains, then good riddance to bad rubbish." Murray, intrigued as usual, looked at Wilde who seemed to take it all in without betraying his thoughts.

"Now, we decided to let this little demonstration of Darwinism at its finest be a lesson to the general public and a deterrent to all of the other prisoners serving major sentences in the American Penal system. We shipped out cargo holds full of inmates to the Andersen Air Base to begin building the two walls which stand today. The rapists, extortionists, armed robbers, and thieves got to build a wall by hand and watch the slaughter simultaneously. Hell, it worked, damn it! And the American public loved it. Sure we had some pot-smoking hippies on the Mall in D.C. but God bless America—free speech! This scum sat on the edge of hell looking down into the ninth level as Hispanic, Black and White gangs—like packs of animals—murdered each other. We would have as many as a thousand inmates at a time on the island working, and they knew if they so much as looked cross-eyed at a guard, they were going over the fence. By God, after a prisoner had visited Andersen and worked on the wall during a landing of a plane, Catholic school girls could run their prison back home. With the three strike policy staring them in the face, and discrimination against former convicts outlawed in the occupational world, recidivism plummeted. A little logos goes a long way in this world." The video ended. The lights returned to full illumination.

"Upon the completion of Operation 'Jack's Release' of the 4,113 death row inmates released onto the island, fewer than four hundred remained," Dr. Carran announced to the crowd. "A modern day Pitcairn Island. The situation stabilized as the racial groups settled into their villages especially since the capital had been ravaged and burned."

"Unfortunately," Dr. Ko interjected, "This happens to be when retired Senator Emma Bowers gained special permission to set up a Mormon Mission on the southern tip of the island she called Lindisfarne."

"Yes," Dr. Carran continued, "That information has been kept confidential from the public. However, as principals, it seems vital for your training." As Murray contemplated the sick irony of two religious communities in history being named Lindisfarne and both being massacred, Dr. Ko approached the microphone and commenced to divulge the history of the ill-fated Mormon Mission.

"The story of Senator Emma Bowers can only be described, in the logical sense, as misplaced faith. If your religious persuasion loves martyrs, well then, possibly no greater martyr has lived, and died, since Senator Bowers' disastrous Mormon Mission established on L.O.F.I. in 2028; even the Catholic Church would not follow this expedition. The public knew of her death in Guam, but it had been attributed to a flying accident where her plane went down in the sea and bodies were not recovered. The flight recorder and black box, all forged, solidified the ruse. By special request, not to mention her clout with the Inklings, the Mormon senator swayed the group to allow her to attempt to convert the heathen. Bowers and her party landed in Achang Bay on the southern most tip of the island and headed in toward the little town of Menzo, which at the time still had been abandoned by the population and not occupied by the inmates. Bowers mission group consisted of nearly one hundred missionaries. After they established themselves, they began forays into the three camps on the island. The only cooperative groups turned out to be the roving bands of Orientals and Middle Eastern peoples who were never welcomed into any camp and had to perpetually subsist in 'No Man's Land.' Once conversions began and some inmates from the various camps not only became Mormon, but also moved down to Menzo with the Bowers' expedition, the true brutality of America's exiles exhibited itself. The Blacks, Whites and Hispanics made a truce to raid the Menzo Mormons and capture their converted people. Though the camp had perpetual surveillance by drones, Bowers insisted on no guns and no guards; this, as she stated, would be left to the will of God. The murderous groups moved in on the village in a three pronged attack which would have impressed the likes of Attila the Hun,

Genghis Khan and Harald Hardrada. The groups put to sword, for they had beaten their plowshares into weapons, every Mormon soul in that camp, and the inmates made it back into the jungle before any military response could be attempted even though the island lacked the troop strength to 'go in.' The most heinous aspect occurred days later when the inmate groups met out on the AB Won Pat runway in full view of the long ago abandoned Church of Jesus Christ of Latter Day Saints building, still standing but half burned in the razed capital from the Race War, and beheaded all of the inmate converts—hence execution alley. Still to this day between the groups for executions, the truce holds on the runway, for that 'sanctified' land those animals hold dear."

Murray ruminated upon the fate of the Mormon Mission. Though Catholic himself, he had a fond impression of the Mormon students he encountered at Mayfield. Always congenial and reverent, they generally exerted themselves in the most studious manner and possessed the great ability to accept that much of the world around them embraced values not near their own. Moore remembered a heated class debate over the issue of the passage of laws concerning gay marriage and the 'moral' issue of gay couples adopting and raising children. Though his Mormons this year addressed the historical event with their religious instructor during their theological studies after school, the DeGraw triplets, with their friend Brittany Simpson, came and picked his brain one evening during his office hours which he kept for students to get assistance on homework and the like. Murray often laughed when he thought of his occupation, only half of his job required teaching in the class; the rest of the job resembled a coagulation of the following fields of study: psychology, sociology, criminology, and anthropology.

"Mr. Moore," Brittany had asked, "As a Catholic, how do you passively sit as a clear violation of our shared faith seems to be ignored?" Though the law had been around for half a century, that did not mean that all had accepted it. It took full-blown inter-racial marriage to all but eradicate racism—a span of nearly one hundred years after the Civil Rights Act of 1965. Every year, various religious groups marched against the law, but without much traction. The public seemed satisfied with the compromise and the law—same with the eighth amendment the leftist groups marched against. Society viewed these marches as extreme. However, the Mormon students never embraced the radicalism, never wished to march, only to learn and teach. Murray remembered as he spoke, he could see them sitting, Jeffrey, Curtis and Sarah, along with Brittany, silent, taking it all in. "Well, you are correct. This represents a moral conundrum for the religious, myself included. To debate the law of God here from the Old Testament would be futile—Leviticus and Deuteronomy are unequivocal. When presented with the teachings of Christ, then we are called to work with the sinners are we not? The church has not condoned the actions of same sex couples; besides, Christians are supposed to spread the word, and remember, 'and whosoever will not receive you, when ye go out of that city, shake off the very dust from your feet for a testimony against them.' Christians can do their job; the gay community can decide their path and God can be the judge of it all; no one gets hurt." Murray had no problem with that philosophy; he could not even be confident in himself as to the logical merits of his pontifications; however, it worked for him.

"How then do you feel about gay couples raising children?" inquired Curtis of the DeGraw triplets.

"That question can be easily solved via ethos, logos and pathos my friends—at least in this educator's mind," Murray grinned.

"How so?" asked Sarah.

"Might I direct you to the Reverend Jonathan Swift?" Now, the group smiled. When students came to Mr. Moore for spiritual guidance, it would be a toss up as to what text he would cite from first, *The Holy Bible* or *Gulliver's Travels*. To Moore, both were divinely inspired. "First, my friends let us evaluate motive. 'Men and women are joined together like other animals, by motives of concupiscence,' and since most children are beget from lust, that would exclude the gay couple. Their desire for a child reflects a human desire to raise and nurture. When that beneficent need goes unsatiated, the pathos of a person should extend some empathy or sympathy." Murray scanned his small group, "Plus, remember the other words of Swift, 'Considering the miseries of human life' being born altogether would prove, 'Neither a benefit in itself, nor intended so by the parents, whose thoughts in their love encounters were otherwise employed.' Face it guys, most heterosexuals are overcome by lust, then have nine months to contemplate parenting. The couples in question come to this decision without their minds clouded with licentiousness; thus, with a proper application of logos, common sense should prevail in predicting that these people, no matter their moral depravity as believed by some, will at the very least be benevolent parents. Until I see airplanes full of gay couples bound for L.O.F.I. for multiple child removal felonies, my mind seems rather comfortable in this philosophy."

Murray stepped off of his proverbial soapbox. He looked around at his religious crew estimating their feelings upon their countenances. He wrestled with the concept quite often, being of a Catholic mindset. He came to the same logical conclusion over the birth control debate which periodically flared up in America. He just thought of the countries without birth control: Yemen, Saudi Arabia, Iran—no women's rights—and then he thought of the plethora of countries making up first world civilization that included women's rights and birth control. America's logical compromise seemed to work. When abortion became illegal, birth control, which had reached perfection in 2030, became available for all—life therefore became protected before and after birth. As for parenting, all adults were held to the same standard—a felony for the abuse of a child. Murray decided that concluded the extra lesson.

"You guys have any other questions?"

"No," came back the unified reply.

"Well, I hope this helps you understand America's position on the matter, and my own I suppose. Don't let it rattle the foundations of your faith. I realize this social conundrum sits hard in the laps of the faithful, but try and think of it from this perspective; it represents the final rung on the social equality ladder. Remember, the Catholics and the Mormons were once persecuted in this country for their ways of life. I guess we all need to live and let live. If Christianity proves correct in the end, then God shall judge them harshly. Let the Almighty judge, not us. It must be the price for a free society." Religious conversations always walked a fine line in a public teacher's world, but during the after school tutoring or office sessions, the instructors were afforded greater latitude. "I hope you guys have fun this evening."

"Are you kidding me?" chimed in Jeffrey, "Ms. Gladish piled on the Spanish homework for tonight. We all have work to do!" Murray had found once again that his wandering mind had drifted from the profound task at hand—listening here in Guam—back to his days in the classroom which now seemed so terribly far away. Today proved a monumental day for his mind: Mormons, Lindisfarne, carnage, murder, slaughter and mayhem; he could only speculate as to what today's news meant to his privately ailing compadre, Jacob Wilde.

CHAPTER TWENTY SIX

Days of training occurred, historical videos ran ceaselessly concerning information on the island, and the principals learned how to utilize data mining while working with field agents. The schedule seemed arduous, for the candidates were constantly moving with little time for reflection. July insisted urgency: the Academy wanted them trained and comfortable so that by the beginning weeks of August, they could be shipped to their new schools to ease into the transition. Due to the bunking arrangement in dormitories, any type of inquisitive and insightful conversation could not be had with Jacob Wilde. They sat in numerous class settings, inundated by a deluge of information, history and new found powers of government that Congress at the Great Compromise took (and principals now have as a result). Murray still felt intrigued. He spent an entire hour listening to Dr. Spencer Carran explain how they used an army of young naval statisticians to chart every form of carnage witnessed on the island in order to ascertain and determine if a pattern could be established. Dr. Ben Ko lectured the candidates on how man outside the walls of civilization settled into a routine somewhere between barbarism and animalism. With animalism, man proved to be the top of the food chain and the sociologists, psychologists, and anthropologists all marveled at how their numbers were maintained like a herd. When the number of inmates increased due to an influx of prisoners, wars would spike, battles and murders all rose drastically. When the number of inmates disintegrated, the inmates settled down. William Golding's perception of mankind went from a mid 20th century novel, to regarded almost as a textbook. Though Dr. Carran lived the life of a straight-laced pure scientist, Dr. Ko had a touch for flair and panache. Ko convinced Lieutenant Colonel Weeger to make a special Predator drone drop in the inmate zone. Three care packages, including copies of *Lord of the Flies,* a conch shell and a book on parliamentary procedures made it to all three camps. One of the shells ultimately had been used as a horn, the other two were spotted being wielded as weapons, gaining one confirmed kill. The novels and rules of decorum were used as toilet paper in all three camps. All of these types of lectures only served as fodder for Murray's conviction that the ends justified the means.

The day that Murray Moore had longed for finally arrived— the tour of the Great Wall of Guam. After being choppered over to the Andersen Air Force base the night before, the candidates were on the tarmac as a C-130 prisoner ship flew into, and touched down on the island. Moore chuckled internally for he could hear in his head that hippie song from the steps of the Lincoln Memorial about the "plane a coming; landing at land's end, and all I have seen would be sunshine since I don't know when"; *Ha, damn straight,* he thought, the rabble of society will be stuck in L.O.F.I. prison till they don't know when. Most candidates sternly observed the inmates file off the plane after the landing hatch in the rear dropped. Wilde stood erect, stoned-faced; Moore, intrigued, smiled as they waddled past like penguins manacled at the ankles. Today would consist of a tour by Lieutenant Colonel Weeger on the Great Wall of Guam and a visit to the bridge affectionately known as the "Plank."

While the refuse of society shuffled by, a roofless electric bus pulled up at the end of the runway to pick up the candidates to usher them along the coast to the road behind the Great Wall of Guam. Murray quickly moved to be the first on, and he hustled to the back to look over at the wall as the bus, for the moment, pointed toward the sea. In the class they took yesterday evening prior to bed, Weeger addressed them about the wall, its function, defensive capability and most importantly—for Moore danced with intrigue—the expulsion process. Moore could not wait to see the mechanisms that made it all work. Wilde, taciturn again, seemed indifferent to the process. Moore could see Weeger all puffed out with pride discussing this edifice that she guarded with predator drones, a company of marines, and the United States Navy on the other side of the island.

"Tomorrow after an arrival of inmates bound for the colony," Weeger spoke without emotion, "I will lead this group on a visit to the O.D.W.A which you should know now as Outer Defense Wall Alpha. From this structure, we shall move along the wall to conduct an aerial surveillance of the surrounding area." Lieutenant Colonel Weeger displayed pictures up on the projection screen of the structure. "When we arrive at the vertex of the wall, we shall deploy the Retractable Vertical Insertion Unit otherwise referred to as R-V.I.U. (she pronounced it 'r-view') and proceed from the forty foot O.D.W.A across the R-V.I.U. over the twenty-five foot mote and onto the Inner Defense Wall Beta or I.D.W.B."

Murray chuckled internally and leaned over to Wilde while Weeger flashed pictures and murmured, "Why doesn't she just say we are going to walk on the Great Wall of Guam, cross the "Plank," and step out onto Hadrian's Wall to gander in at the bloody Picts? Why all of the military jargon and other rotgut?"

Jacob, still unamused by the gravity of all of his recently acquired knowledge, simply retorted without looking Murray's way, "Protocol."

"After we have verified the security of the area, we hope to deploy the sling and expel an example into the inmate zone." The rest of the class consisted of the dimensions of the two walls in length and breadth. All of Murray's focus, since being a logo and anglophile, revolved around the Hadrian nickname for the inner wall. How apropos he thought, since the Romans located at the proverbial end of the world in Northumbria constructed this edifice to seal out the bloodthirsty savages of Scotland. The only difference between the Picts and the inmates of L.O.F.I. consisted of clothes, which were worn by the latter in battle.

Turning the bus around and heading past the north runway and rambling down the newly constructed road to the back of the Great Wall of Guam constituted the extent of the ride. The forty foot wall consisted of sheer concrete, which according to the class, had reinforcing on an unprecedented level. An outdoor elevator lifted the crew to the top, and the candidates finally got to view what they had seen in endless pictures and digital images—the interior of the Penal Colony. Murray had vicariously endured the horror of those in the colony now for a couple of days with a veritable flood of information, facts, videos and digital images; he felt disappointed when gazing out into the calm abyss. Though he could distinctly see the outline of the village of Dededo to his southwest; his view of the former capital city in ruins could not be discerned for the distance turned out to be too great. He had hoped to see an inmate, though he must admit that his opaque knowledge of the area left him uncertain to his expectations.

Though this field trip appeared informal with only Lieutenant Colonel Weeger as guide, the one hundred or so Marines lined up along the wall in a formation which seemed to indicate they were either standing at attention for the candidates or manning a guard position; or both. Murray glanced down over the Great Wall of Guam into the twenty-five foot mote which separated it from Hadrian's Wall. He remembered reading the list of nastiness which occupied the mote; every device within served not only to be utilitarian in nature, but deadly in effect. Though the inmates could easily climb Hadrian's Wall with hand made thirty-five foot ladders, the traversing of the Sea of Tranquility (for that served as the mote name) would prove suicidal as Marines gunned the inmates down from the Great Wall and predator drones mounted with 60 caliber machine guns hosed them down from the air. Furthermore, the Great Wall consisted of enormous flood lights every twenty five yards which Murray suspected, when lit, could be seen from the many space stations. His level of intrigue only magnified when they reached the Retractable Vertical Insertion Unit and there stood waiting for them the familiar faces of Colonel Nutt, Dr. Carran, and Dr. Ko.

"Welcome," Colonel Nutt greeted the crowd.

"Alright," Hannah Weeger looked over the twenty-three candidates, "We are going to deploy the R-V.I.U. and proceed down to Inner Defense Wall Beta." Weeger paused; Wilde brooded; Murray scanned the horizon hoping for any sign of inmate life. "Sergeant Keith," called out Lieutenant Colonel Weeger, "Please deploy R-V.I.U.!"

"Yes ma'am!" Sergeant Keith turned and waved toward a control tower located a hundred yards from the angle of the wall which served as watch for the inmates, but also the flight control for the air force base. The towering device reaching for the sky above began to lower, much like a drawbridge, extending over and touching down on Hadrian's Wall. Murray, intrigued as usual, much to his consternation, had great difficulty discerning the nature of the contraption located at the end of the "Plank." This transient moment, Murray wished would not end, for here he stood, literarily and figuratively, on the threshold of the wall marking the end of civilization; a wall which served as a buttress against anarchy. After the "Plank" touched down, Lieutenant Colonel Weeger moved behind the device and up the two steps and began marching down towards Hadrian's Wall located not only twenty-five feet south beyond the mote, but five feet lower in elevation thus giving the "Plank" a slight declivity. Sergeant Keith then bellowed, "You will proceed in single file fashion behind the Lieutenant Colonel!"

Murray bolted toward the front, trying not to skip down this fifteen foot wide contraption which traversed a pit of razor wire and soft sand which he knew to contain a wide assortment of land mine devices. Since he proceeded down the "Plank" with only Weeger in front of him, Moore received a full view of the Retractable Vertical Insertion Unit. The device, simple in nature, stood erect at the end of the "Plank" and therefore extended out over the edge of Hadrian's Wall into the interior of the island, about seven to ten feet—Murray could not discern for sure. Two rods extended up toward the sky about six and one half feet and out at about a sixty degree angle. At the center of the platform, a contraption of some sort existed on the floor at the very edge—nothing else.

As the group of candidates made it to the end of the "Plank," Weeger directed them to either side. The rear of the twenty-three consisted of Colonel Nutt, Dr. Ko and Dr. Carran; as they passed the candidates on either side of the "Plank," they greeted them with salutations. Nick Kues stood to his left, while Wilde faithfully stood on his right. Moore, ever more intrigued with the interior, continued to scan the island looking for any sign of an inmate, or better, impending bloodshed. Instead he felt nothing but the gentle zephyr off the ocean, heard only the swaying of the trees and singing of the birds and saw a visual delight of perceived peace and tranquility.

"Look," Jacob hissed toward Moore's ear. Moore swung his head around and looked up the "Plank" to see a contingent of Marines surrounding, in an escort formation, a prisoner that Moore could only hope would be tossed into the abyss of anarchy. Kues, chuckled a bit, "This should be good." The force-marched captive neither looked over-come with fear nor remorse, only stolidly stone-faced. All of the candidates witnessed him, for now they could make out the gender, waddle down the bridge for he had been fettered not only on the wrists, but also at the ankle. The movement of his body seemed completely idiotic and unnatural, much like the videos from his college years of the generation of "thugs" from pre-Great Compromise days who wore for some inexplicable reason their pants drooping down strapped to their thighs and undergarments in full exposure. Murray recalled an entire lecture hall at Northern Kentucky University that erupted in raucous laughter at the sheer and immense impracticality of the dress first, but also the two-fold ridiculousness of the look for it denoted toughness to the youth, yet sang human offal to the adult. Moore wondered how many of that type of ilk found their way to this island over the past half century.

Reaching the foot of the "Plank" the procession halted. Two Marines simultaneously held the man's manacled arms out as a third scanned a device that held the wrists together. The scanning released the connection allowing the two Marines to stretch the fetters up and attach them to the extended rods giving the visual of a Christ-like figure spread out upon a cross. As the young man hung there, arms stretched to the heavens, Murray could make out two tattoos on the inside of his biceps since his loose fitting shirt slid down to his shoulder blades—on the right an outline of the state of Kentucky and on the left, the words "born & raised!" The third Marine bent down to the inmate's feet, being joined by Sergeant Keith and commenced to hook an elastic device about the man's ankles and afterwards disconnecting the chains. Murray chuckled inwardly, for he reflected back to elementary school, where he felt sure the last remaining teaching nuns on earth still taught. Sisters Mary Jude of Providence and Patricia Maria of Turin had to be the oldest, meanest and feistiest nuns still in a classroom. Moore found himself perpetually at odds with these two relics of a pre-Vatican II world, and they always told him that one day he would, "suffer like the Lord." Murray, while looking at this poor bloke strapped up in front of God and creation, figured that Sisters Mary Jude and Patricia Maria would love nothing more than to see him take this criminal's place. As the fumes of Saint Anthony faded, he wondered, as he inwardly enjoyed seeing this guy in front of him about to get his "just dessert," how much of the benevolent, yet stern, nuns' teaching he had embodied?

"Private Preda! Private Trautwein! Stand guard!" Colonel Nutt exploded, "Marines, fall back!"

The Marines moved out and all but two marched to the back of the crowd. One stood sentinel on either side of the doomed man. Colonel Nutt stepped forward and pulled out a tablet and began to read, "For repeated felonious crimes against the humanity of the United States of America, Franco Mudey you have been tried, convicted and sentence by a jury of your peers to be exiled into the United States Federal Penal Colony of Guam. Felony, the first: possession of illegal pernicious narcotics. Felony, second: distribution of illegal pernicious narcotics. Felony, the third: assault on officers of the law." Upon completion, Colonel Nutt paused, looking up above the tablet to see the candidates' reaction, if any. "Therefore, by the power invested in the Guam Penal System by the federal government of the United States of America, your citizenship has been revoked because you have clearly forfeited your right to live freely in society; therefore, you are hereby sentenced to exile on the island of Guam until you are dead, dead, dead!" Colonel Nutt scanned the candidates for reaction. None.

"Marines, remove arm restraints!" Without a word, the two Marines, Preda and Trautwein, simultaneously removed the man's wrists from the shackles leaving him fettered at the ankles only.

"Sergeant Turner, do your duty!" Without a word, Sergeant Keith Turner approached the rear of Franco Mudey, held his palms open behind the prisoner's shoulder blades with elbows akimbo, then briskly shoved, thus hurtling the excrescence of society into the abyss of anarchy. Franco Mudey bounced a couple of times at the end of the elastic rope and came to a gentle rest. "Sergeant Turner, expel the pariah!" Turner, raised his hand, indicating to the tower behind the congregation to disengage the electronic restraint, and the inmate fell onto the floor of L.O.F.I., gathered his senses then began moving toward the jungle.

None of the candidates moved because all of the dignitaries and military brass stood silent. Murray glanced at Jacob who had fixated his stare at the Mudey inmate as he attempted to collect himself with as much moxie as he could muster. The inmate began to move at a brisk pace towards the jungle when he stopped and turned his head—clearly having been hailed. Out of the woods stepped a black man of respectable build and then a revelation hit the crowd of candidates. Growing up in a largely color blind society, for most people were some hue of brown, they had failed to notice that Mudey clearly manifested a swarthy skin tone. As Franco and the black man took strides toward one another, Murray sensed distraction out of his peripheral vision—a white man exploding out of the jungle into the clearing hurtling a spear. From that distance, thirty feet up and at least seventy-five yards out, depth became tricky. As Murray expected the white man's spear to plant into the bi-racial Mudey, he found himself flabbergasted as the spear sailed passed a startled inmate and into the side of the large black man who had, moments prior, decided to run for it. The prodigious white man accosted Mudey by the arm under the elbow and hurled him into the bushes in front of him and they disappeared. Wilde sat incredulous; Moore felt intrigued.

"Well candidates," Dr. Ko spoke relishing the moment, "I hope this little exercise proved fruitful."

"Whoa!" Jacob exploded. "What just happened?"

"I think I can explain," Dr. Carran inserted, "due to the shifting demographics of the United States, the inmates on the grounds are at an impasse. With profuse numbers in 2025 of Blacks, Whites and Hispanics, social scientists pontificated that the inmates would indeed draw themselves into groups segregated by race. Due to the incessant inter-breeding of the multifarious races and ethnicities in the United States during the last two generations, anthropologists and sociologists have become uber excited to study the demographic shift on the island since it originally established itself on primeval human instinct—race."

"In layman's terms," Dr. Ko interrupted, "Blacks, Whites, Orientals, Middle Easterners, Indians, and Hispanics have melded into a genetic amalgamation of humanity. The proclivity of the old cliché, 'birds of a feather, flocking together' seemed to render a discombobulating rift amongst the tribes on the island, for you see, most inmates now are multi-racial or bi-racial. Very few pure racial specimens exist in the United States today; however, in 2025 the hardened criminal world, being much older, basically fit into neat pigeon holes of racial demographics."

"This represents the subject of our studies: man's evolutionary challenges on a Darwinian level," inserted Dr. Carran.

"Indubitably!" Dr. Ko smiled. "The racial tribes have had to choose: form new groups or reconcile their differences. At first nearly all of the bi-racials and most of the multi-racial groups opted for the black camp; however, when the numbers tipped heavily in the black favor and both the whites and Hispanics felt a disrupted balance of power; they brokered a peace accord and waged war on the blacks knocking their numbers down, but taking enormous losses."

"We are truly blessed to witness the depravity of humanity in its most instinctive form in a completely controlled Petri dish," Dr. Carran grinned from ear to ear. "What we are witnessing here amounts to nothing less than the anthropological recapitulation of man's incessant violence towards one another. Since the balance can be altered by the department of Homeland Security, we can test the mercurial affect of overloading a type of racial group or ethnic group." Murray became more and more intrigued; Wilde grew more and more pallid.

"The scientists here are caught in a paradox. Man's very nature makes him pugnacious and perfidious exhibiting a propensity to judge along racial lines. We haven't conducted enough experimentation to conclude matter-of-factly; consequently, we have a severe lack of pure racial groups anymore and this phase of the study shall cease I am afraid in the upcoming decades. The paradox lies in this; the United States, with its penchant for improvement and high ideals, has worked diligently to overturn the laws of nature and remove us from our instinctive primordial violent unthinking nature. We do not want to overturn the progress man has made in America to rid itself of the wretched racism and violence of the world. We only wish to preserve the status quo in America; furthermore, it demonstrates that Man's true nature, without restraints, would be evil incarnate." Dr. Ko guffawed, "We really are worse than animals for we have higher level thinking skills, the ability to utilize ethos, logos, and pathos, but left unchecked in a world of anarchy, man devolves into the beast."

"The science community has been excited about the progress of it all," Carran finished, "It truly marks the anthropological and sociological genius of William Golding."

"Ostensibly candidates, we here on the island of Guam have validated our data mining from the schools, along with our targeted assassinations—which admittedly represents the dark underbelly of American freedom. We as a nation no longer need to vacillate upon the turpitude some claim exudes from a place like Guam; human evil must be controlled and squashed. Besides, here in L.O.F.I. the animals and inmates roam free."

CHAPTER TWENTY SEVEN

After the expelling of Franco Mudey the day before, the candidates were escorted back to the air base via the bus and flown back to the naval base. After dinner, Murray found himself summoned to the Academy of Principals office which held not only Colonel Nutt, but her full entourage: Dr. Ko, Dr. Carran, Lieutenant Weeger, and Vice Admiral Timmy Truong of the United States Navy. The moment Jacob exclaimed for all of the candidates to hear, "Doesn't anyone see anything wrong with this?" Murray feared that a conversation such as this in front of him would be bound to occur. As Moore scanned the room, he noticed a painting of the ill-fated Titanic and immediately thought of her engineer, Thomas Andrews, who had to tell the captain that the ship ultimately would be doomed to sink within hours. The grim melancholic reality that Titanic and Wilde may share the same fate rattled Murray to the core as he thought of Andrews leaning in a smoking lounge with a pipe and a port awaiting the cold black abyss of his error.

"Murray, we have a problem," Colonel Nutt wasted no time. "Your colleague's statements walk a dangerous ideological line which has efficaciously been eradicated in this country. His words upon Air Force One certainly raised the awareness of more than just those present at your bunk. Furthermore, you must remember most of the structures in this complex are bugged, along with the aircraft."

"Mr. Moore," interrupted Dr. Ko. "We had hoped that you being his close friend could reel him in."

"If I may," now spoke Dr. Carran, "I would like to clarify that this man has certainly slipped through the cracks going undetected. His students obviously didn't know he held nothing but liberal views. The staff here have been flummoxed as to how the man could be this idealistically liberal, teach for ten years in front of staff and student—not to mention the battery of psyche tests administered— and not reveal his true dogma."

"Mr. Moore?" questioned Colonel Nutt.

"Yes?"

"Did he not reveal his idealistic views to you?"

"Well, uh," Murray choked on his own remembrances. Sure they had talked, endlessly in many instances about politics; however, they constantly challenged one another. Sometimes Wilde did exhibit all of the qualities of a leftist ideologue, but he always landed in the middle with logical, moderate practicality. Murray had received a 'C' in psychology in college; how in the hell would he know the real from the rhetoric? He did his best to explain that to the panel.

"Mr. Moore, we have a video we would like you to view."

"Sure, Dr. Ko." As Dr. Ko pointed to the wall, Dr. Carran used a remote to cause the screen on the wall to come to life and lo and behold the old curmudgeon himself, Senator Johannes Schmitt appeared again, much more grizzled, further aged, but still chomping upon a cigar. "Mr. Moore, if you could please watch this."

"Well," Schmitt began his pre-recorded edict, "It seems I have been informed of a minute dilemma in the Academy of Principals. No matter how simple a man tries to make things, someone or something always comes along to muck it up. Apparently, even though we have developed a fairly elaborate and thorough vetting process, we have had some candidates fall through the cracks. The Academy doesn't have teachers observed and evaluated by principals for a decade, then run through the ringer by a series of egg heads from the university and field tested by social psychologists to make it to L.O.F.I., then wig out on us. By God if they get this far, the geniuses with master's and doctoral degrees should be confident they have a principal in their midst who can fulfill his or her duty. Well, the best laid plans of mice and men apparently do go awry. I have been informed that we have now for the first time a candidate deny his duty—refuses to enforce the edict from the Academy and could possibly go public causing some sticky hullabaloo. America ain't got time for that type of hogwash. No sir! Teachers have been warned repeatedly to back out of the process if they are not 100% comfortable. The only recourse that the Academy of Principals has for candidates who decide to renounce their calling and commit complete apostasy would be to remove them as a potential threat for the way of life we have toiled so industriously to provide. Yes sir, if they choose that direction of action, then I am sorry to say, but the aforementioned candidate would be bound for L.O.F.I." Johannes Schmitt then symbolically, for he certainly reeked of panache, crushed the cigar into the ashtray as if to offer finality to his verdict.

Murray Mallory Moore surveyed the room with all eyes upon him. Nothing needed to be stated; he knew the situation. His best friend, his compadre, his buddy would be tossed into the penal colony if he couldn't conform; or maybe his fate reached inevitability. Moore stewed upon the idea of Jacob Wilde being tossed head first into L.O.F.I. How would he survive? What would happen if they discovered he came from the teaching ranks? Or that he had been a principal candidate? Would they exact vengeance upon him to avenge their perceived wrongs? Or would they elevate him to a prince or martyr to further their cause? One thing he did know, he did not want Jacob to have to face what he knew would kill his friend.

"Has his fate been chosen?" Murray asked.

"Not entirely," spoke Colonel Nutt.

"Mr. Moore," inserted Dr. Ko. "He must be won over or the panel will be forced to commit an act which it has not performed in over two decades."

"I loathe this option," returned Colonel Nutt, "But too much would be at risk."

"I think I can help."

"Help us Murray Moore; you are our only hope."

Murray Moore and Jacob Wilde did not take long on the Guam Naval Base to find a bastion of solitude. Though it did not quite replicate the teacher cloister back on the grounds of Mayfield High School in Ohio, it surely sufficed in this new world of theirs. On the western edge of the southern peninsula of the Guam Naval Base, land's end of the American Empire found itself ironically marked by a place called "Spanish Steps." Just like Wilde knew back at Mayfield that Moore needed a secluded spot and a six pack to pray over, so too Murray could recognize that need in his dear friend, Jacob. They had walked the desolate road in silence, back through the brush to the cliff and down to Spanish Steps which emptied into a picturesque oasis of eddying surf against a pebbled beach with the cliffs of Guam looming behind and small islands dotting this miniature cove—complete paradise.

Murray led Jacob to a spot on the small, tight beach at the water's edge, marked only by a cooler obviously pilfered, borrowed or bought from the base. Murray hoped that a tête-à-tête over some beer, like they always did back home when their minds needed straightening out, would prove fruitful, for Jacob had drifted off the reservation and the powers-that-be had not equivocated to Murray that Wilde's actions had been noticed. Murray worried over some of the various items Wilde had said to him lately, virtually questioning all that they were doing. However, the two of them questioning

life, the universe and everything—though not a diurnal event—
certainly had been a topic to be touched upon briefly every couple
of weeks throughout their career together. Murray's predicament
stemmed from one major reversal in this process; usually Jacob had
his resolve intact and Murray needed life's compass read for him.
Now, since Jacob had stated for all to hear, his disquiet with the
entire process, Murray had to right the ship.

"I suppose the powers that be are pretty upset with me?"
Murray walked his friend, Jacob, to the beach, sat him down,
and reached into the cooler of beer producing and opening for
Wilde a green bottle of Tsingtao. "Holy cow man! Where did you
find this?"

"I did not find it; I smuggled it here on the plane."

"How?"

"I put them in my sock!"

"What!"

"Yeah, I stuffed six bottles into my socks buried in my duffle
bag. I know that they are your 'special occasion' beer; however, I
had hoped to have a more auspicious and celebratory beer night
by the beach."

"They are mad at me, aren't they?"

"Jacob, the situation can only be viewed as grim." He ruminated
a moment looking around at this veritable garden upon the beach
where he agonized at what information he must divulge to Jacob.
A surreal miasma swept over Murray. The juxtaposition of the grim
situation, with that of his picturesque location, made it difficult for
all points to register. Here he sat in a tropical Eden, overcome with
sublimity, and yet, now, he must attempt to walk his friend back
from the abyss—earthly damnation. He could not fathom how to
even begin the conversation; fortunately, Jacob took the pressure
off of him.

"I can't do it. I cannot go along with this." Jacob quaffed a size-
able percentage of his bottle, burped then continued. "This does
not reflect the America that I teach. We are no better than third
world countries with totalitarian dictatorships—death squads and
scientific experiments upon our citizens." He pulverized the rest of
the Tsingtao.

"You are wrong. We are better. Much better," Murray did not state this out of trepidation concerning this situation, but out of conviction for the ideology. Throwing murderers, rapists, child molesters, drug dealers and all the rest of that pernicious ilk out of the country into the "wild" troubled him no more than putting down a rabid animal. He received no pleasure from it; it reflected a harsh reality. And as for the students that principals turned into Homeland Security as potential threats to society, the decision reflected a proper interpretation of student data—after all scientific data could and should determine everything. Besides, the principals were not pulling the trigger; they simply listed the soured students as potential threats, and Homeland sent an agent to follow, to analyze, and to quantify the data sent to them; if the opportunity manifested itself, the former student would be put down, saving society an enormous amount of pain from their crimes and money spent convicting them. Murray reiterated all of this to Jacob again.

"What can I do?" Jacob had popped open the next Tsingtao and attacked it.

"Look, I would rather you be a live donkey than a dead lion."

"What does that mean?"

"Simply this," Murray took a swig of his beer, "Deal with it. Go along with everything. Lie, damn it. Tell them you are over it; you get it now. I can help you come to terms with it all later."

"I don't know if I can."

"If you don't, they are going to toss your ass into L.O.F.I."

"What?"

"You heard me, L.O.F.I." Now, Murray drained his bottle. "We aren't sitting back at school my friend in the teacher's cloister burning zombie and vampire sex novels, man. You have been admitted into a secret society which controls America and ostensibly the world. Through this educational setup, America controls the economy at home. Think of it man! The school data we collect on students determines how many go to vocational training to be a plumber or the university to become an engineer. Our teaching and vetting numbers are sent to the INS. Our data then gets sent to the Statue of Liberty Stations worldwide, and America lets in what America needs. You don't think our steady 3% economic growth comes naturally from all of those Founding Father documents do you? Keep that in mind because they are not going to play around with your silly, romantic, liberal ideology that you have kept neatly hidden your entire life and career. They will hook you up to that expulsion device and toss you in. I will do it myself!" It pained Murray to state the last; however, what choice did he have? His resolute conviction in this system, which had recently been fully revealed to him, only solidified his duty. He hoped to save his friend, but would not go down with him for foolishness.

"Why have you forsaken me?"

"I have not! You have forsaken yourself. We love this country! We believe in this country. How many nights have we sat, just like this, sipping beers, stoking a fire, talking about any and everything and thanking God Almighty that we are teachers and that we would not do anything else in the world? We bought into the ideology because we believe in the results. We live in a country where the poor are employed and insured, everyone gets a free public education, everyone receives a job based upon their intellect, racism has all but been eradicated, religious freedom flowers, our global economy booms, the military has become defensive, the debt has nearly been paid off from the pre-Compromise days, and we continue to drain the talent of the world; all because our country legislates from the middle. By draining the world of talent, America consequently keeps them not only beneath us, but in need of us for trade and protection. Why do you think the world exists in a relative state of perpetual peace? Our government works most excellently. The mighty moderate! How many times have I heard you teach about the glories of the Great Compromise? The Inklings? The radical moderate?" Murray paused, drank, then continued, "Now you sit here whimpering because your paradisiacal view of the country comes with a dark underbelly. Suck it up son! We have a country to run."

"I don't know what to do."

"Tomorrow when we head back to the walls, you need to complete the last test, no matter what that task may be! If you can shoot a mule in the head, certainly you can do one more exercise. I will help you. You must conform." The beer flowed.

"But don't you see? This government, our government, which controls the schools, controls the bulk of the industrial production, regulates much of everything, including apparently who lives or dies, represents nothing more than fascism!"

"Yes, however," Murray felt set to deliver a comment of finality, "More like a benevolent paternalism tempered with assassination or as I refer to it—happy fascism."

CHAPTER TWENTY EIGHT

"Proceed."

WINSTON CHURCHILL TO ERNEST SHACKLETON – AUGUST 1, 1914
*ON WHETHER TO CONTINUE THE ANTARCTIC
EXPEDITION OR CANCEL TO FIGHT IN WORLD WAR I*

The final trial had begun. Murray felt he had scourged Jacob as politely as possible the night before in the garden-esque area around the Spanish Steps. He could do no more for his friend; Jacob either had to capitulate upon his semi-radical liberal ideology or face a lifetime in the United States Federal Penal Colony on Guam. Murray knew Jacob would not last in the colony as long as Piggy in *Lord of the Flies.* As Murray stood at attention on the Great Wall of Guam looking out over the tropical paradise with the other twenty-two candidates, he muddled through his mind in befuddled admiration for the die-hard liberal. Over the past fifty years, when the radical left tried to speak up or out against something, the majority of the populace, radical moderates, or as Wilde called them, the militant middle, had shouted them down with quiet compliance from the remaining right wing of the political fringe. As Murray waited for the final test to begin, he quiescently recalled one of his final class Socratic Seminars covering the subject of politics in 20th century literature—one of his favorite topics.

"Mr. Murray?" The class had assembled in the commodious community room to allow the students to spread out and speak out upon their given topics. His seniors, generally of unimpeachable character, leaped at the chance to hone their political sabers on the whetstone of discussion. He would assiduously abstain from jumping into the conversations and debates though admittedly at times; that proved extremely difficult.

"Mr. Murray! Mr. Murray!"

"Yes, Kimmie."

"We need your help in our circle." Moore divided the Community Room into four concentric circles allowing the students to move between the groups debating their novels, politics and research. Kimmie reminded him of his little sister, but worse, more exacting and demanding; the type of student that generally exasperated him due to the inundation of questions.

"What seems to be the issue, Kimmie?"

"Scot and I disagree on a point, and we wish to have your opinion."

"Okay, but what about the other three in your group? Waldeck? Flick? Mitchell? You three can't help settle this dilemma?" Murray already knew the answer. Kimmie, unafraid to debate anyone, entangled herself with the precociously intellectual giant of the high school known to all as Kaeff—the only name to which he wished to be referred. The other three had enough common sense to adhere to a silent approach when Scot Kaeff got rolling on his favorite topic, political morality.

"Mr. Murray," spoke up Alec, "Anthony and Joe tried to debate Kaeff, but they were hammered."

"Politely, I hope," Moore's gaze sidled over toward Scot.

"Dude! Your argument could be placed somewhere between lame and vacuous. And your lap dogs couldn't even whip together a whimper for a rebuttal. Mr. M, I need an intellectual rival!"

"What started the debate?"

"Well, Mr. Moore," Joe Mitchell cut in, "Kimmie said society would run smoother if the radical liberals would just shut up. The country seems to be running fine."

"Good one! I feel like Montag, 'Hey Kimmie! Go ask the white clown!' Mr. M, this seminar group could be best described as a copious stream of pontifical semi-anonymous mugwumpery," Scot Kaeff completed his efficacious group evisceration quoting one of his favorite lines from Sir Winston Churchill.

"Easy Scot," Moore attempted a soft tone in order to placate the group. "Please, give me the subject of debate."

"Uh, I think," broke in Anthony Flick, "It had something to do with the lack of conservative fundamentalists and leftist's radicals."

"Yes," Kimmie defended herself, "You never see radical right wing nuts any more, only in history books. Plus today, radical liberals are everywhere."

"Scot, your response?"

"Ah, Mr. M, you know I like to be called Kaeff."

"Okay, Kaeff, and by the way, I like Mr. Moore." Protocol restored for both.

"Sorry, dude." Murray furrowed his brow, "I mean, sorry Mr. Moore."

"Please," Murray now exasperated, "Your answer."

"Yeah, well it will be quite simple to explain." Scot Kaeff rose up in his chair, "You don't see right wing zealots because they sold out for thirty pieces of silver, the non-principled swine! All they cared about could be summed up in a few pithy phrases: low taxes, no abortion, no welfare, ruthless punishment for criminals, and periodic aerial bombardment of third world dictators. They got all they wanted, honey."

"See, Mr. Murray!" cried Kimmie.

"Mr. Murray," interjected Alex, "Did not the liberals get stuff? Like gay marriage, health care for all, a livable wage for the working class, free education, and a reduced military budget?"

"Correct, dillweed!" Kaeff came after them again. "The problem lies with this, the liberal will always search society, go to the lowest common denominators and try and lift them up, whether it be women's rights, the out of work, the minorities, the homeless, the poor, the oppressed. If you right wing nuts have your tax money and gated communities, you say piss on the rest!" Kaeff paused. "Sorry, for my language Mr. Moore." Murray nodded.

"So, Mr. Moore," Anthony Flick smiled, "Your take please."

"Hmmm," Murray did not have to think long, "Kaeff happens to be correct." He chuckled inside. He hated to admit the fact, but Scot Kaeff—outspoken genius—hit the nail on the head. Sure the conservative hated birth control and gay marriage, but they got abortion outlawed and three states were granted immunity from the Gay Marriage act, Mississippi, Alabama, and Georgia. At one time, most of the South obstructed the law, but when South Carolina's and North Carolina's economy tanked because the rest of America boycotted their beaches, the almighty dollar once again trumped God's law. Soon after their secession from the law ended, Tennessee, Louisiana and Arkansas followed suit. The aforementioned three remained the only holdouts against the Gay Marriage Act. America tolerated it because it worked. The radicalized Christians headed south and the gays headed anywhere but there; all seemed content. Though Kaeff may have been a tad invective in his diatribe, conservatives have a simpler, more myopic view of the world, thus easier to palliate their concerns, but the liberal will always fight. The liberal always finds a niche of society not getting what the rest receive and they jump into the fray. The liberal will always find a cause. The liberal will never be content; thus, the liberal will never be happy.

Now Murray, Jacob and the other twenty-one candidates stood upon the Great Wall of Guam awaiting their final test. The weather exemplified perfection—tropical breeze, warm sun, the smell of eternal summer. All seemed the same this day as the day before with one major exception. The expulsion device used yesterday attached to the end of the "Plank" or R-V.I.U. as they called it did not sit alone today. On either side of the device an additional expulsion unit rested with its hooks extended toward the heavens making it a total of three upon the wall. Murray felt intrigued. For the moment, the only people on the wall happened to be the candidates led by the stolid Lieutenant Colonel Hannah Weeger. Jacob stood in front of Murray with the Kentucky candidate, Nick Kues behind.

Opposite the candidates, there stood the numerous dignitaries, military brass and Homeland Security Agents. Moore realized this test would serve as the crescendo of all of their activities—the consummation of their dogma. He could make out numerous people he had met recently: Crazy Eddie and Uncle Tom from the Grand Canyon, along with Kristin Fortunski. He could see special Agent Gruenschlaeger and Louis Cottonwood with his probationary agent, Zack Hatfield, along with his young buck Luke 'Top Gun' Kues who came to see his brother initiated. All of the elites from back in the states: Colonel Nutt, Jennifer Alliston and Dr Hauer. More and more people kept streaming out onto the Great Wall of Guam: Dr. Carran, Dr. Ko and Vice Admiral Timmy Truong. All would exacerbate the internal conundrum percolating in Jacob Wilde's heart.

As the evening had concluded the night before, Murray felt sure that he had convinced Jacob to abandon all of his romantic liberal ideology for fear of the punitive repercussions if he did not. The two men had finished the beers and muddled their way home. Murray had become exasperated, for Jacob had become maudlin due to his excess of alcohol. They had all but stumbled toward the door when both men staggered, Murray forced to adjust his half mooned spectacles, when he noticed the agony and suffering in the eyes of Jacob. Murray knew, though he denied it, that the carousing on the beach and the surprise Tsingtao may have gone for self-gratification only. He could see the intransigence in the mawkish eyes of Jacob as if he could see clear down to his soul. A maelstrom of ideology would be hurtling toward his friend soon, and Murray feared Jacob's Lord Jim conviction would send him over the edge.

The immutability of his romantic ideals manifested themselves with abject lucidity. Murray did not wish to forsake him.

In keeping with geographical regions, the trinity of Kues, Moore and Wilde had been formed to represent the Mid-West region. Whether by chance or planning, Moore felt dubious, but his group had been called first to mount the "Plank" and walk toward the three expulsion devices upon Hadrian's Wall. Kues looked anticipatory, Moore intrigued, and Wilde apprehensive. Due to Wilde's clear tremulous demeanor, Moore felt confident that the order of the test did not occur due to happenstance. The Academy of Principals wanted him on that wall first; they needed him on that wall first.

A military band began to strike up a song. Murray stood dumbfounded and incredulous, for he did not notice in the throng of people on the Great Wall of Guam, though the ranks were copiously filled, that a fairly efficiently sized band had occupied the space with what appeared to be the entire Air Force Base. The song he recognized, but not immediately. Though Murray felt sure that the rest of the candidates busied themselves trying to comprehend the pomp and circumstance juxtaposed with the verdant and lush jungle of the island, Moore felt a pang pierce his very soul as a military tenor began to sing, and the gravity of the song reached him as he recognized the lyrics of "Danny Deever." The sonorous voice undulated through Moore's soul; his emotions exploded as the melodious voice erupted over the heads of the crowd. Murray had no idea if the voice reflected baritone or tenor, in his soul the anglophile in him rose up from his depths to the edge of his eyelids in the most unmanly aqueous fashion. Moore blinked back his tears as Kipling's ballad rang toward the heavens when he noticed three penguin waddling criminals, who represented the most undesirable of the American society, heading toward the plank.

The song wailed incredibly, the prisoners were marched down the plank and hooked up to the expulsion devices. The movement of the prisoners quickened with the help of the Marine escort, and the three hung their eyes, glazed-looking, out over the wall toward the eyes of numerous denizens of the penal colony nestled in the bush. Moore, too enthralled with the song and singing, "They are hanging Danny Deever in the morning!" to notice the absolute horror projected upon the face of Jacob Wilde who stared into the eyes and countenance of a young man who had sat in his classroom less than a year ago. As the song lyrics ended, the music stopped, and Moore's reverie broke, the audible sound of a whimper could be heard coming from the mouth of Jacob Wilde as he stood horrified looking into the face of Sam Wolfe.

Murray, whose nostalgic fog had lifted, realized that Sam Wolfe did not represent the only recognizable visage strung upon the expulsion device. Looking into Murray's eyes glared one of his most irascible young flunkies, Jake Neyer. Moore, who recognized Wolfe immediately, and taking into the fact that he knew Neyer, glanced up at Nick Kues who looked equally aghast. This test would truly cut to the core of the candidates to see who would comply, who would dither, or possibly, who would self-destruct. Each teacher-to-be-principal, so clearly as events stood in front of them, would have to hurl their own student into the societal abyss. Like the executioner of the middle ages, or the hangman of the Western American Expansion or so many others who in the course of human events have had to exact a sacrifice as deemed necessary by society, Kues, Moore, and Wilde, along with the rest of the candidates behind them immediately and those to follow in their proverbial footsteps, would each have to toss their own students over the wall and into a certain death.

The three former students hung on the edge of oblivion, arms outstretched, with Wolfe in the middle, Neyer to his right, and the unknown student to Murray and Jacob on the left. Murray looked at Jacob in hopes to throw a modicum of moxie his way in order to build enough resolution in him to survive this last test. Weeger and Nutt strode to the forefront, Dr. Carran and Dr. Ko drifted toward the candidates; Moore felt sure the medical men were there to observe the candidates' reactions and not the actions of the inmates. Murray knew the entire setup served to goad anyone on the fence to rebel or capitulate; a capitulation which would serve to crush any contemptible feelings or notions a candidate may have—make the intractable, tractable.

"Attention candidates and convicts!" shouted Colonel Nutt. "The three former citizens of the United States of America who stand hung before us, Sean Starke, Sam Wolfe and Jake Neyer, stand here convicted by a jury of their peers for multiple or egregious felonies and are bound for expulsion. Do you have anything to say for yourselves convicts?"

"Yeah, piss off!" shouted Jake Neyer.

"Dude, shut up," shouted the Sean Starke inmate.

"Who are you telling to shut up?" belted out Neyer.

"You convict! You know why you are hanging there. You did your three crimes; now prepare to do your time. I accept my punishment," added Starke.

"You can piss off, too," retorted Neyer as Wolfe remained quiet.

"Silence!" Nutt bellowed. "Candidates! Each of you knows these former citizens who have been condemned to the island. After I read their convictions, your job as former teacher and future principal will be to expel them from our midst!"

Wolfe looked at the Starke inmate, "In a couple of minutes, I will be with you in L.O.F.I." Wolfe shook his head with a sense of approbation for Starke's shouting down of Neyer. Lieutenant Colonel Hannah Weeger stepped forward and flipped on her tablet.

"Sean Starke, of the state of Kentucky, for murder in the first degree, you have been tried, convicted, and sentenced by a jury of your peers to be exiled into the United States Federal Penal Colony of Guam." Weeger continued to rattle out legalese, all the while Moore wondered if Wilde would have the strength to put logos ahead of ethos, "You are hereby sentenced to exile on the island of Guam until you are dead, dead, dead!" Nick Kues never hesitated, but sent his former student hurtling into the inner realm of the penal colony. As he stepped back following the thrusting of his inmate over the edge of the wall, the crowd noticed Starke, the convict, falling and then bouncing up and down. Alternating, Colonel Nutt turned to Jake Neyer and began to read his verdict as he glanced around for any eyes of sympathy from the crowd.

"For repeated felonious crimes against the humanity of the United States of America," she continued counting out his felonies which exceeded three, for after his second conviction he apparently continued his crime-ridden ways, racking up three more at one time involving robbery, assault and distribution. Nutt kept reading, "Citizenship has been revoked." Murray listened to the list and could not wait to chuck this vial vermin into the abyss. When Nutt annunciated the last of the three "deads" at the end of the verdict, Murray thrust his open palms violently into the shoulder blades of Neyer, his former-slacker-turned-criminal, and sent him convulsing into L.O.F.I., bouncing helplessly awaiting the last of the pariah currently on display.

Finally, there came the verdict of Sam Wolfe, who while in high school, teachers use to exult for his potential greatness and extol his talents to benefit society. He completely went awry and both Jacob and Murray felt a bit culpable because Sam's collapse occurred the year both taught him. Murray would find out later that Wolfe attempted to escape three times since he had been sentenced to L.O.F.I. There he stood on the scaffold, three felonies read and Weeger finished, "You have clearly forfeited your right to live freely in society; therefore, you are hereby sentenced to exile on the island of Guam until you are dead, dead, dead!"

Jacob Wilde stood stone still.

Murray Moore felt intrigued. Would his friend be pliable?

Colonel Nutt scowled at Wilde. She waited. Moore coughed.

"Mr. Wilde," cried Lieutenant Colonel Weeger, "Do your duty!"

Jacob Wilde stood stone still. Clearly manifesting itself from his countenance, Jacob Wilde had no intention of sending his former student into the gloom of the island. Wilde stood resolute, determined and liberal. The stereotypical liberal modus operandi had overcome the logos of Jacob Wilde; for his implacable ethos would not allow him to accept anything except the romantic idealism in which he so sycophantically believed.

"We must not continue this practice!" He bellowed. All were silent.

"Mr. Jacob Wilde, do your duty!" Colonel Nutt exclaimed.

"I cannot. I will not!" He looked around searching for a hint of approbation from anyone in the crowd. He received nothing; the crowd proved impervious to his antics. "These are not the ideals of our Founding Fathers! Brutal punishment! Murder and mayhem in order to produce laws! Surely, you cannot tell me you close your eyes at night and are not haunted by the visions of the horror in which our government has engaged in order to provide the façade of liberty and freedom. These disreputable practices of allowing these convicted felons to be tossed into this labyrinth of anarchy to be at the mercy of their fellow man cannot but burn your conscience. Have you no compunction? Everyone who knows the Constitution and understands justice, hear my voice!" Again he looked toward the crowd but only felt its repulse.

"Mr. Wilde," interjected Lieutenant Colonel Weeger, "This represents the country and how it works."

"Then my country must not be of this world! If my country were of this world, then intellectuals and patriots would fight the injustice. We cannot deliver these three criminals this way into the jaws of death and continue the practices of our warped covenant."

Murray Moore stepped toward the crowd that started to ebb toward his friend. He had sympathy in his heart for Jacob Wilde but daggers in his eyes. He looked toward Nick who shouted, "Expel him!" Nick had never hesitated when he stepped forward and shoved his shackled prisoner right between the blades and sent his inmate Sean Starke hurtling into a bouncing free fall awaiting his release into the wild. Why couldn't Wilde? What part of reality did his good friend not fully comprehend? Wilde must comply.

"No," Wilde, nearly inaudible, muttered toward Moore, "You have forsaken me again." Murray spoke not a word, but went straight to his work. He had already demonstrated his leadership by outperforming his teaching friend when he had shoved Neyer off with a jerk. Now only Sam Wolfe remained as Neyer and Starke dangled and bobbed up and down at the end of their cords. Moore, turned back toward the crowd, then furtively spoke toward Jacob, "You have only this chance left."

"Please forgive my comrade. His mind at times becomes clogged by fastidious ideology from an over active romantic, idealistic heart." Murray looked at the military brass, the other candidates, the soldiers on the Great Wall of Guam, and he shouted, "Tell Jacob what he should do!"

"Expel him!"

"What?" Murray shouted hoping against hope that fanaticism and peer pressure would save his friend.

"Expel him!"

Murray stopped and moved toward his friend. Jacob looked down at his feet, the convict, Wolfe, had turned his head nearly 180 degrees to watch. Moore stood arm's length from both Wilde the teacher and Wolfe the inmate. Wilde noticeably wept for he knew he had crossed the great barrier which sealed his fate. Wolfe, noticing that Wilde could no longer save him from his own fate, had decided to take matters into his own hands.

"Wait!" Wolfe surprised the crowd. All observed patiently.

"What?" Murray began to sniff out a ruse from the prisoner. However, since he knew not what direction to take and understood that his friend would be banished, he found himself being jarred by an epiphany that though Wilde had most assuredly failed the test, he, himself, had yet to pass it. He stepped toward Sam Wolfe and placed his hand on Wolfe's left shoulder and pressing, asked, "What do you want?"

"Before you expel me, I wanted to address the crowd. I wanted to address you and Mr. Wilde."

"No," Moore had suddenly realized that he had taken control of the expulsions from the wall, no military people intervened. Surely, this represented his final test, "Absolutely not."

"But," Sam Wolfe pleaded, "I just want you to know who I am!"

Moore, with complete antipathy for the criminal and total apathy for his possible plea for forgiveness, shoved Sam with great force in the left shoulder blade, and Wolfe became the last of the three human projectiles to be banished from the American Society. Murray Moore then grabbed his close friend Jacob Wilde and walked him past the military brass up onto the "Plank" and toward the Great Wall of Guam in hopes that he could possibly save this man, who ostensibly represented the only family he had.

CHAPTER TWENTY NINE

Murray Mallory Moore sat quietly next to his friend and colleague, Jacob Wilde on the beach at the bottom of the Spanish Steps on the edge of Guam and at the geographical end of the United States of America. The day had proved an unparalleled challenge in both the lives of Moore and Wilde. Moore ruminated about the day, the events, the endearment he extended toward his friend for his ideological flaw—along with the stalwart determination he exhibited in front of the other candidates as he expelled two of the inmates over the wall to become the new denizens of

L.O.F.I. He knew he would love to be able to emulate his friend's beliefs, but never his actions. The lack of practicality that Wilde displayed on the wall discombobulated Murray to the core for he had never ideologically believed in anything strongly enough to risk exile and banishment onto an island of lunatics, murderers, rapists and thieves. Maybe the feeling of conviction exhilarated the individual making the stand. Murray Moore never cared about anything in the world enough to risk all of his earthly comforts. The only romance he ever experienced on the globe derived from his reading of the accounts of Shackleton, Mallory, and Scott. Man defying the odds, challenging death, all to embrace the fleeting moment of bliss reflected his only romantic ideal. Maybe Moore's myopic ideology reflected a queer romanticism, but nevertheless, he could not shake the notion. It probably explained his pure disdain for that dog eating Norwegian Roald Amundsen—no romance in his conquest of the pole. Regardless, Murray never could conceive of being crucified for a belief.

As Murray led Wilde through the crowd up the "Plank," back onto the Great Wall of Guam toward the elevator to the ground level, he felt sure that the two of them would be stopped by soldiers, sailors, or someone. Moore wished to put Wilde in a safe room in hopes of exonerating Jacob with the Academy in some fashion. He knew neither whom to nor how to approach this conundrum. Surely, they would not toss a teacher in with the wolves? Once they reached the ground, two phlegmatic soldiers stood on either side of Jumbo, the Marine One pilot, they rode with a couple of days ago.

"Well boys, needless to say, the brass called down to have you brought in." What could they do?

Still silent at his side, Murray glanced away from Jacob taking in the beach, the fading dusk, the cooler of beer and chuckling about the tranquility of it all. He struggled with the circumstances, and how a man who perfected nuance, like Jacob had as a teacher, could not figure out that the dark underbelly of America reflected nothing more than a nuance of the two realities America faced fifty years prior with the Great Compromise and now in their present world. Sure, the penal colony and citizen extermination seemed, up front, brutal upon the surface, but so did euthanizing a dog or cat. Moore would not lose sleep over the reality; he could not. He believed in it. Now Jacob had ruined it all: his career, his life and his future. There would be no clemency; the Academy of Principals could not grant it. The candidates knew too much and had gone too far. They would have to make an example out of him. Murray put down the pad of antiquated paper and reached down for his beer, taking a hardy gulp. Moore hoped he could take Wilde to his new school and put him back into the classroom. There had been that ephemeral moment when they had met with Colonel Nutt, Lieutenant Weeger, along with Dr. Ko and Dr. Carran about the possibilities of adjusting Wilde's quixotic dogma, but the quartet explained to Moore unequivocally that the options were limited and none of them included Wilde leaving the island again.

Moore initially stewed with enmity for the Academy with its principles and rigidity. He presumptuously surmised that the L.O.F.I. option for Wilde not conforming would prove only to be an idle threat. After the brief discussion with the cadre of four following Jacob's refusal to conform on the final test, that transient illusion gave way to a bleak reality. Murray crushed the can, tossing it as he reached to the cooler opening another without hesitation. Thank God the island had Coors for this occasion—Moore's beer of choice for conquering mountains.

Now the darkness fell completely, Murray could address Jacob finally. He looked over at his silent friend lying splayed out on the ground face pressed down into the beach where he fell after the bullet pierced his skull. Darkness would save Murray from seeing his good friend's brains blown all over the beach, the foliage, and the cooler. He could not let Jacob be expelled into L.O.F.I.; he would not survive a day, if lucky. Moore feared what would happen if the denizens discovered he came from the ranks of educators, an institution that may have had a hand in placing them there. He exhorted Weeger and Nutt to allow him to live here or come back to the states with him; they were unflappable, for the laws and rules about the Academy could not be manipulated. Dr. Ko and Dr. Carran had offered a few ways that Jacob could commit noble suicide. Nothing so violent as the Japanese version of Seppuku, just a series of pills. Murray, indignant with their callous proposition, told them that he would take care of the matter his way.

"Mr. Moore, whatever do you mean by taking care of it?"

"Look, I won't let you toss my buddy into L.O.F.I.; they will torture or kill him. Besides, he will be in over his head. His liberal ideology, though noble in civilization, won't serve him any good in there with the animals."

"Well Mr. Moore," continued Colonel Nutt, "The other option represents a level of finality that…"

"I know the other option," Moore cut her off, "I will need gun."

"What do you plan to do?" inquired Dr. Ko.

"Look doc, I am not going to have you four put Jacob in a room, put the light in his face and tell him his options are suicide or L.O.F.I. A man shoots his own dog, not a stranger." He indignantly scowled at them, "Jacob Wilde has been my best friend for the last ten years; if anyone has to present his options to him, it will be me."

Moore promised Jacob a way out if he met him at the bottom of the Spanish Steps. Initially, he could not contrive a plan, but then, realizing his buddy just needed hope for a distraction, an idea engendered itself within his mind. A few beers with the talk of an exile island surely would fit the bill. Thankfully, Jacob, though astute in all matters concerning the government, history and political ideology, never read the classic pieces of literature from which Moore relied as much upon for lifetime guidance as the Bible. He could thank Aldous Huxley for this idea.

"There happens to be an option," he told Jacob.

"What? The Lawrence Oates option? I won't do it. I can't do it."

"No," assuaged Moore, "Not the Lawrence Oates option, though that offer found its way to the table in our meeting."

"You are kidding me!"

"No man, this happens to be a rather serious matter, Jacob." Moore handed Jacob a beer. "The Academy does not like to look foolish. You slipped through the cracks. When you get to Guam, you should have no reservations." Moore suddenly felt culpable; he recognized the moral antagonism that Wilde felt prior to hitting Air Force One. He witnessed it first hand in Washington, D.C. A now bitter sense of naivety hit Murray in a most visceral way. He had wished, had hoped, and had ignored the signs for the simple reason that he wanted his long time friend with him. Wilde had been crying out for help, and Moore had let him down. Peer pressure gone awry—in middle age even. "Look man, I should have 'outed' you when you began to show signs of weakness."

"No, don't blame yourself. I am my own man." Truth be told, Jacob Wilde did not hold his friend culpable; he should have been more vociferous in his qualms. He would have been removed. Jacob's problem stemmed from not wanting to disappoint Murray. With each recognizing their errors in judgment, they surmised they both fouled it up. Murray's and Jacobs' policy of running into a classroom with the same vigor as up a mountain caused them to miss warning signs. That same impetuous drive they exerted upon each other had caused them to find themselves underdressed on a snowy mountain and soaked on a rainy summit more than once in life. Up until now, they managed to escape with only a great story for their students. Being raconteurs both, it only propelled their capriciousness.

"The other option, do you want to hear it?"

"Yes."

"The USS Cypress!" Murray laughed to himself drawing upon Huxley's *Brave New World,* knowing full well Wilde never read this, but the familiar allusion would be useful in keeping his story straight. "Simple, you can board a ship and patrol the island with other teachers who did not complete the training."

"Really. Why are you telling me this now?"

"They don't like to use this option. Highly top secret." Murray handed Jacob a second beer even though he had not quite finished the first.

"What do you do?"

"Patrol the island and ensure that no one makes it off in some type of make-shift raft. America can't risk any of these clowns getting home." Moore could not risk too many questions; Jacob may be slack on the literature, but he possessed none of the qualities of Lennie Small and his rabbit distraction could only hold out so long. Jacob needed to drink the beers. Murray thought of the irony of sitting on *Lord of the Flies Island,* utilizing Steinbeck and Huxley to shoot his best friend in the head. Strange. He had always taught his students the value of one book equating to the author's lifetime of knowledge. He thought of the novels he had devoured in life; that should have made him fairly intellectual and wizened.

"I can do that. How long?"

"Jacob, you can never go home. Boat, L.O.F.I., or suicide; I would say the answer seems axiomatic."

"You are right. The best option." Moore mused deeply as he sensed the relief overcome his friend's disposition as they opened their third beer. This entire predicament contained fifty shades of gray. Would the powers that be accept the premise that Jacob shot himself in the head? Did it matter? They would probably accept any story so long as they did not have to chuck a teacher in with the animals. They idly chatted over the third beverage, and Moore knew that Jacob had fixated the idea in his mind that he would be safe. He visibly relaxed and hammered his third beer, inquiring if Murray wanted to go for the fourth. Though the first three had always been perfunctory when they drank, numbers four, five or even six moved into the realm of capricious self-indulgence. Moore knew that after the third beer, Wilde's esoteric mind became distracted and muddled; thus the perfect time for him to play the Judas and betray his friend with far worse than a kiss. When Jacob Wilde leaned forward to grab two beers from the cooler, Moore swung out the cocked and loaded Colt 45 pistol, raised it to the level of Jacob's head as he eased back down to his right. As he settled down on his own backside fully expecting to turn to his left to pass a beer, Moore delivered the long anticipated bullet through Jacob's brain. Hopefully, Jacob's last thought had contained naught a modicum of fear.

Now, Moore had finished his beers and worked on Jacob's, awaiting complete darkness. He could not look again at the destruction he had wrought upon his friend and colleague. Murray read the suicide note he had written, "I hope this action will demonstrate that the spirit of nobility, and the power to lead by example has not passed out of the teaching profession. I fear I must go. I have been to the edge of my existence, and I have decided to die like a gentleman—an educator. I regret only for my true friend, Murray Mallory Moore, who I leave behind. Finally, for God's sake, take care of my students." Moore polished off his beer and leaned over Jacob, carefully looking nowhere near his head and pinned the suicide note upon his shirt breast. Murray then best placed the gun, carefully inserting it in Jacob's now stiffening hand and made an approximate drop, imitating a self-inflicted gun shot wound.

Would the Academy of Principals believe the story that they had drank the beer, and Murray convinced his friend about the nobility of suicide? Would they believe he left his friend alone to kill himself? Would they spend the time to calculate the angle and distance and all of that other forensic mumbo-jumbo to ascertain that Murray actually murdered his friend? Or would they call it a mercy killing telling him "a guy got to sometimes"? He doubted it. His only fear, which struck him ironically with humor, came when he could envision the Academy determining that he did indeed shoot Jacob Wilde in the head and then wanting him to be a superintendent.

Slowly, extremely slowly, Murray Mallory Moore's head rotated like an erratic compass needle, the head turned right; north, north-east, east; left, south-east, south; all scanning to see if anyone would be responding to the report of the fired hand-howitzer. Moore doubted anyone would. He glanced down at Jacob Wilde knowing that the long-hoped-for bullet had entered his brain, subsequently putting his friend out of his heterodoxy of doublethink. Murray felt cruel; Murray felt kind. Two salt tasting tears trickled down the sides of his nose into the corner of his mouth. Trepidation had not driven his mercy killing; conviction served as the spur in his proverbial side. Moore knew he would miss his friend. That did not matter though. Moore's metamorphosis had become complete. Patriotism. Nationalism. Jingoism.

All infected Murray. Imprisonment, exile, murder, though contentious, propelled his country, this utopia. Murray's conviction, palpable. Murray's resolution, tangible. Questions, none. The means justified the end. He would never wonder, never question; Murray Mallory Moore knew. He felt it. He embraced it. He loved this Ameritopia.

AFTERWORD

To be clear, I want no reader, after the perusal of my novel, to even contemplate that I believe in all or any of the governmental structures presented in Ameritopia. I know that the representative democracy currently employed by the United States of America manifests to the world the path which will lead all people to freedom. Infallible in practice. Perfect in union. We always have been perfect and always will be perfect. Or nearly perfect. Furthermore, I would never wish to advocate for any society where the citizens are held responsible for their actions. I think a person's accidental birth in America followed by eighteen years of languishing in apathy accomplishing nothing, and then voting for bread and circuses represents the type of government which could be nothing but the envy of the world.

Made in the USA
San Bernardino, CA
09 July 2013